PARK AVENUE
PRINCE

LOUISE BAY
USA TODAY BESTSELLING AUTHOR

D1016476

Published by Louise Bay 2017

Copyright © 2017 Louise Bay. All rights reserved

This is a work of fiction. Names, characters, businesses, places, events and incidents are either the products of the author's imagination or used in a fictitious manner. Any resemblance to actual persons, living or dead, or actual events is purely coincidental. The author acknowledges the trademarked status and trademark owners referenced in this work of fiction, which have been used without permission. The publication/use of these trademarks is not authorized, associated with or sponsored by the trademark owners.

ISBN: 978-1-910747-43-8

Sign up to the Louise Bay mailing list

http://eepurl.com/bjHtfH

BOOKS BY LOUISE BAY

PARK AVENUE PRINCE

KING OF WALL STREET

love unexpected

Indigo NIGHTS

Promised NIGHTS

Parisian NIGHTS

The Empire State Series

*H*OPEFUL

*F*AITHFUL

Read more at www.louisebay.com

CHAPTER ONE
SAM

"It's huge, Sam," Angie said as she walked into the empty living space with high ceilings and views of Central Park and across the city. The sun was so bright I had to shield my eyes as I looked out the windows on the west side. I sucked in a deep breath as I took it all in. Did I really own this place? I knew it was my signature on the paperwork but sometimes it felt as though I were leading someone else's life.

"That's what they all tell me." I chuckled. Like most men, I still had the puerile sense of humor of a fifteen-year-old boy. But after fifteen years of friendship, Angie expected nothing more.

"You're disgusting. I'm not talking about your penis, for crying out loud."

"Who said anything about my penis?" I held my arms out wide. "*I'm* talking about this place. As usual, your mind is in the gutter."

Angie shook her head, but there was no denying the size of the new apartment I'd just bought. It was seven thousand, two hundred eighty-six square feet of the Upper East Side and I lived here now. "The view will ensure it keeps its value," I said, looking out at the Manhattan skyline.

"The location alone will make sure that happens. It's 740 Park Avenue, Sam." She was shaking her head, incredulous. I didn't blame her.

The address had been important. One of the most sought after listings in New York made my purchase one of the safest real estate transactions in America. A victory for me, but also a good place to put my money, or some of it, anyway.

"Do you ever think this isn't your life at all?"

"Sometimes." I'd made every dollar it took to buy this apartment in the last decade. When I'd graduated high school, I'd left the group children's home where I'd spent the previous six years with nothing but two pairs of jeans, two t-shirts, a sweatshirt and some underwear. For me, leaving my old life behind, getting to start again, had been liberating. The only thing that'd tagged along from those days was Angie. We'd met the first day in my new school after I went to the home. She was in the girls' home nearby and must have recognized a fellow orphan. We'd been best friends ever since.

In fifteen years, I'd not managed to shake her off. All the odds had been stacked against me. But here I was, standing in my apartment on Park Avenue overlooking the whole of the city. I'd always known, even when I wasn't sure where my next meal was coming from, that if I was in control of my life, things would get better.

And they had.

"You thinking about Hightimes?" Angie asked.

I shoved my hands into my pockets. "How could I not be?" The group home where I'd spent the last part of my childhood couldn't have been further from Park Avenue. And it was where I'd developed the drive and determination that had me standing right where I was.

Just under a decade ago I'd graduated high school on a Friday and started my job at a sportswear retailer Saturday morning—the same day I'd moved out of Hightimes and into a rat-infested New Jersey studio. I'd never gone to college, but I was pretty sure today counted as my graduation.

"How many bedrooms?" Angie asked as I followed her through the apartment. The place was bare, but the old moldings, the mix of refinished hardwoods and brand-new marble managed to make it feel warm somehow. The real estate agent had been quick to point out the original details and high-end finishes. But what had made me say yes was the tile in the main kitchen. It had reminded me of my mother—she'd loved to bake and I'd sit on the counter next to her, passing her utensils and tasting as she came up with peanut butter cookies and carrot cake. Her bread was my favorite—even now going by a bakery would conjure up my mother's smile in my memory.

"Five. And two kitchens. Why would anyone want *two* kitchens?"

"One is for staff," Angie replied. "Come on, keep up. You'll need people to help you with this place."

I snorted. "Don't be ridiculous." I wasn't about to pay someone to cook for me when I could make the best PB&J sandwiches in the state of New York.

"You can't just eat peanut butter and jelly sandwiches now that you live here."

I grinned, amused at how Angie could read my mind. "What, like there's a rule? I like them."

"You can't *still* like them. You ate nothing but for two *years*."

After I'd started working, I'd saved every penny I made. I'd begun with buying and selling everything from knock-off sneakers to small pieces of electrical equipment in the hours I wasn't at the store. I'd since moved on to real estate. From my perspective, just because I could buy whatever I wanted didn't mean I would. As far as I was concerned, there was no point in putting money into something that didn't make money. So, no staff. And no more rent checks.

But all the PB&J I wanted.

"But now that you have a home, things can be different," Angie said.

Home. Images of my childhood bedroom—before my parents died—flashed into my mind. It was the last time I'd ever thought of the place I slept as home. I spun, taking in the space. Would this place ever feel like home?

Angie ran her hands along the creamy gold wall opposite the windows. "Even this wallpaper feels like it cost a million bucks. You're going to need to spend some money. I think Ikea stuff is going to look a little weird in this place. I don't even know where you'd shop for things for a place like this." She spun around, her arms out wide. "What are you going to do for furniture?"

"I have my couch being delivered tomorrow. And I bought a mattress and some kitchen stuff from Ikea. I'm done."

I glanced at Angie when she didn't say anything. "That

disgusting couch you got on Craigslist a hundred years ago?" she asked, staring at me blankly. "You're bringing it here?"

"Well, your husband wouldn't help me move it, so no, *I'm* not bringing it here. It's being *delivered* tomorrow morning."

"Unbelievable." Angie threw her hands in the air.

"What?" I could tell she was about to lose her shit, but I didn't know why.

"This place must have cost you ten million."

She was out by eight figures, but I wasn't about to tell her that and make myself sound like a total douchebag. "And you're buying an Ikea bed and having a fifty-year-old Craigslist sofa delivered? What the fuck?"

Angie was always telling me to enjoy my wealth, and I did . . . kinda. I just didn't need expensive stuff.

"Furniture doesn't make me money. This place is an *investment*—one I can live in so I don't have to pay rent." I shrugged. I wasn't being entirely honest. I could rent this place out and live somewhere a lot smaller, but there was something about that tile in the kitchen, about the way the sun came through the huge living room windows in the afternoon, something about the sheer amount of space that made me want to stay. It was almost as if living here would lead to something better, something happier.

Angie had her hands on her hips. "Seriously, you need some stuff. Like vases. Or pillows. Something to make the place . . ."

"If it makes you feel any better, I've hired an art consultant and we're going to a gallery this evening."

Angie scrunched up her face. "A *what* consultant?"

"Someone who's going to find some pictures for the

walls." I nodded once as if I'd just presented her with a royal flush in poker. She couldn't complain about that.

"Because art is an investment, right?" She rolled her eyes.

"So?" I shrugged. "Doesn't mean it won't look nice."

"I think it's a good idea, but you can't just sit on your beat-up sofa in this huge apartment with expensive art on the walls. If you're going to do it, go for it."

"I don't care if it looks weird." Angie was being a little hypocritical. She was notoriously careful with her paycheck. "Surely all that matters is that I have what I need."

"Need? You don't *need* an apartment on Park Avenue or five bedrooms or two kitchens. But that's okay. All I'm saying is relax a little." She pushed me out of the way and I followed her into the kitchen where she began opening and closing cupboard doors. "You've earned it. You don't have to be overly indulgent, but get some things that will make your life more comfortable. This is New York fucking City. If such a thing as an art consultant exists, there must be someone who buys furniture for rich dudes like you."

"My life is very comfortable." Was she serious? "This is Park Avenue, for Christ's sake."

"Okay, what about when you bring women back? You can't fuck them on a mattress you threw on the floor," she said as she hopped up onto the counter.

"I've never brought a woman back to my place. Why would that change now?"

"That's because you've always lived in a hovel," Angie said, staring up at the ceiling as if she were checking for cracks. "Now you don't have to be ashamed of where you live."

"Hey, I've never been ashamed of where I live. I've always paid my rent—that's nothing to be ashamed of. And I don't bring women back to my place because it means I can get up and leave any time I want. There's no way that's going to change."

"Just think about it. Please," she said.

I would, but only because I trusted Angie. Still, I wasn't planning on changing my mind anytime soon. I didn't need *things* to make my life better.

The more you had, the more you had to lose.

CHAPTER TWO
GRACE

Glancing around the gallery, I couldn't help but grin. There was a lot of preparation still to be done before guests started arriving tonight, but things were shaping up and I was so proud and excited that my gallery was holding its first exhibition.

I whipped my head around at the tinkle of the bell that sounded every time anyone came into the gallery. My best friend walked through the door, ignoring the people buzzing about everywhere, and came straight over to me.

"You know you're not the painter, right?" Harper asked, looking me up and down.

"I'm touching up the walls where they're scuffed," I said, holding a can of white paint and a paintbrush. "And I don't want you resting on your laurels." I nodded toward a broom in the corner. "We don't have long. Get busy."

I needed the first exhibition in my newly opened gallery to go well. I was prepared, but the adrenaline racing through my veins had me jumpy. I glanced around the large white space. The catering staff were in the process of setting up and two pictures still rested against the walls.

"I need to decide where to hang those," I said, putting down the paint by the door and pointing at the two paintings. "But I can't decide where they should go." Yesterday, the order had seemed so obvious. Today I kept changing my mind—I wanted everything to be perfect.

"Does it matter?" Harper asked, her face totally blank. "We don't want his shitty work to sell anyway, do we?"

I chuckled and a layer of stress lifted from my body. Harper was right, part of me wanted this exhibition to bomb. The artist I was featuring this evening had been my boyfriend up until about four weeks ago, when I'd returned to the gallery to find him fucking his assistant. In *my* office. He was no longer my boyfriend. Unfortunately, I was still going to have to spend the evening telling everyone how special his art was.

It wasn't the first time I'd been disappointed by a boyfriend. I liked men with talent. Painters, musicians, writers. At school, I'd always done work for extra credit, and as an adult dating struggling artists was the same. Being a girlfriend came with additional responsibility—encourage and support your man until he makes it big. The upside was supposed to be I'd be there when he did. Except they never made it big. Until Steve. He was the first guy who, when I told him how talented and amazing he was, there was no voice at the back of my head saying, "Really? Is he good or do you just like banging him?" Steve was going to have a glittering career.

I hated that his exhibition at *my* gallery would be the start of it.

Unfortunately, opening Grace Astor Fine Art had taken more money than I'd expected and I couldn't afford to take a craft knife to his canvases and kick his cheating ass out of my life.

The bell tinkled again and Harper's sister-in-law, Scarlett, stepped into the gallery. "This is so exciting," she said as she hugged me and then Harper. "Shame about the artist."

"Hey," I said. "You can't say that. I need the place to be a sellout. I have this quarter's rent to pay next week."

It didn't matter that Steve was a dick. I still had to make a splash with this exhibition. I'd already sold a Renoir my grandfather had left me to open this gallery. It had broken my heart; he'd often told me stories of the girl in the painting as if it were me, off having adventures of my own in Paris. Letting go of it had nearly killed me, but my grandfather had left me a letter in his will that said the Renoir should be used for my own adventures, whether they be in my imagination or in real life. So I'd sold it with his blessing but a heavy heart. Still, this gallery was my real-life adventure and something I'd been working toward since college. I wasn't about to let me or my grandfather down.

"You can always ask your dad," Scarlett said. "If it gets too much."

Things were tight, but not *that* tight. I just needed tonight to be a success.

"She's not asking her father," Harper replied for me. "She's doing this on her own."

I'd been so determined to prove to my parents and to myself that I could do this without help, I'd taken out a loan rather than ask my father for money. He wasn't an ATM—even though my mother thought differently—and I'd fail before I treated him like one.

"I just have to separate how I feel about Steve personally from my business goals. I'm not going to like every client I have." I had to cling to that thought and focus on how Steve was going to make me money and attract other artists to the gallery.

I just had to push aside the memory of his pants around his ankles while he fucked an eighteen-year-old against the cabinet in my office.

I put on my white cotton gloves, drew a deep breath, and picked up the canvas in front of me. "This needs to go here." I moved it so it would be one of the first pieces people saw as they came in. "It's the most expensive." I was going to turn on my charm, maybe even exaggerate the little bit of an English accent I had from being born across the ocean, and sell the shit out of these paintings. The sooner I wasn't dependent on Steve, the better.

"And this," I said, picking up the piece I was replacing, "should go over here."

I just needed to get through the next few hours and everything would be *fine*.

"Are you shutting off the back?" Scarlett asked.

The back of the gallery had works by other artists that I'd acquired and a small section, hidden behind a false wall, of my particular favorites. People would have to come right to the end of the gallery to see it. It wasn't that I didn't want anyone to know they were there, but that little collection didn't really belong with the rest of the work. They were more traditional drawings and paintings—portraits and nudes and a pair of photographs of Central Park by a completely unknown photographer. My favorite, the La Touche I'd bought at auction five years ago, had hung in my bedroom before I opened the gallery. It was of a woman sitting at her desk writing a letter. So simple, but I wanted to know who she was writing to, why she seemed to be hiding her paper. It was art like this and my Renoir that had made me want to have my own gallery in the first place. But none of it was "hot" and I needed to go where the money was, at least for now.

"I think I'll keep the whole place open, just in case anyone's interested in anything else." I didn't owe any loyalty to Steve, now did I?

I finished rearranging the paintings and set the handymen to work so I could come back and hang the pictures up when the fixtures were on the wall.

"Right." I put my hands on my hips. "Can you help me move the tables so there's more of a flow into the back?" Hell, not only was I not going to block off the back, I was going to encourage people to take a look at the rest of the gallery. Tonight had gone from showcasing Steve to showcasing Grace Astor Fine Art. I was done pushing men forward, wanting them to shine. It had gotten me precisely nowhere. I was going to put myself first from now on.

It was just good business.

———————

"You look great," Harper said as I stared at myself in the bathroom mirror at the back of the gallery. "Are you ready?"

I was as ready as I ever would be. My red dress fit like a glove and my five-inch nude heels felt like a power source—like I was wearing weapons on my feet.

I checked the time on my phone. Just a few minutes before the exhibition opened. "Yeah, I'm ready. I just hope people come." When I'd envisaged opening a gallery, I'd focused on being able to showcase up-and-coming talent, influencing consultants to choose certain artists for their clients. I'd thought it would be all about the art. But I'd learned that was only the tip of the iceberg. The *business* of art—trying to make sure I had enough money to pay the rent, getting all my tax documents filed, organizing cash flow—took up so much time. I'd really not understood that making a profit would have to be my primary focus. Art was simply how I did that.

"Of course they'll come," Harper said. "You have an eye for talent." We strode back into the gallery space. There was a bar set up toward the back of Steve's paintings and a tray of champagne glasses that had already been poured. "Can you go stand over by the door with that?" I asked one of the waiters. "People should be arriving any minute."

I hoped.

The bell over the door tinkled. It was Violet, Scarlett's sister who she'd gone to collect. Okay, so at least when potential customers came, the place wouldn't be empty. I greeted them and sent them on their way to look at the paintings.

The door chimed again. "Melanie, so nice of you to come," I said, kissing an old friend of my mother's on the cheek. She bought a lot of art and liked to say she'd seen new artists when they were still unknown. If I could get her interested in the gallery, then I'd feel like I had some momentum. She knew a whole lot of wealthy people across the world.

"Of course, I wouldn't miss it." She glanced around. "This is a great place you have here, darling."

"Thank you." I'd finally gotten what I'd been working toward all these years, but women like Melanie would never really know how that felt. She worked by going to charity luncheons and donating money to the needy. It was the work women like her and my mother did. And the kind my father would feel more comfortable with me doing. The idea that his daughter had to concern herself with things like profit and loss distressed him. He wanted me to remain his princess.

"Let me show you this artist's work," I said, picking two glasses of champagne off the tray and handing one to Melanie. "I think you're going to love him." My stomach lurched. Like it or not, I had to convince buyers he had a gift and launch his career despite what he had done. I had to keep reminding myself I was really selling Grace Astor Fine Art, and Steve's success was just a by-product.

Luckily for me, over the course of cocktails, people kept arriving. I moved through the throng of people from one person to the next, encouraging enthusiasm for Steve's work and trying to cement contacts.

It wasn't until Steve crashed through the door an hour after doors opened that I realized he hadn't been around. His eyes were glassy, his overly-long brown hair a little greasy. He had his arm insensitively slung around the shoulders of his assistant. Standing at the door, he clearly thought people had been waiting for him and he was expecting to get a round of applause, but no one knew who he was.

It was my job to effusively introduce him to people, and then his job to charm them. But the images of walking into my office and finding him there stopped me from approaching him. My business savvy could make me fake it when I didn't have to look at him, but I didn't want to hang out with him.

He caught my eye and moved toward me. I quickly made an excuse to the art dealer I was speaking with and escaped, almost knocking down Nina Grecco—one of the most influential art consultants in the city.

"Nina, I'm Grace Astor," I said as I held out my hand. She gave me the same tight smile I'd been dishing out all evening as she took my hand. "I'm so pleased you could come."

I understood the role consultants played. I got that the art world was difficult to navigate and that sometimes people needed an education when they were shopping. But most of Nina's clients just wanted to know what was going to make them money. They weren't interested in the art, only the dividends it could pay. Art had been an investment for hundreds of years, but I still hoped that rich romantics were going to fall in love with everything this gallery had to offer. I wanted clients who would have an *emotional* investment in what they were buying. Art wasn't stocks or gold bullion—it was far more personal, or at least, it should be.

"Ms. Astor, this is my client, Sam Shaw." Nina put her hand on the arm of the man standing next to her.

I trailed my eyes up to see a man who was around thirty, with dirty blond hair and deep brown eyes staring back at me. "Mr. Shaw, it's very nice to meet you." He smiled but it didn't reach his eyes. He looked bored, as if the evening was something to be endured rather than enjoyed.

"Grace, this artist tonight is just on the cusp of breaking out, isn't he?" Nina asked, while still gazing at Mr. Shaw.

An eye roll nearly escaped me but I managed to rein it in. "That's right. There's a real buzz about him at the moment and some very important collectors here tonight." I slipped into the rhythm I'd developed along the course of the evening. "He's a very painterly painter who clearly has his roots in abstract expressionism." Mr. Shaw didn't meet my eye. He stared at the canvas wearing a confused expression. Nina was wasting her time.

"Gracie," Steve's voice boomed out behind me and caught Mr. Shaw's attention.

I tried not to let the uncomfortableness I felt show. "Let me introduce you to the artist," I said.

Steve's arms went around my waist and I squirmed. "Hey, Gracie."

"Steve, please meet Mr. Shaw and Nina Grecco." As subtly as I could, I pushed against his chest, trying to break free from his grasp. He ignored me, holding me tightly. "I was just going to tell them about this piece." I pointed to Nina's left. "Do you want to give us some more background?" I smiled and caught Mr. Shaw's eye. He looked between us

17

as if he were trying to figure out what was going on.

Steve began to talk about his inspiration for the collection while I tried to wriggle free from his clutches.

"Ms. Astor, would you please show me around your gallery?" Mr. Shaw asked, interrupting Steve in full flow. I smiled. Intentional or not, I couldn't have been more grateful for his rescue.

"Do you want me to come?" Nina asked.

"We'll manage just fine," Mr. Shaw replied before I said anything. "Lead the way." Steve released me and I headed to the back of the gallery, Mr. Shaw following.

I stopped as the crowd thinned out and turned to him. "This space at the back has a mixture of artists," I said, and Mr. Shaw shoved his hands into his pockets and nodded. "What kind of art do you like?" I asked taking an opportunity to look at him more closely. Instead of being able to decide whether or not he was handsome, I was struck by his expression—the way he was looking at me. It was almost the way a person might look at a painting—first to get an overall impression and then more closely at what the painting was trying to say.

Our eyes unlocked as he looked around.

A frown formed on his face. "I have no idea."

While he was otherwise occupied, I looked at him closely but I couldn't place him. The wealthy in New York was a pretty small number. Everything from the watch hanging heavily on his wrist to his soft leather shoes told me this guy clearly had money—he was an Upper East Sider. But I'd never met him before. I would have remembered. He was tall, well over

Steve's six feet. Broad shouldered, Mr. Shaw filled out his suit very nicely. The slight curl of his hair in his otherwise perfect façade suggested something a little wild about him. The sound of someone's deep belly laugh made me realize I was staring at him and I turned away.

Mr. Shaw began to walk farther away from the exhibition, toward my secret space, and I followed him as he poked his head around the wall. "Is this part of it too?" he asked.

"Part of the gallery? Yes. But the work behind the partition doesn't really fit with the rest of the pieces. I just like them."

He glanced at me and then turned his attention back to my hidden works. I followed his gaze. "This is a La Touche. An impressionist oil painting. And this"—I pointed at the Degas—"is an original lithograph, signed by Degas, who, as you probably know, was famous for painting ballerinas. He was a contemporary of La Touche."

"And these?" He nodded to the pair of photographs.

"These are recent and not particularly valuable, but the photographer was homeless for a period of time, and I think you can see it in his work. He takes pictures of New York through the eyes of someone who's slept on the street. He sees the contrast between the beauty and the harshness this city offers."

He refocused on me, his eyes narrowing slightly just before he spoke. "And you like them because of his story, or because of the photographs themselves?" he asked.

I thought about it for a moment. "Both." I shrugged. "The photographs stand on their own—they're both pretty and gritty at the same time." I glanced at Mr. Shaw, who was still inspecting me. "But I think knowing the artist's story adds something to them. He knows this city like most of us don't and I think you can tell."

I lifted my head a little, not wanting to be found lacking under his inspection.

Silence pulsed between us. Did he like what he saw?

"As I said, these are kinda passion projects for me. They're not necessarily meant for people to buy. The rest of the gallery is more contemporary."

"They're not for sale?" he asked, his tone a little confused.

"Well, yes they are." Of course it was great if people liked them, I just didn't expect people who liked the work in the front of the gallery to like this stuff. "I guess it's not the main focus of the gallery."

He looked at me again and it was as if his stares had built up into something more—into something tangible and I had to stifle a shiver.

Something in his non-response was intriguing, almost as if he were keeping something back—maybe there was a little Batman underneath the Wall Street façade.

"You don't like the rest of the work in the gallery?" he asked, looking over my head. "Just this little section here?"

"Of course I like all the things in the gallery. Steve's very talented and the pieces back here are all very collectable." Had I talked myself out of a sale?

"But you're not passionate about them." His eyes were on my mouth as he spoke, and I swept my finger over my lips, almost feeling the burn of his gaze.

"It's not that." Wasn't it? He'd summed it up pretty well. "I just need to wear a business hat. Everything can't be about what I'm passionate about."

He nodded and I smiled awkwardly. I'd not explained myself very well, but I hadn't been prepared for the question. I hadn't really expected anyone to come back here.

Silently, we wandered back toward the edge of the crowd where Nina was waiting for us. When she pulled Mr. Shaw back into the exhibition, I went to find my friends. I needed a five-minute break from the constant smiling and I wanted to be able to breathe again after holding myself so tightly under Mr. Shaw's inspection. When I reached Scarlett and Harper, they both squeezed me tight and congratulated me. Over Harper's shoulder, I found Mr. Shaw ignoring the art and looking straight back at me, his stare unrelenting. He wasn't embarrassed to be caught, but the glance wasn't flirtatious either. I couldn't decide if he was trying to communicate something or he was simply still studying me. "Do I have my skirt tucked in my panties or spinach in my teeth or something?" I whispered to Scarlett and Harper.

They both looked me up and down. "No, you look perfect," Harper said.

"Beautiful," Scarlett said. "Why?"

I shook my head. "Just, that guy over there is staring and I can't work out why."

Harper looked around and found Mr. Shaw in the crowd immediately. "That one?" she asked. "The really tall, hot one who wears a suit almost as well as *my* man?"

"He's not that hot," I said. He *was* handsome, just not someone I found attractive. *Normally.*

"He's extraordinarily hot and it looks like he's hot *for you*."

"He looks angry," I replied. "And anyway, definitely not my type." Our exchange had been a little odd—less small talk and more existential.

"That's for sure," Harper said. "He looks like he pays his own rent and goes to the barber regularly. You wouldn't want any of that, would you?" Harper's and my taste in men were polar opposites—a prerequisite of a friendship that was going to survive teendom into adult-hood. Too many friends had fallen over the hurdle of the same man.

"Different strokes," I said. I'd always resisted the kind of man my parents wanted for me. Someone safe. A doctor, a lawyer from the right family, someone from the Upper East Side.

I'd never seen the appeal of a suit in the way Harper did. While there was no denying Max King, her husband, was handsome, he just wasn't my type. I liked a guy I could daydream with, who was spontaneous, someone bohemian who could constantly surprise me. I didn't want some guy who thought they could buy and sell people just like stocks and bonds—or art.

But Batman? He didn't seem to fit into either mold. He dressed in a suit, but the questions he asked, the way he looked at me—it was as if he wanted to strip away anything inconsequential and dig deeper, into my soul.

Maybe I'd like to let him.

CHAPTER THREE
SAM

One week since the exhibition at Grace Astor Fine Art and I couldn't remember a single piece of art that had been featured that night. Grace Astor, however? With her full mouth, curving waist and confused smile? Her I couldn't seem to forget. My office was in midtown so when I'd finished for the day, I decided to take a walk and pay Grace a visit. The only art I did vaguely remember were the pieces she'd hidden away. I wanted to see them and her again.

The bell above the door dinged as I entered the gallery, seemingly at odds with the modern paintings on the wall. Despite my distaste for the work, the little red stickers below each painting told me the exhibition had been successful.

I had no interest in anything at the front of the gallery, so I strode toward the back to find Ms. Astor's hidden stash.

"Good afternoon," a woman called from behind me over the clip of heels. I turned to find Ms. Astor walking briskly toward me wearing a tight blue dress that hit just below the knee and thick, black-rimmed glasses. She was like a fantasy Lois Lane, though something about this woman's frown, the determined look on her face, told me she was the hero of her story, not the sidekick.

"Ms. Astor," I said, hoping she'd remember me.

She slowed and surprise replaced her frown. "Mr. Shaw, isn't it?"

I put out my hand to greet her. "Indeed." I flashed her a grin. Angie had told me my smile could make a woman's panties drop from ten yards away. Unfortunately, Grace didn't look impressed, just confused. She took my hand, and I gripped it tightly, holding on a little too long.

"How can I help you?" she asked, as she glanced down to our hands. I released her and she exhaled.

"I came to have another look," I said, pointing to her hidden collection. "Do you mind?"

"Not at all," she replied as we walked toward the back.

"Did the exhibition do well?" I asked, hoping she'd give something away in her response about her relationship with the artist. His hands had been all over her before she'd given me a tour of her gallery.

"Yes, almost everything sold that night or in the following days once the reviews were published."

I nodded, trying to leave space for her to say something more. Wanting to watch her mouth curl around the words she spoke.

"I have four pieces left if you'd like me to show you?"

"Like I said, not my thing."

We stood in front of the hidden collection.

"You like your art more classic," she said as we both stared at the art. It wasn't a question.

I stuffed my hands in my pockets. "Honestly, I don't know. I'm new to all this." Ordinarily, I was very careful about what I revealed to people. I'd learned quickly that business and Manhattan were full of bullshitters who didn't want to be reminded of their own flaws and weaknesses, which meant you couldn't reveal yours. It was a game—if everyone kept pretending, no one would be found out. As much as I was an outsider, I proficiently played the role of someone who belonged.

"New to what?" Grace asked.

"Art," I replied. "I'm not sure what I like."

"But you like these?" She nodded her head toward the paintings we were looking at.

I nodded. "I guess." I was drawn in by their intimacy and mystery, but I had no idea whether or not they were investment pieces.

My attention wandered from Grace to the art. These works were small, discreet, personal. Although it didn't seem as though any of the pieces were connected—they were clearly by different artists—they were subtle, almost as if not meant for an audience. The intimacy of them made them all the more compelling because they seemed to tell me about the person who created them. The rest of the gallery was full of loud, attention-seeking pieces that shouted their importance the moment I walked in—there was no mystery in them.

But these told me much more about Grace. Four nudes, all drawings; what looked like a proper painting—Grace had said it was done in oil—of a woman at a desk; a small painting of a harbor and the two photographs of the city.

"It's a bit of an eclectic collection," Grace said, tilting

her head to the right as she stared at the woman at the desk.

"Yes, but I like that." It was as if I could sense they were her choices—they felt personal. "They're for sale, right?"

Grace captured the corner of her bottom lip between her teeth before answering, "Yep, they're for sale." She sounded unsure, reluctant. Was it that she didn't want to sell the artwork at all? Or did she just not want to sell it to me?

I bent to look at the nude on the right.

"Well, like I said at the opening, they don't really go together. The photographs are the most modern of the selection. The photographer has had some attention recently, but he's not got a huge following at the moment."

"Tell me a little more about his pieces?" They were the only photographs in the gallery that I could see.

"Well, they're beautiful."

I wanted her reason to be more than that. I liked what she'd told me about the background of the photographer. "And?" I asked. I was taken in by each of the pieces in this section, but the photographs were the most interesting. Grace had liked the artist's story. Her interest in a homeless photographer indicated an empathy I didn't come across very often.

She glanced up at me quickly. "I like that he still looks for the beauty, despite having seen such darkness. And I think you can see the tragedy in them but also . . . *hope*."

My breath caught. This woman was someone who saw beyond the surface, and I wanted to know more about her.

"And with these nudes . . ." She circled her fingers toward the two on the left. "At first glance, they're almost carelessly put on the page, but if you look closer, and you notice the turn of her head, the artist is fascinated by her."

I knew that feeling.

"But I don't know if they're any good," I said.

Grace transferred her weight onto one leg, pushing her hip out and emphasizing the curves of her body, and crossed her arms, almost as if I'd offended her. A small grin tugged at the corners of her mouth. Had I managed to chip away at that armor she wore? She shrugged a shoulder. "If you like them, why does it matter?"

I drew in a breath. "Because I don't want to lose money."

"Of course," she said, her tone suddenly more professional. "Well you won't. Not on any of these."

"I'll take them," I said, straightening up.

"Which?" she asked, her frown returning.

I smiled at her, and I thought I saw a hint of a pink in her cheeks in response. Did my attention make her blush? I could only hope. "All of them."

"All of them?" she asked, breathless. "Are you sure?"

I tilted my head. Why was she hesitating? Did she think I wasn't good enough to buy them? "Is that a problem?"

Pushing her glasses back up her nose, she said, "No, not at all. I just thought you'd come to see the Steve Todd exhibition."

"That was Nina's idea," I said, stepping toward her. "Not my thing." Not that I knew what my thing was. "Seemed like a big gamble to spend money on something I didn't understand and felt no desire to know more about." Without thinking, I brushed a strand of hair away from her face.

Our eyes locked and Grace's eyes narrowed slightly as if she was considering her next move. She was trying to figure me out and I liked that.

"So, you want these instead?" she asked even though we'd established that I did. She stepped back, her eyes flickering from my face to my feet almost as if she were trying to decide whether or not I was coming on to her. As if I wasn't making it entirely obvious.

I knew from experience what it felt like not to be important to anyone and instead of letting that eat me alive, I used the knowledge to make myself powerful. Attention was seductive. Angie kept telling me I should insure my face, but I knew it wasn't my looks that made me so successful in the game of seduction. Women understood I'd do whatever it took to succeed—in or out of bed—and were pulled in by the attention and focus. It was the same in business. When I wanted to make a deal, it was flattery, puffing up egos, that got them across the finish line. People liked to feel important—men, women, in business or the bedroom.

I kept my eyes on her and she fiddled with her glasses. Usually I'd elicited a smile by now, a coy tilt of the head. But Grace Astor was still unsure.

"Okay, well if I can just ask you to follow me."

"Anywhere," I replied.

She hesitated just long enough that I knew she'd heard me and turned on her heel and clipped back toward a desk. Maybe she was married. I glanced at her left hand. No ring. I watched her full, tight ass sway as she walked. Boyfriend?

She fumbled about in the drawers below her desk,

giving me an even better view of the curve of her body and her breasts falling forward, pressing against the opening of her dress. "Here," she said, pulling out a pad of paper. "If I can just take some details, I can arrange to have the pieces delivered. You live in the city?" she asked, shutting down just as I'd thought we'd begun to have a conversation.

"Park Avenue."

At that revelation, I got an eye roll. "Of course."

Jesus, did she know she was being rude? "Is that a problem?" I asked.

"Oh, no, sorry. I just . . . When would be a good time to arrange delivery?"

"I presume you'll be there to oversee installation?"

Her mouth opened slightly, her generous lips almost inviting me to stroke my thumb over them. For a second I thought she'd say no; instead she smiled. Not the genuine twinkle of the smile she'd worn when I confessed I didn't know anything about the paintings I was buying, but a fake, have-a-nice-day, pleasure-doing-business-with-you smile. "Sure. Of course, Mr. Shaw. When's convenient?"

I never pushed for something I wanted when I knew I wasn't going to get it. But I wanted to know more about Grace. Perhaps she could replace Nina and be my art consultant. If I asked her now, she'd say no. So I'd wait. When she came to my apartment, she'd have all my attention and focus and I'd make sure she said yes.

CHAPTER FOUR
GRACE

I stood outside the building I'd grown up in, this time at the goods delivery entrance, waiting for the van with Mr. Shaw's paintings to arrive. I'd been determined not to just be a spoiled Park Avenue princess and spend my life going to charity luncheons, but somehow I'd still managed to find myself back here. But it was on different terms. I had my own business and I was making my own money. I checked my phone. No message. I folded my arms in front of my chest. How was it taking the driver this long to come from the gallery? I didn't want to keep Mr. Shaw waiting.

While it wasn't unusual for a gallery to oversee delivery, I had expected Nina to be involved with this part. If Mr. Shaw was paying her, then why did he need my help? I shouldn't complain. He'd been a good customer. Steve's exhibition had done well, but because he was just starting out (and because I'd been sleeping with him), I'd agreed to only a quarter of the commission I'd normally take from the sales.

We hadn't put anything in writing, and all the money had been paid to me, so I *could* insist on taking a standard cut, but a deal was a deal. Even though I hated him, I didn't want to lower myself to his level. I'd be careful not to be so stupid again. Steve had offered me no apology, no explanation. He hadn't tried to patch things up, either. He just acted as if we'd never been more than friends, as if I was just the gallery owner where he'd had his first exhibition. He'd switched so easily and effortlessly I wondered if he'd ever had any real feelings for me. We'd been dating exclusively for over nine months. He'd been living in my apartment for all that time.

Maybe he'd just been using me all along.

But ruminating on how bad of person he was wasn't going to get me anywhere. I needed to move on and concentrate on the future, on Grace Astor Fine Art, and on clients like Mr. Shaw. Mr. Shaw who I was trying not to find attractive.

The truck pulled up and I texted Mr. Shaw to tell him we were on our way up. I'd hired three delivery guys to help me; one to stay with the truck and two to deliver the work. None of the art was big enough to need two people, but it would be good to see how this delivery arrangement worked. Hopefully this would be the first of many across Manhattan.

"Hey, guys. Let's get this door open and make sure nothing's damaged," I said.

"It'll be fine. We know what we're doing." The older guy rolled up the back shutter to reveal the pieces securely fastened to the sides of the truck.

"Good. If you hand me that one," I said, pointing to the Degas, all packaged in paper and bubble wrap, "and you take one each, that'd be great. I don't want you bringing up more than one at a time, okay?"

We walked into the service entrance to the building, and Victor, the security guard, held the door open for us.

"Thanks, Victor."

"No problem, Miss Astor. I just saw your mother come through the lobby."

I hadn't told my parents I'd be in the building today. My father would be at work and I avoided one on ones with my mother as much as possible. "I'm actually here to deliver these paintings to Mr. Shaw."

"Oh, the new guy." Victor nodded. "Okay, well you know this place as well as I do. If you need anything, let me know."

I smiled at him and made my way to one of the service lifts.

As we arrived at Mr. Shaw's apartment, the door was already propped open with a box. Was he just moving in? Victor said he was new, but anyone who'd not been in the building at least twenty years was new to Victor.

"Hello?" I called from the threshold.

"Come in." Mr. Shaw's voice boomed from the other end of the corridor. I turned briefly to the two men behind me and stepped inside. The hallway looked devoid of any signs of life. There was nothing on the walls. No console tables or rugs or furniture of any kind. Perhaps he *was* just moving in. I walked toward the light, unsure where we'd find Mr. Shaw.

As I reached the doors to the living space, I found him facing the New York cityscape, the sleeves of his white dress shirt rolled up, his hands stuffed in his pockets. Okay, Scarlett and Harper had been right, he *was* handsome—in an obvious sort of way. He might not be my type, but I still knew a good-looking man when I saw one. And the way he'd studied me at the gallery was . . . perhaps I'd been imagining it but it was almost like a physical touch—like his focus had mass. Watching him look out onto the rooftops, he was tall and broad and his ass was a little tighter than I remembered. I liked the way the ends of his curls shimmered in the light. I'd thought he might be flirting with me when he'd come to the gallery but I hadn't been sure. He spun and I gasped, worried that somehow he'd know I'd been breaking him down piece by piece, as if he were a painting I was passing judgement on.

"Grace," he said as he walked toward me, his heavy gaze coating me until I looked away as if I'd been staring directly at the sun.

I turned toward the two delivery men. "Just put those down and bring the rest up, one at a time."

As they walked out, I turned to Mr. Shaw, who was still staring at me. I took a step back. There was an intensity in his attention that was unnerving and uncomfortable. But at the same time it felt good. It felt like I wanted to stand in his way a little longer.

Should I have one of the men stay?

"I thought Nina might be here," I said, glancing around. If Nina had been involved, she wouldn't have had Mr. Shaw buy such a mixture of artwork. But I wanted to know why, if he was focused on keeping his money safe, he'd made these purchases without her. The room was completely empty of furniture apart from a beaten-up leather chesterfield set opposite the windows. There were no rugs, no TV. Not even a potted plant.

"I fired Nina."

Wow. Nina was the most sought after in the business. I doubt she'd ever been fired before. "I'm sorry to hear that." I put down the small print, concentrating on keeping my expression neutral.

"Don't be. She told me what I wanted to hear. I prefer people who tell me the truth." He revealed his values and where he put his energy with every sentence he spoke.

"She's very sought after." Although he'd satisfied my curiosity, and he'd given me more detail than he needed to, I still wanted to know more. But not about Nina, about him. "She doesn't often accept new clients."

"You think I made a mistake?" Did he really care what I thought about him firing Nina?

"No." I shrugged. "I mean, I have no idea. You can choose who you work with."

"Exactly," he said, holding my gaze and I felt it slip over me, like warm water.

I shivered.

"Are you nervous?"

"No." I rubbed my arms as if I were cold.

He grinned and nodded. "I see," he said. He knew I was lying.

I frowned. I wasn't sure I wanted to know what he saw. "Where did you want these?" I had to focus.

"Aren't you here to tell me that?"

"You have no preference? Bedrooms, living space?" Why buy paintings if he didn't even have a table to put his coffee cup on?

He offered no explanation for the emptiness.

"Not really. You have free range."

"Okay, well I'll get them unwrapped and then we can decide together. You'll know the light better than me."

I bent down and began to unwrap the Degas I'd brought up. I hated to see my secret collection of paintings go—particularly the La Touche—but I was a business-owner now. These works weren't for my enjoyment, and though Mr. Shaw clearly wasn't a connoisseur, I liked that in a way. There was something about the art that had drawn him in. Maybe Grace Astor Fine Art had triggered a passion for art in Mr. Shaw—perhaps I *would* be touching people with my gallery and not just making money.

As the delivery guys brought up the rest of the paintings, I unwrapped each piece from their cardboard, bubble wrap and tissue paper trying to concentrate on something other than Sam Shaw. Eventually, all eight were lined up against the wall opposite the windows.

"So, are you planning to buy anything more?" I asked. I wanted to make sure I didn't take up space earmarked for anything else.

"I don't know," he said as he stood next to me, so close I could feel the heat of his body. "Maybe. I need to find someone to help me. Like I said, I don't know anything about art."

"But you like these pieces," I said, glancing at his sharp jaw as he fixed his stare on the paintings. "Art doesn't have to be about what critics say is good. You can just have an emotional reaction rather than an intellectual one."

"Passion over logic?" he asked.

I couldn't stop my grin. "Is such a concept so alien to you, Mr. Shaw?"

"Call me Sam." His tone was slightly curt. "You think I'm not passionate?"

The conversation seemed to have veered off course. I hadn't meant the comment to be personal. I felt as though I was tumbling down a rabbit hole into unknown territory. "I don't know you," I replied, wondering if I'd created a dead end in this conversation.

A beat of silence passed between us.

"I think the combination of the two things is where I'm most effective," he said. Again, it seemed like an unnecessarily personal revelation. But it drew me to him and I couldn't be sure that he hadn't designed it that way.

He turned to face me. "Is your reaction to art emotional or intellectual?" he asked.

"It can be either or both."

"And this?" He swept his large tan hands toward the lined-up works.

"Both," I said simply. I felt as if I was giving something away by admitting it, and it seemed he knew it.

"Ahhh," he said. "Passion and logic."

I didn't respond and he didn't ask any more.

"In your gut, which is your favorite?" I asked. I needed to get these pictures placed so I could get out of there. The way he got so personal so quickly made me feel uncomfortable. It wasn't just his nearness, or his intense stare. It was as if he were trying to unmask me without me noticing. But I had noticed. And my uncomfortableness existed because I wasn't sure that he'd like what he found when he looked underneath. And for some reason that mattered. I wanted him to like me, find me attractive.

"I like all of them."

"Or you wouldn't have bought them, right?" As soon as the words were out, I realized how sarcastic they sounded.

He chuckled and I relaxed. "I'm not sure about that. Like I said, I'm new at this art stuff. I really want to make sure I make good investments."

"But you fired Nina." I crossed my arms in front of me. I didn't know what I was doing wondering about this man. I should focus on my job not his hard body or deep brown eyes. "She's the best at finding great investment pieces."

"I did."

"And you don't know whether what you bought here," I said, tilting my head toward the unwrapped works, "is a good investment."

He drew in a breath and shoved his hands in his pockets, turning away from me. "You're right. I'm not following my own logic."

Silence stretched between us. I needed to get better with clients if I was going to make this work. I was insulting him and he was taking it. I was testing him—trying to elicit a reaction from him I wouldn't like so I could turn away from him.

His eyes flickered around my face and finally he said, "I'd like you to be my advisor. To replace Nina."

It was the last thing I was expecting him to say. "I can't," I blurted.

He didn't react. I wanted to apologize, to explain that the

gallery was all-consuming and I was under a lot of pressure to turn a profit so I could make my loan payment. And I didn't want to piss Nina off—she could ruin me if she told people I stole clients. No consultant would want anything to do with me. And him. I couldn't spend more time with *him*. He took up too much of my energy, my thoughts.

"I think the nudes would be good in your dressing room," I said, pretending he hadn't just asked me to help him, and that I hadn't so rudely refused.

"Won't that make me look like a pervert?" he asked.

I laughed and my whole body relaxed. "I hadn't thought of that. Well, can you show me around or are we hanging everything in here?"

Without a word, Mr. Shaw headed back into the hallway and opened the first door on the right. "That's a study." The room was empty other than for the taupe rug and blinds.

On the opposite side of the hallway, he opened another door. "This is the second guest bedroom." Empty, again. Did anyone actually live here?

Another guest bedroom was the same as was the room he said would be used for storage. But of what?

He opened the final door nearest the entrance and held out his arm, inviting me inside. I glanced up at him as I stepped forward, but he was looking at the ground, almost as if he were bracing for my reaction.

It was a huge space. Silver-gray carpet covered the floor and under the window was a mattress—no frame—with plain, pale blue sheets and a stack of books next to it. I glanced at him but he wore a blank expression.

I walked farther into the room and looked more carefully at the books, desperate to get more information about this man who at times seemed so controlled and all about business and then wanted to talk to me about passion and made me laugh. There were some thrillers I'd never heard of, and a copy of *The Count of Monte Cristo* sat on top, dog eared and clearly read over and over.

Who was this man?

I turned full circle to make sure I hadn't missed something, but, no. There was nothing in this apartment but a couch that should have been donated to the Salvation Army, a mattress and some books.

Mr. Shaw lived like a squatter.

And yet the man owned an apartment at one of the most expensive addresses in New York and paid me for the art I sold him with an American Express black card.

"And your dressing room?" I asked.

"Through there." He pointed to an archway. I stepped through to find his wardrobe full. Custom suits. Handmade shoes. But no wall space where I would want any of my paintings to sit.

"I think the office would be good for the nudes," I said, absentmindedly reaching out to feel one of the suit jackets.

"Sure, whatever you think."

"Do you have any idea where you'll put the furniture?" I asked from over my shoulder as I made my way back up the corridor.

We stopped at the doorway to the office and he shook his head, glancing again at his shoes. "No. Not yet."

With an empty apartment of blank walls, it wasn't difficult to find space for any of the pictures, and within twenty minutes I'd decided where everything should go.

"And the La Touche, I think that should be in the dining room." I'd saved the best until last.

He nodded. He'd offered no opinion or information as I'd moved pieces from one resting spot to another. He'd just watched me. We hadn't shared pleasantries, or talked about the weather. I'd worked in silence. But somehow it became more comfortable the more time I was there, as if we were getting to know each other even though we weren't speaking.

I held the frame against the wall. "What do you think?" I asked.

"I like it," he replied with a nod. We'd had a breakthrough—I'd managed to coax an opinion from him.

I grinned, pleased that he seemed to like my favorite piece. "You have a beautiful smile," he said and I looked away. Our interaction had felt oddly personal since I'd met him but this was the first time it felt as if a line had been crossed.

"Thank you." I put the painting on the floor, resting it carefully against the wall.

"You ever wonder who she's writing to?" he asked as he stepped closer to my side.

I couldn't dampen my smile. "I think she's writing to a lover, or someone she wants to be her lover."

"What would she be saying to someone who she wanted to be her lover? Is she trying to seduce him?" he asked. I wasn't sure if he was talking about the painting.

41

The air between us thickened and the heat of his body warmed me. This was more intense that just flirting. I could feel the weight of him almost touching me. Was that why he'd insisted I bring the paintings and advise on where to hang them? Did he want me?

"Whoever the painter is, he's trying to figure it out as much as we are," I whispered.

"I think *you* like trying to figure people out," he said, brushing a strand of hair from my face and tucking it behind my ear. He'd done the same thing at the gallery. This time it wasn't enough. I wanted more than his fingertips scattering across my skin.

But he *was* right. I'd been trying to figure him out from the moment I'd seen his empty apartment. He was rich, handsome and confident, but there was an undercurrent of sadness about him, reflected in this echoey place, that I couldn't explain but I was drawn to.

"I'm going to kiss you now."

To someone watching a video of us, not having experienced what had been passing between us since I arrived, his declaration would be out of place and inappropriate but being here with him, when he said it, I realized he was always going to kiss me.

I liked that he'd given me warning but not asked my permission. Perhaps in his lips I'd understand him more.

Towering over me, he took my face in his hands and pressed his mouth against mine once, then pulled back and kissed me again, harder this time. His touch created a hum across the surface of my skin and my body sagged despite the voice inside my head saying, *Who is this man? I don't find men like him attractive.*

But I wanted him to kiss me.

My arms circled his waist, stroking up his broad back, over the muscles tight under his shirt, so different from the slight men I was used to dating. Instead of finding it strange or uncomfortable, it felt right, like every other man's touch had been erased by his.

He stroked his thumbs over my cheekbones, then reached around to the small of my back and pulled my body against his. I gasped and he smiled against my mouth. In that moment he had all the power, not because he took it, but because I gave it to him, willingly.

His tongue pushed between my lips and I tilted my head back, wanting more of him. My knees weakened and my mind and body became unsteady as if he were taking all my energy—all my self-control.

He gripped my waist and pulled me up. "You okay?" he asked, his stare boring into me.

I nodded, fixing my gaze on his chest, his broad, hard chest. What was I doing? How had I ended up in this man's arms, and why did it feel so good?

"Can I ask you a question?" I asked.

He chuckled and released my waist. Cool air hit my shirt-covered back and I was pissed that I'd caused him to pull away. "You've been dying to since you walked in."

"How do you know?"

Scraping his fingers through his hair, he took half a step back. "I'm good at reading people."

"Oh yeah? So what questions have I been desperate to ask you then?" He clearly thought he knew everything.

"You're trying to work out who I am, and why this apartment is empty. Why there's a beat-up old couch and a mattress on the floor, yet the closet is full of custom suits."

I concentrated on the curve of his mouth as he spoke. Each word seemed so deliberate, pushing out of those perfectly full lips.

"Oh yes, and you're attracted to me, but for some reason you're fighting it." He smoothed his hand around his neck. "I've yet to put all the pieces together on that one."

I shivered. Who was he to think he could dip into my brain and tell me what I was thinking, even if everything he'd said was completely accurate? Arrogant but accurate.

"I have to leave," I said, making my way toward the hallway. "I'll send the handyman around tomorrow to put the pictures up. I've marked exactly where they should go."

I glanced back to see him shove his hands into his pockets, his smile dimmed. "I meant what I said about wanting you to help me add to my collection."

"I can't do that," I called over my shoulder.

"Don't let a kiss, even if it was the best kiss you've ever had, get in the way of business."

What a piece of work. Did he just go around flirting with strange women, telling them what a great kisser he was? I stopped at the hallway entrance and turned to look at him. "You think it was the best kiss I ever had?" He might have been right. I couldn't remember a kiss that reverberated through my whole body the way his had. It'd literally weakened me and made me want more.

"I know it was the kiss of *my* life. So I'm thinking it can't have been so bad for you, either." His tone was teasing and confessional at the same time—it almost sounded like he meant it.

I rolled my eyes in the most obvious and exaggerated way I could. "Do women really buy that?" I turned back to the door, desperate to get out of there. What was I doing, kissing my clients? Wanting to kiss them a little longer?

"I'll call you tomorrow about the consultant thing. Sleep on it." That didn't justify a response. I'd told him no. I was grateful for his business, it meant I could make rent this quarter, but it didn't mean I should spend any more time with him. I'd kissed him and that was bad enough. Who knew what would happen if I had to work with him more closely?

He could find another art consultant.

CHAPTER FIVE
SAM

"You seem distracted," Angie said, staring at her menu. Despite it being busy, we'd still managed to snag the best booth at our favorite old-school diner in downtown. Angie's husband was working so we'd used the opportunity to eat out. There was something about the familiarity of this place that kept us coming back. That and the burgers.

I shook my head. "Nope, just hungry. Why are you studying the menu? You know exactly what's on there. Hasn't changed in like ten years."

Fact was, I *was* a little distracted. Grace had left my apartment yesterday before I'd gotten a chance to organize my thoughts and convince her to become my art consultant. She was beautiful, and I'm sure had her fair share of admirers. I couldn't figure out what was stopping her from letting go with me.

Angie looked up and set the menu down. "You're working something out," she said.

"Stop trying to read me, it pisses me off," I snapped, waving a waitress over. "Let's order." When we were teenagers, Angie and I used to sneak into town on the weekends. We'd walked the streets of midtown, our heads tilted back so we could take in the skyscrapers. I'd always said I'd own one of the buildings one day. So far, I had three in midtown, two in downtown and now my place—my first investment into residential property. After our long walks around the city, we'd always ended up at this diner and ordered a milkshake to share. Those days of daydreaming were how I'd survived—I'd had to believe the future would be better than the present.

"Yeah, it's not like you do that to me and everyone else, all the time." Angie rolled her eyes. Grace had made the same gesture when I'd told her she was the kiss of my life.

She'd thought I was trying to seduce her, and she was right, but that didn't mean it wasn't true. Most people would have asked me straight out why I didn't have any furniture. Why I was living in 740 Park Avenue but sleeping on a mattress on the floor. And although I usually didn't give two shits what people thought about me, for some reason having Grace walk around my empty apartment had been a little uncomfortable. I shouldn't have to explain that I didn't care about filling my home with lots of fancy furniture, or that I liked my beat-up old sofa and I didn't need anything more than a mattress on my floor.

And yet, I'd wanted her to understand.

"I'll have a cheeseburger, fries and a chocolate milkshake." I ordered first out of self-defense. If I didn't, Angie would never make up her mind.

"I'll have the same, but can I get a side of onion rings and the mac and cheese?" The waitress scribbled down the order. "Oh, and can I get extra tomato?"

"Am I going to have to roll you home?" I asked. "Your

husband hates this place, so I know you aren't ordering for him."

"I'm hungry." She shrugged. "Stop avoiding my question and tell me what's on your mind."

"I bought some paintings," I said, trying to deflect her attention.

"Just the stuff your consultant told you to buy?"

"I guess." I slid the menus to the side and traced my fingernail around the metal surround of the table. I couldn't remember the last time I'd lied to Angie. I was always completely honest with her. But we never discussed women in any detail because they were rarely on my mind. Unlike Grace.

"And are you going to buy some furniture? I know you're sentimental about the couch but maybe put it in the office or something." Angie's nails tapped on the countertop.

"I'm not sentimental about the couch; what are you talking about?" I wasn't sentimental about *things* at all. That's why I didn't have much.

"Then why on earth do you still have it? It's falling apart."

"It's perfectly okay," I replied. "If you make sure the cushions are the right way up, you can't see the holes. There's no reason not to hang on to it."

"Whatever."

Our food arrived and Angie pounced on the mac and cheese as if she hadn't eaten for weeks. She always had a healthy appetite but even for her she seemed a little overenthusiastic.

"Buying furniture is like burning money. The couch I have is fine." I didn't need to live any differently just because my address had changed. Although it would have been nice to have been able to offer Grace a drink. Maybe I'd order some wine glasses. I didn't even have silverware at the moment. I'd taken a couple of the office mugs and brought them home with me, but I was a simple man. I didn't need much.

"You don't want a house warming?" Angie asked. "Seems a shame to have such a fancy place and no one to show it off to."

"A house warming?" I chuckled. "Who would I invite? I only know you and Chas." Angie and her husband were my only friends. I didn't have drinking buddies. I'd not gone to college. And aside from Angie, there was certainly no one from my past I wanted to stay in touch with.

"A business party, then?" she asked.

I took a bite of my burger, chewing slowly to give myself time to think. I didn't want the people I did business with in my home. It shouldn't matter, it was just an investment after all, but I didn't want a bunch of strangers standing around the place judging me. "No. I'm not a party person."

"What about a TV then? Surely that's not too extravagant?"

While it would never be an investment, it didn't seem too much to own a television. "Will you get off my back if I buy a TV?"

I might even get a new couch. That would show Angie that I wasn't even a little sentimental about a piece of furniture. Not a couch, not anything.

"Jesus, Sam, I just want you to enjoy life a little. Don't you see? You made it; you don't need to hang on so tight. At least go and get laid."

I wiped mustard from my mouth with my napkin. "You think I'm sexually frustrated?" I tossed the paper onto the counter. Angie knew I didn't go without.

"I'm just saying that you should have some fun. Spend some money, get a girl."

"With a face like this, you think I need money to get a girl?" I chuckled and Angie started to laugh.

"You're a prick."

"But a handsome prick, right?"

"With your money, you never need to worry about looks."

I picked up my napkin and threw it at her. She grinned. "So you got your eye on your latest victim?" she asked.

"I'm not a serial killer, for Christ's sake."

"You're a serial heartbreaker, that's what you are." She took a huge bite of her burger, as if afraid it might disappear if she didn't disable it immediately. I guess it was a habit formed in group homes when you had to eat quick or risk having your food stolen by the kid next to you. Angie had moved on from her past—meeting Chas had helped. But the scars were never too far below the surface.

"The girls I have fun with understand it's just that— fun. None of them stick around long enough to get their heart broken."

"That's because you don't call them." Angie was riding my ass a little more than usual. I wasn't in the mood.

I shrugged. I would never marry. What was the point in stringing a girl along just to dump her a couple of months down the line when she got serious?

Angie's eyes dropped and I could tell a sympathy smile

wasn't too far away.

"Don't even," I said. Whatever she was thinking, I didn't want to hear it. "Let's go a buy a TV, get you off my back."

"Okay," Angie replied, her voice soft. "I just want you to find happiness."

"I doubt you'll fit through any store doors though, after this meal," I said, ignoring her comment.

"That's okay. I'll wait outside. This mac and cheese is way too good to waste."

———————

I pulled out my cell from my pocket and slid it onto my dark mahogany desk in my office. I had more furniture within these four walls than I did in my entire apartment, even if I did now have a television. While Angie and I'd been out, I'd also picked up some kitchen essentials, including some crystal whiskey glasses I planned on seeing Grace Astor's lips pressed against sooner rather than later.

As she still hadn't called to change her mind about being my consultant, I decided I was going to have to switch up my game.

I leaned back into my leather office chair and pressed call.

"Grace Astor Fine Art," she answered on the second ring.

"Grace, it's Sam."

"Oh, Mr. Shaw."

Mr. Shaw? I'd swapped bodily fluids with the woman. What was with the formality?

"What can I do for you?"

And wasn't that the question I wanted her to answer? Kneel on the floor and take my dick to the back of her throat? Wrap her fingers around the base of my cock and squeeze just hard enough? Strip naked, bend over and feel my solid dick as I pounded into her pussy until we both came, panting and breathless?

No doubt about it—I wanted to fuck this woman. Like Angie'd said, I needed to get laid.

"I need you to come to the apartment. Your handyman hasn't done such a good job with the installation." I swung my chair around so I could take in the view of the city. Could I see her building from here?

"That's not like Mr. Grames," she said. A rustle of fabric on the other end of the line brought her into sharp focus.

What was she wearing?

"What exactly is the matter with them?"

"I'll show you. I'll be available after seven this evening."

There was a second, maybe two, of silence. "I don't think that's a good idea," she said finally. "I can send Mr. Grames back and you can just tell him what you want changed."

"I'm afraid that won't do." I hated having to pull the client card, after all what I wanted from her was entirely personal, and I wasn't about to let her off so easily. I knew she found me attractive, so unless she gave me a good reason for keeping her distance, for not giving into me, I wasn't about to give up. Quitting hadn't gotten me to owning three billion dollars' worth of real estate in midtown Manhattan alone. "Make this right, Grace, then we can discuss what you'll do for me as my art consultant."

"Mr. Shaw—"

"Grace, I've had my tongue in your mouth and your ass in my hand. Please, call me Sam."

She sighed. It wasn't wistful, more of an exasperated exhale. "Sam," she said, her tone deliberate, as if she were addressing someone whose first language wasn't English, "I've explained that I can't be your art consultant."

"It sounded more like a won't than a can't, and I don't accept that."

"Either way, it's not going to happen. I'm happy to give you a couple of names, though. I have a number of contacts who would be more than willing to help you."

"I'm not interested in anyone else helping me." I liked the fact that Grace had tried so hard to hide the most personal art at the back of the gallery because she knew what would make money was at the front. But I'd found her secret art. I imagined she was much the same—hiding the most interesting things about herself—providing the world with a glossier version. I wanted to know *her* secrets.

I wanted to discover more of what she was hiding, physically and mentally.

"Well, I'm sorry, Mr.—Sam, I think it's best if—"

"Do you have plans tonight?" I asked. I wasn't going to back down.

"That's not the point. I'm saying that I don't think it's—"

"So, you *don't* have plans. I'll be at the gallery to pick you up at six thirty."

I hung up the phone. I'd arrive early. She wasn't about to lock up before closing time to avoid me, and if she hadn't come to terms with the fact she'd be coming back to my place by the time I arrived, I was pretty sure that in person I could convince her.

A kiss, maybe, to ensure capitulation.

CHAPTER SIX
GRACE

Sam Shaw had hung up on me. Typical spoiled billionaire, expecting everyone to dance to his tune, do whatever he said. I didn't have the time or the inclination to be his art consultant. I needed to concentrate on the gallery. Steve's show had brought us a lot of attention and I had to capitalize on that. I still had four big pieces of his to sell and there was growing interest in his previous work, which we'd agreed I'd get a higher commission rate for.

Playing nursemaid to a man who wanted nothing but someone to tell him what was going to make money wasn't what I'd opened the gallery to do, even if he had purchased the pieces from me before he knew whether or not they were a good investment. I wanted to nurture new talent and feed people's soul with old masters, not just make rich guys richer. Despite Steve being a terrible boyfriend, and looking back, not a particularly nice person, no one could deny he was talented. And I was proud that Grace Astor Fine Art had been able to launch his career. *That* was the kind of thing I wanted to focus on.

And I certainly didn't want to be near a man I wanted to kiss. It was the last thing I needed. I didn't trust my lips, my body, my heart at the moment. Especially with someone as spoiled as Sam Shaw.

My cell chimed on my desk. It was Steve's new agent, who he'd signed with a couple of days after the opening. I'd never come across her before, which didn't bode well—a bad agent could be worse than no agent at all—but it didn't have anything to do with me anymore.

"Hi, Victoria," I answered.

"Grace, I'm glad I caught you. I wanted to let you know we don't need you to do any more work on Steve's historic pieces," she said, her voice as breezy as if she'd called to tell me my dry cleaning was ready to be collected.

My brain started to whir. "What do you mean 'work'?"

"Just that we've decided to go in a different direction, and we won't need you to sell any of them."

My body tensed. "That wasn't the deal I made with Steve. He said I could sell his older stuff at the standard commission rate."

"Do you have a copy of the contract you could send me?" She knew full well I had nothing in writing. The guy had been my boyfriend. I'd trusted him.

"Steve gave me his word. Is he there? Can I speak to him?"

"He's not here, and I'm sorry, but that's not the way he remembers things. Grace, I'm not trying to be an asshole here, but I need to act in my client's best interests. He needs to be with a bigger gallery."

Jesus, he wouldn't have even met this agent if it hadn't been for *my* gallery. It just wasn't fair.

"I'm not going to take away your commission for his sold pieces," she continued. "I believe there are four works that are yet to sell, and I've arranged for those to be collected this afternoon. You understand, don't you?"

I got that I was being fucked over loud and clear. The commission from the older work would have meant I could relax a little—not have to worry about rent next quarter. I'd thought I was on my way when in fact Steve's exhibition had been a false start. My ex-boyfriend was a moral wasteland. But I'd learn and get everything in writing next time.

I really wanted to tell her to go fuck herself, but I didn't have the energy.

"You better get your guys here fast."

Victoria laughed as if I couldn't be serious. "They should be there any moment." As if by magic, the bell over the door tinkled and two men carrying tissue paper and bubble wrap entered.

I hung up the phone.

"You have four paintings for us to collect?" the taller guy bellowed from across the room. "If you just point to them we'll pack them up and be on our way."

I pushed the breath out of my lungs, trying to calm myself, but as I leaned against the desk, the room rolled as if I was on a boat. I closed my eyes. I needed to keep it together until I'd gotten rid of these paintings, then lose it and drink a bottle of wine by myself.

I opened my eyes, fisted my hands and marched over to the first of Steve's paintings that hadn't sold. I yanked it off the wall and passed it to the little guy. "Here's the first one."

He just managed to catch it, pressing his no doubt sweaty palms across the splashes of color. The second painting was bigger, but I pulled it from its fixtures and set it down on the floor. "And this."

My anger increased with every moment. I wanted Steve out of my gallery, out of my life, and I *never* wanted to be taken in by someone so selfish and egotistical again.

"And you can take these as well," I said, handing over the last two paintings.

I took a deep, resigned breath. "Leave. You can wrap them up in the truck."

The men looked at me, and then at each other, clearly not understanding my anger, but thankfully they didn't argue. I followed them as they left, locking the door and pulling down the cream shade with a snap.

I turned and rested against the blind, tracing my eyebrows with my index fingers, trying to flatten out the scowl I knew I was wearing. What was I going to do? I'd been counting on the sales from Steve's old work to allow me to buy some more inventory. I couldn't just find another artist to exhibit on short notice. Now I had nothing of his to sell; his paintings were just taking up space. I needed to get them shipped out and make room for things I was actually going to make money from.

I'd been so excited to open my own gallery, so proud to put on my first exhibition. Now everything I touched seemed to turn sour.

Someone knocking on the glass interrupted my pity party. Steve couldn't possibly want anything else from me; they'd taken anything of any value already.

I unlocked the door, and found Sam Shaw towering above me.

I caught a whiff of his citrusy scent. It wasn't the heavy cologne lots of Wall Street types used. It was lighter, subtle, more like a body wash. I liked it more than I wanted to and despite my bad mood, my nipples puckered under my blouse. I rolled my eyes. "Oh, it's you," I said.

"It's nice to see you, too." The corner of the left side of his mouth turned up slightly higher than the right as he smirked at me. "I thought I'd come a little early in case you closed up to avoid me. Looks like your plan failed."

"It wasn't you I was avoiding." I turned and headed back to my desk. I wanted to kick off my shoes and get drunk, not go to Mr. Shaw's to rearrange art.

"Oh, really?" he asked as he followed me.

I stuffed my phone and keys into my purse and logged off my computer. I needed to get out of this gallery, and if it meant going with Sam Shaw, so be it.

"Come on, Mr. 'I can buy whatever I want, including people.'" I picked up my bag and stepped back into the storeroom behind my desk to set the alarm. "Let's rearrange your art quickly so I can go get drunk."

"That sounds like the kind of night I was hoping for," he replied.

"Good evening, Miss Astor," Gordon, the doorman at 740 Park Avenue, said, tipping his hat as we arrived. I'd expected Sam to pick me up in his car, but instead when we'd gone outside, he hailed a cab. His driver must be sick or something.

"Good evening, Gordon, how are your girls?" I asked. His twin granddaughters were beyond cute.

"Very well, and more beautiful by the day."

"Be good to them," I said, following Sam through the lobby.

"Always," he called after me as I hurried after Sam.

As we stood in the elevator, facing the tiled mirror, Sam said, "You make friends fast."

Before I had a chance to reply, the elevator stopped at the twentieth floor. "Damn, they need to get this thing fixed," I said. It was as if the west elevator was haunted.

"Get what fixed?"

"For some reason, this always stops on the twentieth floor," I said, pushing the thirty-fourth button furiously.

"Someone probably just called it, then realized they forgot something," Sam said. "You get irritated easily. How many times has it happened to you? Once, twice? Get over it."

"It's been like this for seven or eight years, smartass."

"Seven or eight years? What do you do, ride all the elevators of the Upper East Side, checking they're running smoothly?"

Despite my sullen mood, I couldn't help but laugh. "Yeah, I do, actually. What do you care how I spend my spare time?" I grinned at him and he smiled back and I remembered the way he'd held me, tightly but gently, as if I was something precious that he should be careful with. I looked away.

"Gallery owner by day, elevator rider by night. There's so much to know about you, Grace Astor."

"You have no idea, Sam Shaw, no idea at all."

As we entered his apartment, the lack of any furniture

took me by surprise again, even though it was exactly the same as it had been before. "Okay, so tell me which of these pieces are hung incorrectly." I turned when I didn't get an answer and found myself alone in the living space. "Sam Shaw?" I called out.

"In the kitchen, Grace Astor."

I followed his voice. He was in the kitchen, which, unsurprisingly, was almost empty, pouring whiskey into two crystal tumblers.

"Drink?" he said, handing me a glass.

Hell yes. I threw the whole thing back, thrilled to let the liquid happiness trickle down my throat and make everything better. "Thanks."

He didn't say a word, just grabbed my wrist and held it as he added more whiskey to my glass.

As he took his hand away from my arm, his fingers trailed across my skin. I blinked and looked up at him from under my lashes. He needed to reel it in. Stop his flirting, hold back his kisses.

My heart was bruised, shut down, and if it wasn't it would never be open to a man like Sam Shaw. Too rich, too spoiled, too willing to do whatever it took to get his own way—including show up at my gallery and drag me to his apartment.

At least he'd given me whiskey.

If he'd just stop looking at me like that. I felt the pressure of his gaze all over me.

"Thank you," I whispered.

He eyed me over the edge of his own glass before taking

a sip. His Adam's apple bobbed and I imagined tracing my tongue down his throat.

"One of those days?" he asked.

"Hmmm." I turned and moved out of the kitchen, back into the living space and toward the La Touche.

"Want to talk about it?" he asked from behind me.

That was the last thing I wanted to do. I wanted to forget about my day. Forget what a horrible judge of character I'd been about Steve. He'd always been so humble about his art whenever I'd told him how talented he was. He'd seemed so grateful when I'd agreed to hold an exhibit for his work—concerned he wouldn't do anything for the reputation of the gallery. Most of all, he'd acted like he loved me.

And yet at the first sighting of success he'd morphed into someone so alien it must have been there all along. I'd tricked myself into thinking he was one kind of man when he was entirely another. He'd used me to get what he needed and then when he thought I might hold him back he was gone.

I took another sip, wanting to dilute my realization.

"This looks just as we discussed." The frame was exactly where I'd placed the pencil marks on the wall.

"Do you like it there?" Sam asked, his voice soft from just a few feet behind me.

The whiskey loosened my muscles, and blurred the stress of the day into something more manageable.

"It would look good anywhere." I didn't turn around, just tipped back my glass, wanting more of the day to slip away from me. If I let myself be seduced, just for the evening, just for now, the worries about how I'd pay the rent, how I'd buy more inventory, would all seem less important. Even if just for an hour or two. "The whiskey's good, too."

Sam chuckled and I kept my gaze on the painting as I listened to him retrieve the bottle from the kitchen.

My heart gathered pace as he came closer, his hand going to my back as he topped up my glass.

"Are you trying to get me drunk?" I asked.

"I think you're wanting to get a little buzzed," he said. "And I get the impression that's not a regular occurrence for you."

"You can tell if I'm a regular drunk just by looking at me?" I asked, glancing up at him.

"Not just by looking at you."

What did that mean? What else was he basing that information on?

"But you are looking at me." I turned back to the picture, not making an effort to move away from his hand on my lower back. I liked that we were connected.

"Of course I am. I told you, you're beautiful."

"And like all rich men, you collect beautiful things. Paintings, real estate, women."

Sam removed his hand and chuckled. "Come and see where I think your man got it wrong," he said, heading to his office.

I followed him.

As I turned into the doorway, he nodded toward the wall. "Here," he said. "I'm not sure if you didn't want it there or if it's just off." He folded his arms and stared at three nudes lined up next to each other.

He was right. They looked off. The one on the left was slightly bigger and the background paper a little darker than the other two. It would look better in the middle. I checked the wall for the pencil marks, but they had been put exactly where I'd instructed. "I agree. This one"—I circled my hand at the picture in the middle—"needs to be swapped out with the one on the left." I took two off their brackets and placed them on the floor, leaning them against the wall. "Let's see if we need to change the fixture or if we can just swap them."

"I think this works," I said, moving them around. I stood back, mirroring Sam by folding my arms. "What do you think?" I glanced across at him, his eyelashes curling toward the ceiling, his five o'clock shadow giving his smooth suit a rugged look. Maybe the whiskey was underlining this buzz between us.

"I'm not trying to collect you," he said.

I'd thought we left this conversation in the living room.

"You might be able to tell from my lack of . . . I'm not a big collector of things."

So his furniture wasn't on order or about to be delivered. This was it?

"But you bought this art," I said. "And you asked me to be your consultant, which suggests you want to collect more."

"But buying art makes financial sense. Hopefully."

I sighed. Typical. "I thought you liked these," I said, sweeping my arm in the direction of my secret collection.

"You're right. I do, but I presumed that they'd make

money. I mean, I've heard of Degas. I'm guessing that's a good sign. And you told me I wouldn't lose money. I trust you."

He trusted me? Why? "It was a lot of money to drop on a gamble."

He didn't reply, but I could tell he was thinking about what I'd said as if he were only just considering his purchase.

"No need to be concerned. You made a good investment." I didn't want him to regret what he'd done, no matter the motivation. I wanted anyone who bought anything from my gallery to love and appreciate it. "And bonus," I said with as much sarcasm as I could muster, "they're actually beautiful pieces as well."

A veil lifted and thoughts of his investment passed. "Not as beautiful as you."

I rolled my eyes despite the fact that I wanted to believe he meant it. "But you don't want to collect me."

"No," he replied. "I want to fuck you, make you wild, make you scream down these walls that have you so tightly wound."

It was a more honest response than I'd expected. I had assumed we would continue our dance for a few more songs yet. He'd step forward, I'd step back. But he'd just upped the stakes—stopped the music. And I wasn't *quite* ready.

"What walls?" I said, glancing around the almost-bare apartment, not understanding his last comment.

"You know Gordon, you know the west elevator opens on the twentieth floor." He stuffed his hands into his pockets. "Maybe you lived here. Maybe your relatives have a place in the building. You're a Park Avenue princess."

It was Harper's nickname for me, but coming from her it felt affectionate and silly. From him, the name was like a hair shirt that didn't fit—a punishment made worse, uncomfortable and unnecessary. "I grew up in this building. My parents still live here." I tipped back my whiskey and took the bottle from where he'd placed it on the windowsill and poured without offering him any.

"Not too much, Princess, I need you lucid."

"For the fucking?" I asked, the alcohol making me brave. His analysis of me had meant to provoke and shock but I wouldn't give him the satisfaction.

His lips curled up into a small smile. It was one I'd not seen before—slightly shy mixed with a dash of wicked.

He nodded. "Yeah, for the fucking." He didn't take his eyes from me as if he might miss something if he did.

"Does being that direct usually work for you? You know, with women?" I wasn't trying to provoke. I was genuinely interested. I couldn't remember a man being so blunt about wanting me before. Generally, it was me who made the decision that I wanted someone. Had there ever been a time when a man had asked me on a date? Most of my boyfriends couldn't afford dinner.

I'd never considered it before but Sam's aggressive pursuit of me brought my actions into sharp focus. I'd always given men all the power.

"So, just so I'm clear," I said, "what happens after the fucking?"

Sam's smile turned from wicked to amused. "After?"

I eyed my glass, wanting the illusion of bravery that it

gave me but holding back from taking another sip because I also wanted to be lucid.

For the fucking.

I wanted to find out what it was like to be pursued. To be under a man as big, as confident, as in control as Sam Shaw.

"Nothing. I don't do anything other than fuck."

Oh. So, it was just sex that was on offer. My only other one-night stand had been in college. I couldn't remember if the sex had been good, and that probably meant it hadn't been. Certainly not memorable, in any event. Something about Sam Shaw told me a night with him would never be forgotten.

"I'm not so tightly wound, you know," I said. "I live in Brooklyn." He didn't have me pegged.

He let out an almighty guffaw.

Heat whispered across my cheeks. I suppose it sounded silly, as if I were trying to make out that because I lived in Brooklyn, I wasn't the Park Avenue princess he thought I was.

"I'm not sure you ever grow out of where you grow up," he replied, his voice soft as he stroked the small of my back as if in apology.

I placed my hand on his chest, not knowing if I should push him away or pull him closer.

CHAPTER SEVEN
SAM

"So, Grace Astor," I said, taking her whiskey glass and placing it on the windowsill next to the bottle. I wanted to kiss her. Touch her. Fuck her.

"So, Sam Shaw," she replied, looking up at me from under her lashes. Her body had become more and more receptive to me as our conversation progressed. I could tell she was weighing up the pros and cons of sleeping with me.

She was a Park Avenue princess—I'd met plenty since I'd made my money—but I liked her. Grace didn't fit the stereotype. Most people cared far too much about things that didn't matter and not enough about things that did. Grace jibing me about buying art when I knew nothing about it was an interesting position to take when it was her job to sell art. It drew me to her. Like the photographs she had next to the Degas—the juxtaposition didn't make sense, but worked at the same time.

I circled my arms around her waist and pulled her toward me. She didn't resist, but she kept her hands cautiously on my forearms. She wanted me—she just didn't know how to be okay with that.

"I don't want to get fucked on a mattress on the floor,"

she said, her eyelids flickering.

"We really don't have to do this at all."

"I want to." She looked away, nodding. "Just not there."

"You want to go to your place?" I asked. "Or a hotel?"

She pulled the corner of her bottom lip into her mouth, then slowly released it. I couldn't stop myself from rubbing my thumb along the reddened flesh.

"Here's okay. Just not on the mattress."

I wasn't quite sure what her issue was. Was it the mattress, or the fact I'd had women there before? I hadn't, but she couldn't know my MO was to go back to a woman's place. I didn't mind. I just wanted to get her naked. Where wasn't my concern.

She slid her hands up my arms and rounded my shoulders, as though tracing her hands over my body so she could remember me in another time or place. I removed one hand from her waist, tucked her hair behind her ears then pressed my fingers around the back of her neck.

Her entire body seemed to sag with my every touch as if I had some kind of power in just my fingertips. She was soft—her skin, her hair, the way she spoke when she was embarrassed. She felt good to hold, but I knew she'd feel better beneath me.

I turned us around and walked her backward until she was pressed against the drywall next to the La Touche. There was as many unanswered questions surrounding the woman in the painting as I had for the woman in front of me. My hands circled her waist, my thumbs dipping below her waistband. I felt her desire in the quick twist of her hips and it fueled mine. I ducked my head, my lips finding hers.

She locked her grip to the back of my neck, holding me in place—as if I'd go anywhere. I took her hands in mine and brought them over her head. I wanted to kiss her, to find our rhythm, our mixed breath, before things went any further.

Her tongue was as soft as the rest of her, but not as confident as I'd expected. I liked it. I wanted to guide her.

She tasted like cherries—sweetness with a hint of sour—her edges disappearing under my fingers and my tongue. I pulled back to look at her, wanting to see her reaction splashed across her. Slowly, she opened heavy eyes, as if she were coming out of anesthesia. Her lips were red, her normally sleek blonde hair mussed.

Perfect.

"Hey," I said.

She twisted her arms, trying to get free.

"Let me look at how beautiful you are."

She pulled the edge of her bottom lip between her teeth. I wanted to suck on it instead of her. I took over her lips, her tongue, her kiss.

Her pulse under my palms matched the throb in my dick. Another twist of her hips and a small, almost imperceptible moan from the back of her throat woke me from the kiss, pushing me forward.

"Leave your arms up," I whispered against her mouth. She moaned again, and my dick strained against my zipper, reminding me to hurry the fuck up. Despite the alarm bells ringing across my body, I wanted to slow everything down, knew I had to savor every moment. *Nothing* came after the fucking, so I had to draw out the *something* for as long as possible.

"Okay," she whispered, her breath puffing against my skin, pulling me deeper into the moment. I slid my hands down her arms, my heartbeat increasing in pace with every touch.

One hand on her waist, I hooked a finger over the opening of her blouse, and glanced at her. Her mouth parted, her eyes imploring me. With a little pull, the button popped open, revealing the swell of her breasts. I took a deep breath and exhaled slowly. Perfect. I tipped my head back, trying to bring my cock under control, reminding my body I had all night to get my fill of her.

The thought only made my impatient dick throb.

I pulled her shirt apart, the buttons scattering across the floor as I yanked the lace of her bra down to free her breasts. I wanted her nipples in my mouth, between my teeth, hard against me. I plunged my tongue between her milky white tits, then groaned and sank to my knees in front of her.

I was at the perfect height to take in the glory of her—disheveled, wanton—which I knew would be unusual for her.

Her hips bucked away from the wall. I wasn't the only one whose body was racing for the finish line.

I lifted her tits in my hands until they spilled out of my palms. Like something in one of her drawings, they were sumptuous, made to be feasted on. I glanced up to check her hands were still above her head. My dick throbbed when I saw she hadn't moved them. She knew how to do as she was told in the bedroom. Fuck. She deserved a reward.

I took a nipple in my mouth and sucked, bit and flicked,

her whimpers urging me on. Her movements became more jagged. I could stay like this for days, torturing my rock-hard cock . . . but I didn't want to torture her. I wanted to make my mark. Licking up to the top of her breast, then biting and sucking, sinking my teeth into the generous flesh.

"Jesus," she screamed.

He wasn't going to save her. Not now. Not from me.

I released her and, impatient now, alternated between tugging at her zipper and pulling my shirt off. I wanted her skin against mine, her wetness on my fingers, spread across her thighs.

"Bring your arms down, Princess. I want you to lie back." I guided her to the rug, peeling off her shirt and bra as she rested her hands on my shoulders, steadying herself as she sank to the ground.

Fuck, I wished I had a bed for her. A nice couch or a dining room table. All the places I could be fucking her. I groaned, and as if my imagination increased her pleasure, she arched her back against the floor. "You're impatient," I said.

She nodded. "Be careful though," she said, her eyes pleading with me. Be careful? She wasn't talking about the floor or the cut of my teeth. It was her psyche, her soul, her heart she was pleading for.

I wanted to reassure her, to tell her I would be gentle, that I'd never hurt her, but I couldn't make that promise. Didn't even know how. My blood cooled. Growing up as I did had forced me to detach from others. To not care about holes in my soul that would never be filled. I'd taught myself to tune into people—to read them, but not to comfort or protect.

Despite her pull, I forced myself away from Grace and rolled to my back. "We don't have to do this. If it's too much . . ."

She crossed her arms over her face.

"You don't want me?" she asked.

Maybe *too* much. I couldn't ever remember wanting a woman as badly as I did Grace.

"I want you." I pushed the heel of my hand against my granite cock. "But I don't want you to be . . . uncomfortable."

This had to be physical, and only physical, for both of us. But she tugged at something deeper in me.

I glanced at her taut belly and I couldn't resist dipping my fingers below her waistband. I wanted more. Her zipper undone, I peeled off her skirt. "Take your arms from your face. You're too beautiful to hide."

Consequences would have to be dealt with later. Now I had to fuck her.

I stripped naked, not taking my eyes off her, afraid she might disappear if I looked away for even a second. Hooking my thumbs under her panties by each hip bone, I dragged the delicate lace down her body, exposing her pussy to me. Mesmerizing. A small, neat blonde triangle of hair, just as I'd expected. Grace wasn't a girl who would go entirely bare without a little encouragement. I leaned over her, knocking her legs apart so I could settle between her thighs.

"What are you doing?" she asked, twisting away from me. She wasn't enjoying this?

I grabbed her and held her in place.

"No, Sam. Please, no." She fumbled at my shoulders, trying to pull me up her body.

"I want to taste you," I said. "But I'll stop if you tell me why you don't like oral sex."

She flung her hands across her face.

I pushed her thighs wider. "Tell me."

"It's embarrassing. Please."

Jesus. Was she Catholic or . . .

I crawled up her body, hovering over her. "Take your hands from your face and talk to me." If I could, I'd reach inside her brain and pull out each and every fascinating thought.

Her ribcage lowered as she let out a long breath.

"It's just . . ."

She looked me in the eye, then down at my collarbone.

"I'm just overly . . . wet down there."

Huh? Was she a squirter? I could work with that. "And?"

She gave a little shrug. "I don't know. I'm not normally like this. Please, don't go down there."

Jesus, she might as well have told me I had a monster cock and I was the best lover she'd ever had. She thought she was revealing some embarrassing secret, when really all she was doing was turning me on, revving me up.

After that revelation, I wondered if there'd ever be a time when I wasn't hard. "I don't want to do anything that's going to make you feel uncomfortable." I nudged her nose with mine. "But just so you know, there's nothing I would like to do more than lick your pussy, especially if it's never been so drenched in wetness." I placed a delicate kiss on her lips and pulled back so I could look at her. "*I* did that to you and there's absolutely nothing to be embarrassed about."

She tried to fight the grin dancing at the edges of her

lips. Who had given her reason to be embarrassed about what she had to offer? Someone who was less than her, and knew it. Someone who wanted to squash her.

I hated him instantly.

Her fingertips fluttered at my side and she might as well have been sucking my cock, the things her touch did to me. I needed a condom before I came all over that perfect belly of hers. Awkwardly, I reached for my pants, where I'd transferred a familiar square package earlier.

I looked her straight in the eye. "I need you. And given you've told me you're more than ready, I'm going to fuck you now."

She gave me a small nod and I moved to my side as I pushed the rubber over my straining dick, right down as far as it would go. In seconds, I would be buried in her—there was nothing on this planet I wanted more in that moment.

I positioned myself and glanced up to find her watching me, her eyes connected to mine as if she was trying to see inside me.

Don't bother, Princess.

"Ready?" I asked.

She nodded and rolled her lips together. If she was nervous, within seconds that feeling would fall away. I dipped to take another kiss, to reassure her, and found myself unable to pull away entirely. Instead I dropped my forehead to hers. We were so close our mouths brushed every time she exhaled.

I traced the tip of my dick from her clit down to her entrance. Her body was tense but it soon wouldn't be. I'd fuck all the anxiety away.

"You want me?" I asked.

She whimpered. "Please."

Her sounds vibrated across my lips. Such a simple word.

I pushed into her in a slow, controlled slide, but I wasn't stopping until I was balls deep. Jesus, she was so fucking tight. I gasped, letting go of my breath.

I wanted to be fast, to find my climax in the next thirty seconds, but at the same time I liked how we were connected, every part of my body touching every part of hers. I groaned at the thought.

She twisted beneath me.

"You like that, Princess?" I whispered. "You like being pinned to the ground with my body, my dick right up inside you like that?"

Of course she liked it; how could she not?

She wrapped her arms around my neck and pulled me closer, her legs hugging my waist. She felt this connection like I did. I could tell, couldn't I?

I began to make small, isolated movements, keeping our bodies tight against each other while shifting my cock up and down, not too far out—I didn't want to lose her warmth—just enough to. Be. Fucking. *Perfect*.

Everything was just so intense, the pleasure so concentrated. I licked the underside of her top lip. *Cherries.* The taste went straight to my groin, threatening to push me over as she tipped her head back. "Fuck," I groaned, my words spilling directly into her open mouth.

Her fingernails bit into my shoulder. "Don't stop."

"Not ever," I replied. Our bodies were so tightly pressed against each other it was as if we shared every breath, as if we were merging into one. I reached beneath her butt cheek, wanting her closer still.

"Stay there," she said, breathless. "I like you over me. On me. So heavy." She groaned and arched her back off the ground, turned on by her own words. Fuck me, that was nearly too much. I almost let go, but I refused to go before her. I pushed harder and deeper, keeping my movements small, squeezing into her.

My tongue reached for her mouth again in a desperate attempt to have more of her, to give her more of me. This time our tongues crashed together as she gasped. Her fingers on my arms froze and I felt her pulling me into her, her orgasm igniting mine.

It didn't need much encouragement. I managed to pull back just a few inches to see her beautiful face. Her eyes were glassy, but she was looking straight at me as if she knew *everything*.

"Fuck," I cried out as I spilled into her, bowing my head, my cheek resting against hers.

It was just sex, just fucking, but it seemed like so much *more* than I'd ever felt before. As if she'd pricked my skin with that final look and I'd unraveled before her.

Our breaths were uneven, pushing and pulling against each other's necks.

"Jesus, Grace." I hadn't expected that.

She didn't reply, but shifted underneath me.

I moved to her side, discarded the condom and then

rolled onto my back, my breath still stuttering.

Eventually, Grace sat up, giving me a view of her back. She turned her head to look at me over her shoulder. "Why don't you have any furniture?" she asked, her voice unsteady, still recovering from the exertion. It puffed up my ego. I did that to her. "Is it in storage?"

"How long have you been waiting to ask me that?" I missed her warm, soft body beneath mine. And I wasn't ready to let her go just yet. I wanted to feel her surrounding me again. And I still had to make her come with my tongue. So much to do.

She raised her eyebrows. "Have you noticed how often you answer one of my questions with a question of your own?"

"You do it, too," I replied.

She settled back into the crook of my shoulder, respecting the fact I didn't want to answer her question. Which only made me want to tell her everything. "There's nothing in storage. I rented until I bought this place."

"You didn't collect anything on the way?"

"I told you I'm not a collector of things. Or of people. I'm not sentimental that way."

She didn't respond and we lay there marinating in what had just passed between us—the words, the touch, the way she fit so comfortably against my body.

I might not be sentimental, but for the first time ever, I knew there had to be something after the fucking.

CHAPTER EIGHT

Grace

"You're not sentimental at all?" I asked after a few minutes. Why was I still lying here, against his hard, delicious body? I needed to get the hell out of there, not be in his arms. If only my muscles just had a little bit more power in them. It was as if Sam had drained me of all my energy.

It always took my body a while to open up to a new guy, and I never had an orgasm the first time I slept with a man. I wasn't sure whether or not I'd ever felt anything so intense. My climax had rumbled low and deep, in wave after wave. This man, who could have any woman he wanted with his sure smile and easy confidence, had waited for me to come first. It was only after me that he'd come, as if he'd finally been allowed to do the one thing he wanted to do most.

I shuddered.

"Hey, are you cold?" he asked.

I wasn't, but I couldn't tell him it was thoughts of him, of what we'd done together, that had made me shiver. "Maybe, a little."

He pulled his shirt over me like a crisp cotton sheet.

"I'm not ready for you to put on clothes yet. We have plenty to do first."

He couldn't see the grin trying to escape my pursed lips, but I couldn't stay here. My desire to bury thoughts of Steve had made me weak. Momentarily. But, as comfortable as the crook of his shoulder was, I shouldn't settle here. "I can't believe I fucked my first client," I said, then wished I hadn't said that out loud.

He pulled me closer and dropped a kiss on the top of my head. "I think you'll find *I* fucked *you*."

I wasn't going to argue. He was right. I'd had little say in the how, and I found I liked that. I squeezed my thighs together as I remembered his hot breath on my pussy. I rarely let a man go down on me, but as much as part of me hated to admit it, I was pretty sure if Sam Shaw suggested it again, I'd say yes.

His cock pulsed against his belly, as if he was getting hard again. Jesus. I needed to go. I should have left already. Like he'd said, nothing came after the sex, so what was I doing lying here, basking in postcoital glow?

"I need to leave," I said.

"Not yet. Soon. I want to come again. Make you come again."

It was what I wanted, too. Just to make sure it wasn't a fluke, that I hadn't imagined he'd made my body sing the way I thought he had. Even now, just a few minutes later, I was sure it couldn't have been quite as . . . overwhelming . . . different . . . or as good as I thought it had been.

"And you haven't agreed to be my art consultant yet."

I groaned. I'd been hoping he wouldn't mention the art consultant thing again. Now I wouldn't make any money from Steve's earlier work, I needed the cash.

I couldn't say no.

Even though I wasn't qualified.

Even though I didn't have enough contacts.

Even though working with him would be a complete distraction.

The "nothing" after sex would be easy if I never saw him again. But the way he made my body feel . . . Surely I wouldn't be able to be near him and *not* think about it.

"I'll have my office update the contract I had with Nina with your details, and have them send it over."

I stayed silent and kept as still as possible. I should say no, but I couldn't.

"We can start right away."

What was his rush? Art collecting wasn't a sprint. It was something you took a lifetime to do. I sat up and glanced around for my clothes. "There's an auction of Old European Masters at Sotheby's next month." I reached for my bra and fastened it around my chest. "I'll check out the program and see if there's anything I think you should bid on."

"You're saying yes?" he asked. He sat up and snuck his palm under my bra strap.

I shrugged him off as a sadness I couldn't place settled in my belly. "Yes." I stood and he grabbed my hand, trying to pull me back to him. I twisted my arm and he let go.

"Hey, I said I wasn't done."

"Well I am." I continued to dress. He'd been clear there was nothing after the fucking, and I wasn't about to wait for him to kick me out.

"I thought you were sticking around?" he asked.

"I need to be somewhere," I replied.

Somewhere with alcohol.

———————————

Even though Harper was breastfeeding and spending most of her time in Connecticut, she still made sure she made it to Tuesday girls' night. I couldn't have been more grateful. One of the hardest parts of breaking up with someone was the transition period where for a few weeks I had so much more free time. I knew it wouldn't last long, but at the moment I was aware how much I was on my own.

I'd spent most of my time since the gallery opening working. I went home and continued to fill in spreadsheets or research new artists. Periodically, images of Sam Shaw in my secret, sectioned-off corner of the gallery, sliding his large hands over my ass and pulling me against him, interrupted my concentration but I was fighting it.

"You look different," Scarlett said as she pulled away from my hug and slid into the booth next to me.

I rolled my eyes. "No I don't." Maybe I did. Even days later, my body still felt the aftereffects of Sam's touch. The bruises on my breasts had faded to penny-shaped shadows on my skin. I savored each one, more disappointed every day they grew smaller and fainter. No man had ever left a physical mark on me before. I liked it.

He'd left his mark on my mind, too.

"Just tell me you didn't fuck that loser painter of yours."

I cringed at the thought of Steve's soft, spindly body. "No. Not at all." There was nothing soft about Sam Shaw's body. Nothing unsure about his touch. "But you're right. I fucked a client the other day though. Pretty stupid, I guess."

Except that I couldn't regret it. Sam's body gave me masturbation fantasy material for the rest of time. Had he really been that big? Had he really made me come that hard? It was as if he'd reached into me and pulled out the orgasm by sheer force.

"Why was it stupid?"

"Because I need him to still be my client." I didn't tell Scarlett that Sam's assistant had sent me over the contracts as promised. Or that I'd signed and returned them to her. I didn't explain how Sam had called me three times since, or that I'd ignored him each time. I didn't want anyone to know how he seemed to be taking up more and more of my thoughts.

"Was it bad sex?" she asked. "You can't look at him because he had a two-inch penis?"

A small dick wasn't Sam Shaw's problem. I shrugged and coaxed over a waiter. Harper arrived at our table at the same time. "Can I get a virgin mojito and a bread basket, please," she asked before she even acknowledged us.

"Two more margaritas, please," I said and turned back to my friends.

"Move over," Harper said as she slid onto our booth. "What are we talking about? Jesus, is there nothing to eat in this place? I thought this was supposed to be a restaurant."

"Take it down a notch. You just ordered a bread basket," Scarlett said. "And we were talking about guys with two-inch dicks."

Harper grimaced and moved away from us, as if Scarlett had announced we both had herpes. "Who's got a two-inch dick?" she asked.

"No one," I replied.

Scarlett gave Harper a knowing look. "Some guy Grace banged."

"You banged a guy with a two-inch dick?" Harper asked.

"No, his dick was plenty big, thank you." Jesus, how did we get here? I didn't want to think about the size of Sam Shaw's penis, or how it felt slipping into me, pushing deeper and deeper. How I felt it in my toes and finger tips, beneath and through every part of me.

Harper and Scarlett just looked at me, waiting for more.

"So, who's the guy?" Harper asked.

I shook my head, glancing across at the waiter, hoping he'd interrupt us soon so we could change topics. "No one."

"A client," Scarlett said.

I rolled my eyes.

"When did it happen? Could it be a thing?" Harper asked. Trying to get Harper to talk about finding a serious relationship before she met her husband had been almost impossible. Now she wanted everyone to have what she had. It was sweet, but it was annoying.

"No, it's not a thing and it's never going to be. It just happened, but it won't happen again." Because *nothing* happened after the sex.

And that suited me fine.

"I need to focus on the gallery at the moment. I think

I'm going to offer art consulting to people who want it." I twirled the stem of my empty margarita glass.

"Oh, I thought you weren't into that," Scarlett said.

I shrugged. "But with Steve's work gone, I have to do whatever it takes to make it work."

Thankfully, the waiter arrived with our drinks and took our order, taking Harper and Scarlett's attention away from me, giving me room to breathe, to think. I tuned out whatever it was Scarlett and Harper were talking about. Was he in his apartment now? On that old beat-up couch, the TV on, his hand slipping past his waistband to circle his cock?

I jumped at the buzz of my phone on the table. Sam flashed across the screen. Three ignored calls and two margaritas meant it was time to speak to him. "I have to get this," I said, sliding out of the booth.

"Sam Shaw," I answered, placing my finger in my ear as I walked through the restaurant toward the exit.

"I've called you three times, Grace Astor," he replied, clearly irritated.

"You're on my call sheet, but you beat me to it."

"Your call sheet?" he asked, giving me a second to respond. I stayed quiet. "You signed the papers; you're supposed to be my art consultant. I've not been consulted about anything."

"I signed the papers, that doesn't mean you own me."

More silence, but from the few hours I'd spent with him, I understood it wasn't angry, just contemplative. He absorbed what people gave out, learning about it, and then stored it up. For what?

"I went to the preview for the auction I told you about."

"You don't think I should have come with you? I thought you wanted me to like what I bought?"

I ran my thumbnail between my bottom two front teeth to interrupt the smile that threatened. "I thought you just wanted to make money? I'll get the catalog sent over tomorrow and we can decide before the auction on Thursday."

"No. Bring the catalog. Lunch tomorrow. And what time's the auction on Thursday?"

"Oh, no, you don't need to come. We can establish your upper limits and I can have you on the phone."

"I don't think so, but we'll discuss it at lunch tomorrow. Twelve thirty. Come to my office."

And he was gone.

I stared at the screen on my phone. Not only had he hung up on me, he'd ordered me to his office without telling me where it was. He just assumed I knew. Which I did, because of course, since he'd made me come like it was his job, I'd thought it only polite to Google him. But it was an arrogant move. Spoiled.

The problem was, he wasn't as *typically* spoiled as I'd thought when I first met him. Some things fit—he was demanding, confident he'd get what he wanted. But then there was the part of him that didn't have any furniture in his apartment. And the way he listened a little more than he spoke. And most of all, I was *attracted* to him.

That wasn't typical at all.

I went back inside, the rush of the air conditioning bringing me back to the moment.

"I met someone I thought might be good for you," Harper said as I sat down.

"Did Scarlett turn him down?"

I looked between the two of them. Scarlett was single and always dating two or three people at any one time. I couldn't keep up. But I admired the way she picked up and started again after her divorce.

"Duncan and I decided to be exclusive," Scarlett said.

My eyes widened. Duncan was a tool. "Really? Wow. When did that happen?" I asked as Scarlett grinned from ear to ear.

Shuffling excitedly in her seat, she said, "Last night. He took me to dinner and said he'd suspended his online dating account."

No more violins or roses. Suspension of an online dating profile was the grand romantic gesture in New York.

"Well, that's exciting," I said.

"I just think you should keep your options open. I don't trust him," Harper said, which was what everyone else was thinking.

"As long as *you're* excited about it," I said, kicking Harper in the shin.

"Hey, don't kick the breastfeeding lady. I'm only saying what you're thinking."

I shook my head. "Who's this guy, anyway?" Not that I was interested. I didn't trust my judgment at the moment. Sam wasn't falling into my clearly defined boxes, and despite thinking it was the rich who used people, Steve had proven me wrong on that, too. Everything was topsy-turvy. I needed a time-out from men.

"He's a client of mine," Harper said. "I met him last week and he's just divorced his wife. He's rich and I know you hate that, but I swear I'm not making this up, he works at a homeless shelter twice a month."

I chuckled. "He's either not as rich as you're saying, or he's lying to you."

"Don't be so cynical." Harper accusing me of being cynical was like the Queen of England calling me posh. "You should give him a chance."

"I'm not ready for . . ." Anything. I wanted nothing at all, at least for a while.

"You were ready for casual sex with a new client," she said. Harper and I always challenged each other. It was part of the reason we'd been friends for so long. The difference was I nudged and she shoved.

"That was different." I wasn't about to give in.

"Different?" Scarlett asked.

"Yeah, like exercise or something." I hadn't invested anything in Sam, and the freedom felt good. So good I was looking forward to seeing him for lunch the following day.

It was warmer than fall in Manhattan should be at lunchtime. I'd chosen my favorite Chanel skirt suit—black and white and paired with bright red matte lipstick and scarlet stilettos. The skirt was a little shorter than I usually wore. I wanted to see if Sam noticed my legs.

I was looking forward to seeing him. I wanted to check

if I actually found him as attractive as I remembered. I wanted to know whether that jawline was quite as sharp as I pictured. Whether that quiet smile was as beguiling as lived in my mind.

Clearly, being ten minutes late was bad form if this was just a client meeting, but this was something a little more complicated. A business meeting with someone who'd been naked the last time I'd seen them called for slightly different etiquette. If it had been a drink with a casual fling, I'd have been twenty minutes late. Ten was a compromise.

"Grace Astor for Sam Shaw," I said to the receptionist behind the high, shiny maple desk. She was the girl men loved—a younger, hotter version of Jennifer Lopez, if it was at all possible.

"Please follow me, Ms. Astor," she said and she and her fabulous ass led me along a plush carpeted corridor to a corporate dining room. "Make yourself comfortable," she said before shutting the door as she left. Well this lunch was all business, that was for sure. I'd expected to go out to one of the numerous restaurants around midtown that specialized in meals for suits. But it seemed we weren't leaving the building.

The large, polished maple table was set for two, complete with what looked like crystal glassware and china tableware. If I hadn't already been to Sam's apartment, after seeing this I'd assume it to be similarly expensively furnished, no expense spared.

I knew differently.

I was peering at the blue and green abstract painting

on the wall above the wet bar when the door swung open. "Grace Astor, you're late," Sam said.

"Deepest apologies for my tardiness. It couldn't be helped."

He waited for a beat for me to elaborate, and when I didn't, he chuckled. "We'll eat here if you don't mind. Saves time." He held out his hand for me to take the chair to the right of the head of the table.

His tone was friendly, but businesslike, as if we'd met once or twice before, but not as if we'd seen each other naked, as if we'd pulled and scratched at each other, each begging the other to push them over the edge into a soul-blistering orgasm.

Okay, well I could work with that.

"So, this is the catalog," I said, pulling out the glossy book from my tote and placing it in front of us. "I've marked the ones I think are probably going to go for less than their real value with a Post-it." We hadn't really discussed budgets, so I'd labelled absolutely everything I thought would be a good buy. His picks should give me some indication of his budget.

He flicked his thumb down the line of multicolored Post-its and smiled before opening the catalog and regarding my choices.

We were interrupted by three waiters arriving with large white plates. Sam didn't even look up as the food was set in front of us.

The silence bordered on uncomfortable. "Is there anything you like? I mean, if you want to discuss my reasoning behind any of the pieces I've marked, then do ask me questions."

He set the book down and picked up his fork, pausing when he saw I hadn't started eating yet. I picked up my silverware and we began to eat.

"What do the different colors mean?" he asked.

Was he asking me what colors represented in paintings?

"Your Post-its," he clarified.

"Just ignore them, they don't really matter for your purposes."

"But there is a reason they're different colors." He set his silverware down and sat back in his chair, giving me his full attention.

"Not a business reason," I replied, focusing on my plate.

"I think you like the ones you marked green the best."

He was right, but how could he possibly know that? "Why are you always trying to figure people out?" I asked.

"Not always," he said, picking his silverware back up. "Only people who I want something from, or who want something from me."

"And which box do I fit into?"

He looked up from his plate and grinned. "I think you have a box all of your own."

The room was quiet, and I was pretty sure I could hear my own heartbeat. What did that mean? Was he just avoiding my question, or was he paying me a compliment?

I wanted him to touch me because when he had before everything had made sense. I'd been so focused on the moment and the way our bodies worked together, I hadn't second-guessed anything.

"I agree, by the way. I like the green ones, too. But I

want to see them," he said.

I glanced up and he was watching me as if he were checking every reaction I had to him.

"You want to see the green ones?"

"Yes," he replied.

"You should keep an open mind about some of the others. There may be some other good buys among those that I've marked in something other than green."

"I'm good with the green. I think we should go with your gut."

"And you're not going to tell me how you knew the greens were my favorite?"

"It's no secret. I'm getting to know you. The way you like the intimate or unexpected." He grinned. "In your art." He shrugged and took a forkful of food. "And you clearly hadn't marked them on price or period. It's cute. Don't be self-conscious about it."

"I'm not. If I was I would have replaced the Post-its." I didn't want him to think he'd gotten under my skin. "Anyway, it's too late to see the paintings before the auction next week—the viewing closes this afternoon."

"Then we'll go after lunch."

Did this man not have a business to run? "What if I'm busy this afternoon?"

He narrowed his eyes. "Do what you gotta do, Grace Astor."

Almost everything he said could be interpreted a number of different ways.

"Do you always want more from people?"

He paused and glanced away from me. "Not always."

What *more* did he want from me?

"Okay, I can take you this afternoon . . . on one condition. If you get more then I get more." His lack of furniture had bothered me ever since I'd walked into his apartment. And perhaps more so after his half-explanation. Not being sentimental wasn't a reason a rich man didn't have a bed—or a decent couch.

He finished his mouthful of food and placed his napkin on the table. "Name it."

"After the showing, we go and buy you a couch."

He chuckled. "That's the more you want?"

Was there something else on offer? Did I want there to be? I nodded.

"Deal."

CHAPTER NINE

Sam

As I watched Grace wander around the auction preview, I wanted to pull her aside, untuck the shirt from her stuffy, Upper East Side skirt, and slide my hands over her breasts until she was begging me to fuck her. Here. In this room. In front of everyone.

When we'd fucked on my apartment floor, she'd opened up to me and now, here she was, doing it again in a different way. Just by existing.

I couldn't get enough. Her wide eyes, the way she became mesmerized by everything she saw, the way she leaned in to me, whispering secrets about the paintings. "Look at his boot—it seems black, but if you look closer, the paint is green and white," she said, turning to me, checking that I was listening, wanting me to be as excited about the art as she was.

I smiled and nodded. As impressive as the preview was, she outshone everything in the room. Without thinking, I smoothed a strand of hair behind her ear. The rise and fall of her chest stilted, as if she held her breath. "You're even more beautiful like this—passionate, excited," I said.

The seduction was meant to be over; I was supposed to

be done. I always was after the sex. But since she'd left my apartment, there'd been a niggling feeling that I hadn't quite had my fill of her. Was it because I hadn't dragged out my orgasm with her? I'd come a dozen times since by my own hand, but I still wasn't sated.

So who was seducing who?

She smiled and looked down at her catalog, and we continued as if I didn't want to fuck her right there. When we reached the end of the exhibition she tipped her head to the side, indicating we should move away from the crowd. "Do you know which you like best?" she whispered. "We should narrow it down to two or three and then place limits on them all." Flicking through the catalog, she dug into her purse and pulled out a pencil. "You should prepare yourself for not getting anything at all."

I'd made a mental note of the paintings she flagged as green and paid attention as they appeared on our way around. There were three I liked in particular. "I like these two," I said, pointing at a set of two prints by Toulouse Lautrec in bold colors. They were more masculine than the work I'd bought from her gallery—more straightforward.

"Yes!" she said excitedly and then, as if checking herself, she refocused. "For your bedroom," she whispered. The prints were valued in the low five figures, so I was impressed she'd flagged them. She worked on commission and could have gone for the most expensive items. "I think if we can get them for the right price, it would be a good buy. What else?"

I pointed at another picture, marked green. A black background with a vivid bowl of flowers. It was kind of old-fashioned, but something about the darkness and the way the color seemed to break through appealed to me.

"The Brueghel. God, yes. It's so you."

I stuffed my hands in my pockets. It was? "It's me?" I asked. No one other than Angie made that sort of comment to me. No one knew me well enough to.

Her cheeks colored and she shrugged. "Yeah. You know. Dark and stern. But then you get closer and . . ."

I wanted her to finish her sentence. *Then what?*

"It will look good in that apartment," she said, paging through the brochure.

Finally, we decided on another nude. Apparently, she liked them as much as I did. Had anyone ever drawn Grace naked? Or taken photographs of her? A dull pang hit me in the gut. I didn't like the idea of anyone looking at her without clothes. Even more, I hated I felt that way at all.

"Come on, Saks next," she said, leading me out the exit. "How come you don't have a driver?" she asked. "You're like richer than the pope or something." She flagged a cab, but I pulled her away, putting myself between her and the curb.

"Why should I have a driver? Manhattan's full of them." As if to prove my point, a yellow cab drew up, spraying the morning's rain on my trouser legs.

"Well, you could fire a driver if he did that," she replied. "But I'm glad it wasn't me. Thank you."

Grace gave the address, then listed the exact route she wanted him to take. I sat back and watched, still intrigued. She'd seen buying a couch as a victory. I saw it as an inevitability. I didn't want to have to fuck her on the floor again.

101

But I wanted to fuck her again.

I would fuck her again.

Shit. I kept my eyes firmly on the street outside. *I wanted to fuck her again.*

"But you don't want to spend your money on someone permanent?" she asked.

"No, I just don't think it's necessary."

"You say that like you don't buy into the New York lifestyle, but look at your office, or your suits, for Christ's sake." She looked me up and down as if checking that I was actually wearing a suit. Or was she just checking me out?

"That's different. That's business. People expect me to have nice offices, wear nice suits. It's just part of the job."

Grace chuckled. "So you're just doing what everyone expects of you?"

Was she deliberately trying to find flaws in my character? I so rarely interacted with women outside work other than Angie. I didn't understand the reasons behind her questions. Did she have a point to prove or was she just trying to get to know me? "I'm doing what's necessary. Sometimes you have to take certain steps in order to get to your goal." I didn't care about a fancy couch or having a driver because it was slightly more convenient. What I cared about was making sure I'd never have to repeat my youth. I'd do anything it took to avoid that.

"So you do whatever it takes?" Grace asked as we pulled up outside Saks.

"No. That's not what I said. I do things to help me achieve my goal. But that's just common sense. There's no point making life harder for yourself," I said as I followed her out onto the sidewalk.

She was ambitious. She got how it worked, surely. "You were dating the artist of your first exhibition. You wouldn't have got his show if you hadn't been involved, right? You did what it took."

"What?" She spun around to look at me. "*He* was using *me,* you asshole. Steve wouldn't have gotten an exhibition without me."

"That's not what I was trying to say. Don't overreact."

"Did you know I found him banging his assistant on my desk just after I opened?" She turned and flung open the door, not waiting for me to catch it as it swung shut in front of me. I yanked it open and followed her inside. "And how did you know I was dating him?"

"It was obvious. And just because he cheated on you doesn't mean you didn't do what you had to do to further your goals," I said from behind her.

"Whatever," she replied.

We made our way to the furniture department in silence. Every now and then, Grace opened her mouth to speak then decided against it.

"So am I using you?" she finally asked as she took a seat on a huge L-shaped sofa that had room for twenty people.

"I didn't say you were *using* that painter guy." I took a seat beside her. Every relationship was a trade-off. Someone wanted something from you, you wanted something from them—business, personal—it was all the same.

"You didn't answer my question." she said. "When we

had sex, what exactly was I using you for?"

"Let me ask you something." She rolled her eyes. "I'm not asking to be evasive, I just want to answer your question better," I explained, running my hand over a cushion. Of course she was using me. I just wanted to be sure I knew why.

"Go on then," she replied.

"Who was your boyfriend before the cheater?"

She narrowed her eyes, which I was pretty sure she thought looked menacing. Really, it was beyond cute. "His name was Nathan. Happy?"

"But what did he do? What did you like about him?"

"He was a musician, if you must know." She stood and marched across to another, slightly more realistically sized sofa. I followed her. "He was very talented." She inspected the couch, trailing her hands over the black velvet.

"I like this one," I said as I sat down, hoping it was comfortable. It was long enough that I could lie full length on it and Grace would look beautiful lying next to me, her blonde hair a delicious contrast to the black.

Grace came and sat next to me, her eyes facing forward.

"*Using* is the wrong word," I said. "But you have to get something out of a situation, otherwise why would you bother?" I didn't say that I thought it sounded like she had a habit of dating losers, or that there was likely a whole host of reasons why she needed that. "You have a type of guy you normally date. That's because you get something out of dating that guy—just like he gets something out of dating you." If she liked artistic types, I was definitely not the kind of man she usually slept with.

"Okay," she said, "And I had sex with you because?"

"My big cock?" I replied.

She laughed and I found myself grinning not at my joke but at the sound of her belly laugh.

"You like it?" I asked, patting the couch.

"I do. It's masculine and pretty at the same time."

"Okay, well if this is the one, let's find a sales clerk."

"What, just like that?"

I shrugged as I leaned forward, then glanced over my shoulder at her. I was right; she looked beautiful on this couch. "We've found something we like. What's the point in continuing to look?"

"You've resisted buying furniture for what looks like your whole life, but now, all of a sudden, you're ready to pick the first thing we see?"

I stood and held out my hand to help her up. "I told you I'd get a couch. We found one. I like it. I'm going to buy it. It's really not that complicated."

She ignored my offer of help and stood. "Okay. Well that was easy. What about a coffee table?"

I chuckled. Why was she taking such an interest in my interior decorating? "Oh of course," I said. I wasn't so different to the other men she'd been with—the artist boyfriend, the musician before that.

"What?" she asked, looking at me from where she was crouched over a glass table.

I nodded. "You're a fixer." I'd met people like her before. No doubt she over invested in the people around her, coaching them to be the best they could be before they turned around and dropped her.

"And you're a know-it-all," she retorted. "Do you like this table?"

Well at least she didn't pretend to be something she wasn't. "I'm not going to make it that easy for you, Grace Astor. If you want to push at my boundaries, I get to peer over your Park Avenue princess walls, too."

She shrugged and stood up, catching the attention of a sales clerk. "Excuse me, Mr. Shaw would like to take this couch," she said. "And this coffee table."

Jesus, this woman had some balls on her. But I took that as game on. How could I pull her out of her comfort zone? Before I could think too hard about the implications, I grabbed her around her waist and pulled her toward me.

"What are you doing?" she pushed her hands against my chest as I drew her closer.

"I'm peering over your walls," I replied. "I bet you've never, ever kissed someone in public. If you want me to buy that table, press your lips against mine in front of everyone in this store."

She glanced around. "You're blackmailing me?" she asked.

"Hardly. We're talking about a kiss and a table." Truth be told, I wasn't one for public displays of affection; seeing other couples embracing always made me feel a little uncomfortable. But having Grace in my arms, her warmth began to seep into me. Holding her felt as if I were in some kind of secret club, just her and me.

I didn't give a shit about who was looking.

"Okay," she whispered, then put her hand to the back of

my neck, her thumb stroking up my jaw. If I hadn't known better, I would believe that was real affection in her fingers. I bent and she reached up on her tiptoes and very chastely touched her lips to mine. Her mouth was so soft, vulnerable.

"More," I muttered against her mouth, dipping my head lower. She linked her hands around my head and smiled against my lips. I couldn't help but grin back before snaking my tongue inside and kissing her as if it were my last moment on earth.

Without the whiskey, every sense was heightened, and in a matter of seconds I was hard. I pressed my hand against her ass, pulling her toward me, wanting her to feel my cock. Jesus. Being in public and knowing this couldn't be any more than a kiss made it all the more fun. I couldn't remember ever kissing a woman without the expectation that it would turn into something more. This was new. And I liked it.

A small groan escaped Grace's lips and suddenly she pulled away, almost as if she were ashamed she'd gotten so carried away. I released her, but couldn't keep my eyes off her as she glanced around surreptitiously. She smoothed down her hair and turned away from me, then covered her mouth with both hands. "Your . . ." she whispered as if it were *talking* that would draw people's attention. She waved her hand in front of my face. "It makes my face red."

I stroked my face. She meant my stubble. I shaved every morning, but by the afternoon, I always had some regrowth. Her chin and mouth were a little reddened. I grinned, pleased she still wore the aftereffects of our kiss. How would she like my scruff grazing along her inner-thigh, across her pussy? It was my turn to swallow a groan.

How had I let her leave the other day without tasting her?

"You want normal shipping or the expedited option?" the sales clerk asked, pulling my attention away from Grace and her red, kiss-swollen lips.

"Expedited," I replied without really thinking about it, distracted by the blonde beauty in front of me.

"Right, now a dining table and a bed," she said as the clerk handed me my credit card.

"You know how this works, right?" I asked.

"How what works?" she asked, leading me toward some dining furniture.

"You get to push, I get to push. If that kiss was what I get for a coffee table, I'll have to think up something suitable before you pick out stuff for the dining room."

She trapped the side of her bottom lip with her teeth. "Well, let's just look on the way to the exit," she said. Maybe she thought she could convince me. Or maybe she thought I was going to kiss her again. Perhaps she wanted me to.

I followed her as she wandered around an area full of tables and chairs, watching her take in her surroundings. Eventually she spun to face me and shrugged. "Nope. There's nothing here for you." She grinned and I couldn't help but chuckle.

"Scaredy-cat," I said.

She narrowed her eyes. "I'm not scared; I just don't like these dining tables. It's as simple as that."

I tutted and stuffed my hands in my pockets. "I thought

you had a little more grit, Grace Astor. You've fallen at the first hurdle."

She walked toward the exit and I followed her.

"Is this how you get women? You blackmail them into a physical relationship with you?" she asked, her eyebrows pulling together in an adorable frown.

"Yeah." I laughed. "All the time." We waited side by side for the elevator, then rode down in silence.

As the doors opened, she asked, "What would you have made me do?"

"I wouldn't *make* you do anything."

"Okay then, what would have been the pay off?" she asked as she reached out to flag a cab.

I placed my hands on her shoulders and moved her away from the curb. Almost immediately, a cab pulled up beside us. I opened the door and indicated for Grace. As she slid inside, I said, "A tattoo." How far could I push her? How far did I want to push her? All I knew was I'd enjoy the negotiation—the to and fro, her facial expressions as she weighed the pros and cons in her mind. As much as I wanted an art consultant, I wanted to spend time with Grace whether or not it was about art.

"Jesus, no way. That would be permanent."

"Where are you going?" I asked.

"Brooklyn," she replied.

"And you're getting a cab?" I chuckled. "No, you're not a Park Avenue princess at all." I thrust three twenties at the driver and shut the door.

As the taxi drove off, I watched it head down the street.

I'd enjoyed my afternoon with Grace.

Next time, it would be more than a kiss.

"Christ, I'm sorry, Angie, I don't know what to say." I reached across the melamine table of the diner and covered her hand with mine. Angie had called when I'd gotten back to my apartment after shopping with Grace and asked me to meet her for lunch at the diner the following day.

"Fucking hell, Sam, don't get emotional on me," she said as she snatched her hand away. "Since when are you allowed to hold my hand?" Angie and I never did physical affection. No hugs. No air kisses. Nothing. Not ever. In a group home, casual affection was never on offer. As much as I'd teased Grace about being uncomfortable with public displays of affection, to be truthful, I wasn't any more comfortable than she was.

"Fuck off, I'm not getting emotional. I just want you to be happy." All I wanted was for her to be happy, have the family she'd never had.

"I didn't tell you I have cancer—just that Chas has a low sperm count."

"But can that be fixed?" I wanted to fix it. I'd do whatever it took.

Angie dipped her spoon into her ice-cream sundae. "Doctors said we need to keep trying, and if it still hasn't happened in six months, we might have to think about IVF."

"That sounds . . . like a big step."

"It is. And I'm not sure I'd do it. I mean, I hate needles and it just seems a bit against nature, you know?"

Angie wasn't one to worry about what was natural. "Will Chas's health plan cover IVF?" I asked. From what I'd heard, shit like that was expensive and wasn't the sort of thing to be covered by health insurance.

Angie shrugged, which indicated she knew damn well it wasn't covered, which meant she might not have IVF because she and Chas wouldn't be able to afford it.

"You know we're going to have to have a conversation about this, so just give into it now, rather than after three months of arguments about it," I said.

"What are you talking about, you crazy-man?" she asked, her eyes fixating on the hazelnut balancing on her spoon.

"You know what I'm talking about. You hate discussing money, but I'm going to pay for the IVF." It was an old argument—I even lost the battle over the check for cheeseburgers at the diner once in a while. The only reason Angie'd let me buy their house was because I'd told her all I wanted for Christmas was to be allowed to buy them the wedding gift I thought they deserved.

"Fuck off. Chas would never go for it. You're not paying for our baby."

"Of course I'm not paying for your baby. I'm not a human trafficker, for Christ's sake. I just want to pick up the medical expenses." I sighed as Angie ignored me, looking around the small room at the other couples.

"Maybe it's just not meant to be. God only knows what kind of mother I'd be. I sure as hell didn't have much of a role model."

"You're not going to be your mother, Angie. You know that."

She shrugged. "Who's to say? They say we turn into our parents. And if that's true, any baby I have doesn't stand a chance."

I rolled up a napkin and threw it at her. "Don't you dare let your mother steal this part of your life from you. You're not her. Look at the way you are with Chas—was she ever a loving wife in the way you are?" I slapped my palms on the table. Didn't she see she deserved happiness? "You can't let her rob you of your future—she's done enough damage."

She smiled at me and tilted her head. "Thank you, Sam. You always know what to say."

I nodded. "And I'm paying for the IVF. I don't want to hear about it again. In return, I'll buy a new couch."

She looked back, her eyes narrowed. "Did you buy a couch already?"

Busted. But worth a shot.

"I will if you say yes to letting me cover your medical expenses."

"I think you already bought a couch," she said. "What brought that on?"

"Angie, listen, I want—"

"I'll talk to Chas. No promises." Part of the reason I liked Chas so much was that he was a proud man who would do anything for his wife. Taking money from me was difficult, and I respected that.

"Okay," I replied.

"Okay. Tell me about the couch."

I leaned back, stretching my arms across the back of the red leatherette seat. "What is there to say? I bought a couch."

"Just like that?"

"Sure," I said.

Angie's spoon clattered against the glass of the sundae dish. "Where?"

"Saks."

She tilted her head to one side. "*Riiight*. You just happened to decide to go to Saks and buy a couch."

I grinned. "Okay, if you must know, my art consultant took me."

"A woman?"

"Yes, a woman. We were looking at some paintings and . . ." How was I supposed to explain what went down? "I asked her where to shop and one thing led to another." Yeah, that wasn't even close to how it had happened, but I didn't want Angie jumping to any conclusions. "She offered to help."

"Offered to suck your dick, more like," Angie said and I threw a napkin at her. I could dream. Me on that big black couch, her kneeling on the floor, my hands gripping her hair. The pleather squeaked as I shifted and sat forward in an effort to disguise my growing erection.

"You can't assume that everyone who's polite and helpful wants to get in my pants," I said.

"Why not?" She shrugged. "They probably do. Who is this chick anyway? Is she hot?"

"She's my *art* consultant."

"And couch consultant, apparently. It sounds like she's

113

consulting you very well."

I chuckled and shook my head.

"Well," she said breezily. "I think it's good. You need a little 'consulting' in your life. I like the idea of you picking out furniture with a woman."

That was *not* how it had gone down. "We're not setting up house together, for Christ's sake."

"No, you're just picking out furniture together. You've got nothing to hide." She raised her eyes. "Like I said, I approve."

Angie liked to tease me as much as I liked to tease her, but there was something in what she was saying that cut a little too close to the bone and I wanted to change the subject. "And you're going to speak to Chas about the IVF?" I asked.

She grinned. "Better we talk about my womb that your love life, right?"

"There is no love life, Angie."

Her grin dissolved. "Maybe there should be."

CHAPTER TEN
GRACE

I'd ignored only two calls from Sam since our shopping trip last week. The third one I'd answered because I needed to give him the details of the agenda for today. As I walked into the entrance of the auction house, my stomach somersaulted. I'd never bid at any of these things. I'd seen it done but never raised my hand and spent a lot of money in a matter of seconds.

I checked the time on my phone. Ten minutes early. We'd agreed to meet at three thirty, but it was raining and I'd worried about not being able to get a cab. I hadn't wanted to be late. Anyway, at least now I wouldn't have to wait in line for too long to register and collect our paddle.

I leaned against the dark wood paneling of the wide hallway, staring at the royal blue carpet under my feet as I waited. Perhaps Sam should bid? It was his money we were spending, after all.

In the five days since I'd last seen him, I'd thought about him more than I should. I'd also had tattoos on my mind. I'd never understood the appeal of having something permanently etched onto my skin. What if I got bored or changed my mind about whatever I'd chosen to mark myself with?

Nothing was permanent.

So why was I thinking about what design I'd choose and where I'd have it done? Why was I thinking about Sam holding my hand and making me laugh to take my mind off the pain?

"Hey," Sam whispered, the heat of his breath against my skin.

I looked up to find him towering over me.

"You okay?" he asked, frowning, staring at me, analyzing me.

I pushed myself off the wall to stand next to him. "Yeah, fine. Just thinking while I waited."

"Sorry to keep you waiting," he said, his hands in his pockets. How did he manage to have such an imposing presence without even trying? Most powerful men made a point of taking up space in the room. But Sam didn't announce himself wherever he went. He didn't walk without deference to other people, even if they might be in his way. He was so very controlled and contained, but when he was anywhere near me, all I could do was look at him, wishing he'd look at me. He demanded my attention in the most subtle way.

"I like thinking," I said and grinned at him.

"What were you thinking about?" he asked as we set off toward the auction room.

"Just things," I replied. "You know." How could I tell him that I'd been thinking about him?

"I'm not sure I do, Grace Astor. Enlighten me."

"Do you have a tattoo?" I asked.

His mouth twitched. "You've been thinking about

whether or not I have a tattoo?"

As we entered the back of the auction room, a babble of voices interrupted us, thankfully. I'd given too much away.

"Here," I said, pointing at two seats at the end of a row about halfway down the columns of chairs facing the stage.

We sat down, Sam on the outside, nearest the wall, me between him and a woman on my left. "So, we have to stick to our maximum bid on these pieces," I said quietly, leaning toward him. You never knew who was listening. The room was full of collectors—people devising strategies to get the right art at the right price. "We don't want to get carried away."

"Yes, we wouldn't want that. Would we?" he whispered back.

"I'm serious, Sam. The adrenaline will start to flow and a man like you is bound to feel tempted to outbid other people."

"A man like me?" he asked. "A guy with tattoos?"

"Yes. I mean no." He had me flustered as everything he said seemed so personal. "You don't get to be as successful as you are without being competitive."

He nodded but didn't speak. His eyes scanned the room, taking it all in. There was lots of hushed chatter, almost as if we were in church.

I followed his line of sight as he watched people trail in. "So did you say you had a tattoo?" I asked. We should be focusing on the art. At least, *I* should be. But I wanted to know the answer to the question. I wanted to imagine what it looked like.

"Just one," he replied. "I wouldn't ask you to do something I hadn't done myself."

I couldn't remember seeing a tattoo on his body. I took

a sharp intake of breath as I remembered him over me, the scruff of his beard dragging across my cheek as he moved into me, whispering how good it felt.

"You okay?" he asked, reaching across my legs and pulling my knees toward him.

"What is it?" I asked as he released his hand. Better question, *where* was it?

A couple of people walked onto the stage and the room began to quiet. Sam craned his neck. "You'll see it soon enough."

Excuse me? I would see it soon enough? Did that mean he planned to show me? Where was it? What was it?

Next time?

We weren't getting naked again. Except . . . Except I liked the way he touched me. I liked the way he never had to raise his voice to be heard. I liked the way he moved. Even the way he breathed seemed so . . . deliberate, so purposeful. Like everything for him had a meaning. Next time he was naked with me, I'd scour every inch of his body looking for his tattoo.

He nudged me, breaking my concentration. "Look," he whispered, his eyes wide. "He has a little hammer and everything." He squeezed my leg.

I stared at him, and a grin spread across my face. He was excited about this. And I liked the way I got to share it with him.

The lots passed quickly and soon the Lautrec prints were up.

"I like the colors," Sam said as he stared at the prints being put on the stands on the stage.

I really loved these, and I was pleased he did. They were

almost cartoon-like—big primary colors and strong lines. They were fun. "Do you want to bid?" I asked.

He shook his head. "That's why I'm paying you."

I didn't tell him I'd never done it before, but he was right. It was my job.

The room fell silent in the seconds before the bidding started. The auctioneer introduced the prints, telling us a little of the provenance and the composition—nothing that wasn't in the catalog—and then before I had a chance to catch my breath, the bidding began. A bidder on the phone was against someone closer to the front. My plan was to wait until one of the first bidders had dropped out and then raise my paddle. But before we even got a chance to start, and within just a few seconds, our maximum bid had been reached.

"Sorry," I whispered as the bidding continued.

"Don't be," he replied. "This is fun. Reminds me of the old days selling stuff in the street, there's just more money involved. And people are wearing nicer clothes."

"The street?" I asked. "When did you ever . . ."

"And, *believe me*, the people smell a lot nicer."

Had his parents made him work through college or something?

Our next lot, a Degas lithograph of a nude that would go with the others he'd bought from me, was up next. The bidding started high at forty thousand dollars. We'd agreed to seventy-five for this piece. I'd encouraged Sam to be conservative with our limits, but maybe I'd been *too* conservative. At sixty the bidding slowed down and I gripped the paddle, ready to jump in. I could feel Sam's eyes on me, but I couldn't look at him now. At sixty-five I saw my opportunity and raised the paddle. The auctioneer acknowledged my bid with a pointed finger "Seventy-five?" he asked the bidder in front who'd been in since the start. With a nod, and as if we hadn't bid at all, we were outbid and it was over. Jesus.

I sat back in my chair, shaking my head. "It doesn't matter," Sam whispered. "Honestly. This is an experience." There was something about the way he drew out the word *experience* that made me want to feel his tongue across my skin, his hands resting on my hips. I tightened my grip around the paddle.

The Brueghel still life was next, and the most expensive of the three lots we'd agreed to bid on. I didn't think Sam would have picked it out of my shortlist—it didn't have the instant appeal for people who didn't know much about art because it seemed so traditional at first glance. But if you took your time to look at it more closely, it came to life and continued to reveal itself at every inspection. Still, it was a great piece and we had a good chance of getting it with our budget of one point two million.

My palms grew clammy as I passed the paddle from one hand to another. I didn't want Sam to walk away empty-handed from today, and I didn't want him to think I was totally incompetent and had set our limits way too low. Sam placed his hand around my wrist. "It'll be fine. Whatever happens it won't be the best or the worst day of my life."

It was an odd thing to say, but he was right. We weren't about to cure cancer. His words slowed my heart. Whatever happened, it wouldn't be the end of the world.

I forced by eyes back to the stage as the action began. I should be concentrating on what was going on in front of me, but I wanted to know what the best and worst days of Sam Shaw's life had been.

Several phoned-in bids drove the price up, but by eight hundred thousand, all but one had dropped out, leaving a single bidder in the room and the one on the phone to compete with. At a million, only the phone bidder was left. I raised my paddle with a deep breath. *Shit.* I was about to spend *a lot* of someone else's money. I hoped I'd picked right and I wasn't about to buy a turkey. My bid was acknowledged, and I turned to Sam who calmly nodded at me.

We kept bidding, the price nudging higher and higher in increments of twenty thousand until at one million eighty thousand the hammer came down on our bid.

Shit.

We'd done it. My stomach tightened and my body went hot. I hoped Sam was good for the money. I held my paddle in the air as the auctioneer took down my number and Sam grabbed my hand, squeezing his palm against mine.

There were a few mutterings in the crowd and people turned to take a look at the person who'd just dropped seven figures in a matter of seconds. Sam and I sat there as if we shopped like this every afternoon. I pressed my lips together, trying not to show my excitement, trying to stop the adrenaline from pouring out of me.

"You did it," he whispered into my ear and my nipples tightened against my bra as his breath hit my skin. "Let's go."

I understood his need to get out of the auction house. There was something so intimate about what had just happened— from the way we'd been sitting so close, whispering to each other, to the fact we'd both been reaching for the same goal and he'd been silently cheering me on. Yet, here we were surrounded by all these people. I wanted us to be on our own.

He pulled me out of my seat and away from the staring faces.

As we headed toward the door, I tried to stop him. "Sam, no. We have to pay." He grimaced but turned and strode in the other direction. I handed over my paddle and the paperwork I'd been given when we arrived to the woman behind a wooden desk.

"Congratulations," she said without looking up at us. "You have twenty-four hours to arrange collection. Should I use the card details we have here?"

With one hand Sam reached into his pocket and flipped open his brown leather wallet. I tried to pull away to make it easier, but he squeezed my fingers. Awkwardly, he fumbled and then finally presented his American Express.

I glanced up, and found him staring back at me. He released my hand, and I thought for a second he could see what I was thinking—that I wanted him. My body sagged with relief as he snaked his arm around my waist and pulled me toward him. Did he want me too?

"Come with me," he said, turning us and walking so quickly I found myself having to run every couple of steps to keep up with him.

A cab idled at the curb. "Seven forty Park Avenue," Sam told the driver.

"That was a rush," he said, his fingers tickling over my knee.

I nodded. We both had excess energy. Maybe we should down some shots, dance a little, though I didn't see Sam as much of a dancer. "We're going to your place?" I asked. "To decide where the painting will hang best?" I hoped that wouldn't be the only thing that happened at his place.

He frowned. "If you like, but then I'm going to fuck you on my new couch."

I tried to keep my expression steady despite the throbbing between my legs. I wasn't quite sure how to respond to such a blunt declaration. "The couch has arrived already?"

"I tell you I'm going to fuck you and you focus on the couch?"

Only so I didn't have to think about whether going home with him was a mistake. This wasn't my normal MO. *Sam Shaw* wasn't my normal MO, but I wanted him. Every time I was near him, I wanted him.

I found it difficult to look at him as we got out of the car and went into his building. Even in the elevator I studied the floor rather than glance at him and have him see how much I wanted him. He periodically squeezed my hand, running his thumb over my knuckles, sending sparks of lust across my skin.

In his apartment, we stood in front of the couch, holding hands, looking out onto the city.

"Did you feel it?" he asked, keeping his gaze forward at

the skyline as if he was trying not to look at me. "Between us, at the auction house?"

I knew what he was asking. There was a pull toward him, a need to touch him, a desire to be alone, together.

I nodded and he turned toward me. "I wanted it to be just you and me." He released my hand and cupped my face, stroking his thumbs over my cheekbones. "I like you."

His eyes flicked to my lips.

There was nothing but the sound of our exaggerated breathing in the air.

"I like you, too." I shouldn't like him—I should think he was spoiled and indulged. Except that he didn't seem that way at all.

He sighed as if he were disappointed. Slipping my jacket from my shoulders, he didn't take his eyes from my face. Not as he undid my sleeveless shirt, leaving it to fall to the floor. Not as he removed my skirt. Not when I stood in front of him in just my underwear. He stepped back and finally let his eyes trail down my body. Just his glance intoxicated me, each part of my body lighting up as he inspected me. "Sam," I whispered, urging him to take pity on me, to touch me.

My cry brought his gaze back to my face and he stepped forward. "I'm here," he said. "I'm here, Princess."

My fingers fumbled at his shirt but he knocked them away and unbuttoned it quicker than I could have. My body was weakened by him. Relief flooded me as I placed my palms against his chest. I'd been waiting to touch him, to kiss him. He took his pants off and snaked his arms around my waist, one hand smoothing up my back, the other down to my ass, holding me against him. "Tell me what you want," he whispered, his forehead pressed against mine.

"You. I want all of you," I replied.

He groaned as if just my words increased his need for me. "You don't know all of me, Princess. Not yet."

"I don't care," I said. "I want it all."

He pushed his lips against mine, urgent and needy. Our lust had been let off the leash; I just couldn't get enough of him. I pulled at him and he gripped me tighter. My hands went from his neck to his chest to his sides. I couldn't decide where I should hold him, where I could feel enough of him, get enough of him.

He lifted me and I wrapped my legs around his waist, my arms around his neck, our lips never leaving each other's, our tongues pushing and reaching as he walked across the living room.

His hands went to my hips, holding me as he encouraged me to unwrap my legs.

"Bend over, Grace," he said, turning me so I faced the couch. I shivered and leaned over the black velvet arm, the fabric pressing against my warm skin, softly grazing my nipples.

Sam smoothed his palms up my spine, then down and over my ass. "Beautiful," he whispered, then his touch left me. I pushed up on my hands and glanced over my shoulder. "Stay there," he said from a few steps away. He crouched, rummaging in his pants pocket. I took the opportunity to admire his body, his hard thighs, the peaks and troughs of his arms where muscle overlapped muscle. He stood and walked toward me, his thick cock flat against his stomach. *Jesus.*

Strong was the only word to describe Sam Shaw. And it wasn't just his body that earned that description. When he spoke, the way he walked—everything about him exuded strength. Like rock, having weathered a thousand years of the world, Sam was strong inside and out.

"Are you ready?" he asked, stroking his hand across my lower back.

Couldn't he tell?

I opened my legs and turned my head so he couldn't see my smile as he moaned. The crinkle of the condom wrapper delayed the feel of his cock at my entrance. I sagged, relieved he'd soon be inside me, hoped he'd cure this need I had.

"You want more of me?" he asked.

I nodded.

"Talk to me, Princess," he said. "I want to hear it."

"Yes," I said, my voice small and desperate.

"Say it louder," he bellowed.

"Please. I want you deeper. I want all of you deeper."

He slammed into me and I slid against the velvet. He hooked his hand over my shoulder, driving me onto his cock. "That's what you want, isn't it?" He pulled out. "Tell me," he said, his voice soft.

"Yes, I want it. Please, Sam." What was he doing to me? This man had me *begging* for his dick. But as he drove into me again, my questions disappeared and I could only concentrate on the way he filled me up. I had no control over my body. The heat. The layers of pleasure that seemed to settle over me with every thrust. Sam gave me everything and I lay there, feeling like I could give him nothing in return.

His thighs pressed against mine as he continued to fuck me. His hands tugged and pulled at my waist, my hips, my neck. I was covered in him.

I wasn't used to taking from a man. I was used to giving, to concentrating on making him happy, making sure he was getting what he needed. All I could think about was how good this felt. How perfect Sam made me feel.

He withdrew and I reached for him, but his hands left me, too. I snapped my head around, but before I had time to argue, he'd pulled me up and sat my ass on the back of the sofa. "That's better. I can see your eyes," he said, pushing into me again. His pace was less feverish this time, slow and steady and deliberate, as if he'd regained some control now that I'd admitted I wanted him.

He leaned forward and brushed his lips over mine before dipping to kiss my shoulder. His kiss turned to a bite as he increased his thrusts. I wasn't sure I wouldn't tip over the back of the sofa, but just as I became unsteady, he caught me, pushing us closer, his teeth sinking deeper and deeper. The pain heightened my pleasure and with his next push, my orgasm began to uncurl and my nails dug into his shoulder.

"Oh God, yes," I cried.

His movements became jagged, and I pulled him toward me, wanting more of him, not ready for the peak of my climax to fade.

He let out a tremendous groan, thrusting sharply into me as his orgasm collided with mine. He brought his forehead back to mine, our breaths short and out of synch.

It was like he tore the pleasure out of me, then coated

himself in it. As if our orgasms were symbiotic, joined.

One impossible without the other.

———————————

"I knew you'd look unbelievable naked against this couch," he said as we lay side by side on the cushions, where he'd arranged us post orgasm.

I giggled. "Is that why you bought it?"

"Yeah, I think it was."

I shivered. "Are you cold?" he asked, pulling us closer. I shook my head. I wasn't. "I should have a blanket or something. You know, on the back of the cushions like you do in magazines."

I grinned. "You don't even have dining chairs—accessories are a second layer. You need the basics first."

"Have you decided on what tattoo you're going to get?" he asked.

My eyes widened. "Oh God." I'd forgotten to look. "Where is it?" I tugged at his arm, twisting it so I could get a better look.

He stroked my chin with his thumb. "You're very beautiful."

"Where's your tattoo?" I asked.

Without taking his eyes from mine, he lifted his arm toward the ceiling. I shifted up onto my elbow, scanning his skin.

"No, on my side," he said.

Along his body were a few handwritten words. I pressed my fingers next to them and looked closer. "Wait and hope," I read aloud and glanced up at him as he brought his arm down, hiding the marking once more. It was beautiful. The script was curly and pretty and seemed to decorate rather than defile him. Perhaps I *could* have a tattoo. I liked the way it hid under his arm waiting to be discovered, revealed just to people he decided he wanted to show it to. It made me feel special. I rarely took risks, but when I had, they seemed to pay off—the gallery, him . . . "What does that mean?" I asked.

"It's from a book," he said, cupping my face, distracting me from the ink. He kissed me on the nose. "There was something else I wanted to do to you on this couch." He pushed himself up, sliding me to the edge of the sofa until I sat up. "Lie back," he said. "I want to see that blonde hair spread across the cushions." He pressed my thighs open with his palms and fixed his stare between my legs.

Maybe I should have been embarrassed, but I liked watching him watching me. He was so focused and intense. "Even your pussy is beautiful," he said, glancing up and grinning at me as he pushed his hands up my thighs. "Your mouth . . ." He kissed me briefly on my lips, using just a whisper of his tongue. "Beautiful. This, here . . ." He trailed his tongue along my collarbone and I melted into the cushions behind me. "Is beautiful. It's all . . ." He placed kisses down my chest, between my breasts and over my stomach. "Beautiful." He paused and pulled back before his thumbs opened my lips. I lay before him as he spread me wide, and somehow it was okay to be so exposed to someone, to him at least. It felt right.

He nudged his tongue into my folds, then up toward

my clit. My back arched in anticipation. The fire between us that had built during the auction reignited, as though it had only been temporarily quenched by that first orgasm. Sam moaned against my sex, the vibrations scattering across my body. My hands threaded into his hair, urging him on. I wanted more, wanted whatever he could give me. "Yes." My voice came out breathy and begging as he licked and pressed his flattened tongue against my clit. Wetness trickled out of me. We were going to ruin his couch.

The softness of his tongue on my clit mixed with the rough of his stubble on my thighs was too much sensation. I jerked and he placed his large palm on my stomach to hold me in place. Two fingers began to circle my entrance. I wanted them deeper, needed him inside me.

He knew that if he gave me what I needed, I'd be gone, pushed over the edge immediately. He wanted to tease me a little longer.

"More," I cried out. As if my plea was what he'd been waiting for, he thrust his fingers into me, his tongue rounding my clit. It was too much. I gripped his hair, suddenly wanting him to hold off, but he was relentless. The teasing was over and he was going to make me come with a vengeance. The realization stirred my orgasm. I had no control. My body was his. Sensation ran down my thighs and they began to shake. He flicked his tongue over my clitoris and I was gone. I released my grip on his hair, my hands falling to my side as my back arched and I came in a violent wave.

Panting, I watched as he grinned up at me. "You taste

amazing."

I could barely breathe.

I couldn't tell him that no man had ever made me come with his tongue before. I couldn't say that sex with him was so different to sex with any one of my other boyfriends it was like comparing ice and diamonds. He was everything I shouldn't want—everything I'd spent my life rejecting and here I was, wanting him so badly I could barely breathe.

CHAPTER ELEVEN
SAM

Grace seemed to have a rule that she ignore me the first three times I called her. Which was why I was pulling up her number for the fourth time in forty-eight hours. I looked out of my office window and down below at the street. The yellow of the crush of cabs reminded me of the prints we'd bid on at the auction but lost. I hadn't minded not getting them even though I liked them. I'd just enjoyed being with Grace.

After the auction, the sex, the way I told her she owed me a tattoo, she'd left. And I'd wanted to ask her to stay but I couldn't quite find the right words—a good reason. I'd spent the last two days trying to find an excuse to call her. She'd mentioned something about an exhibition she thought I might be interested in and I wanted to know more. About the exhibition. About her.

"Sam," she answered.

"Come to my office at twelve," I said, looking south across the buildings. Was she at the gallery? What was she wearing? Was her hair up or down? I liked the way some escaped when she wore it up. I wanted to see her.

"I'm busy," she said, but I heard the grin in her voice.

She didn't hate the idea.

"Then unbusy yourself and come to my office at twelve." I was supposed to have a lunch, but I could cancel. "I want your thoughts on dining tables."

I needed another place to fuck her. A dining table would do nicely.

"I haven't said yes to the tattoo," she replied.

"You will," I said. "I expect you here at twelve sharp." I hung up.

I'd never had any difficulty walking away from women I'd had sex with. I knew it was better for them, and for me. I had no need to create emotional ties. But with Grace, I just couldn't keep away. If I hadn't called her, insisted on hiring her, I was pretty sure she wouldn't have gotten in touch with me. She'd have made it easy for us to part ways.

Maybe that was why I was chasing after her like a teenage boy.

I busied myself, trying to get enough work done so that I didn't have to come back to the office this afternoon, after I'd taken Grace to get her tattoo. Wanting to prove to myself that it was possible to spend an hour not thinking about Grace Astor.

———

At twelve fifteen my fingers hovered over the buttons on my phone. Should I call and make sure Grace was coming? I looked up at the knock on my office door as my assistant came through, followed by Grace. I stood up to greet Grace but she didn't look at me. Her eyes were everywhere but on me, taking in my office, Rosemary, everything.

"Can I get you a cup of coffee or a glass of water?" Rosemary asked.

Grace smiled and shook her head, a strand of hair escaping from the way she had it fixed up. "No, thank you."

"Nothing for me, Rosemary," I said, rushing her out of my office. "Please close the door."

I rounded my desk, heading toward Grace. How should I greet her? A kiss on the cheek? A nod of the head? Instead, my hand smoothed over her back and I guided her toward the conference table. "Please take a seat."

"So, I'm here," she said, her eyebrows raised as she sat down and finally looked at me.

I sat, returning her gaze. "Thank you for coming." Did she not want to be here? I didn't want her to think I was pressuring her. I wanted her to be as pleased to see me as I was to see her. Perhaps I should focus on our business relationship. "Tell me about the exhibition you mentioned when I last saw you."

Grace paused before she said, "It's for an up-and-coming artist."

I knew she had a proclivity for rising stars. Was this one an ex-boyfriend, too?

"I think this will be his second exhibition out of art school. There was a really traditional feel to his last show, so I'm hoping you're going to like it." She gave a little half shrug as if to say *What more do you want me to say?*

I nodded. "If you think it's worth my while."

"You don't have to come along," she said. "I could go on my own, do a bit of research, take a few photos on my phone and then report back. I don't know too much about the work, to be honest. I have to see it—it could be a disaster. I don't want to waste your time. I know how busy you are."

Didn't she get it? The exhibition was just a reason to spend time with her. The art was secondary. "I'll pick you up."

She frowned. "You don't need to do that. It's not like it's a date or something. I can meet you there."

Not like it's a date or something. The last time I'd been on a date was in high school, and I hadn't realized it was a date until I arrived at the movie theater to discover it was just me and Jessica Warner. I'd kissed her, because why not? To this day, it had been the only date I'd ever been on.

Grace's hands were folded neatly in her lap, belying her sexiness. If I was going to take anyone on a date, it was going to be Grace. "I'll pick you up," I said. "We can research together. Now, what about dining tables?" I asked, not ready for our meeting to be over.

"Maybe," she said.

I didn't understand. "Maybe?"

"If it's small. And pretty like yours."

It took a few seconds for me to realize that she was talking about her having a tattoo. "You think my tattoo is pretty?"

"Pretty wasn't what you were going for?" She grinned at me.

"If you like it, I'll take it," I replied and her cheeks pinked.

"There's a place in the East Village that is supposed to be good, but you'll have to come with me. I'm not doing it alone."

Her wanting me to accompany her anywhere should scare me. I'd spent my whole life determinedly independent but somehow the thought of her needing me wasn't as frightening as it should be. But I had to make an effort to keep the corners of my mouth down—I liked it.

"It would have to be small," she said. "And I like the idea of words. No Mickey Mouse head or anything." She was talking fast like she did when she was nervous.

I hadn't expected her to say yes to the tattoo. And now she was offering it, I wasn't sure it was the right thing to do. I'd buy whatever she wanted—tattoo or no tattoo. I liked her just as she was. She didn't need to add anything to her already beautiful body.

"What about this afternoon? I'm sure you're busy around here, but I might lose my nerve if I wait." She curled a strand of hair around her ear. "So?" she asked. "Are you busy?"

"Always," I replied. Her shoulders sank a little. Relief? Disappointment? I wasn't sure. "But I'm the boss, so I can—"

"Okay then," she said. "We should go."

"We don't have to," I said. "I mean, it was a big ask—too much. I never thought you'd actually—"

"You need a dining table, Sam Shaw," she replied.

"I'll buy one, but you don't need to get a tattoo. It was a stupid idea." If she'd never wanted one, who was I to tell her she should permanently mark her perfect skin?

"A deal is a deal," she said, her hands squeezing together on her lap. "And it seems the risks I'm taking in my life are paying off." She took a breath and nodded. "So why stop now?"

Grace trailed her fingers along the thick blue binders of designs set against the back wall of the tattoo parlor. "Any idea of what you'd like?" the guy behind the counter asked. There were only two people in the shop. One guy was easily four hundred pounds with a long gray beard and a pirate-like hoop earring through his left ear. He sat in the corner, minding his own business, while a younger guy with a ponytail watched Grace as if someone so beautiful had never crossed his path.

Grace turned and looked at me. "Your choice," she said.

What? She couldn't be giving me such a responsibility. "No way. I'm not choosing your tattoo. You have to live with it . . ." I nearly said "until you die" but I didn't like to be so cursory with those kinds of words. I knew how close death was to us all. Did my parents have tattoos? I'd never noticed any. And now I'd never know. My chest grew tight. I didn't like to think about them, about the impermanent nature of life. Jesus, this seemed like a bad idea. "This is too permanent, Grace. We should go."

She took my wrist, pulling my hand from my hair. "I don't do things I don't want to. Please, Sam." The lilt of her words and her skin against mine soothed me. "Choose something." Didn't she realize that what she was asking me to do was too much? I could imagine Angie maybe asking. Or perhaps a married couple, but I'd know Grace such a short time and we were nothing to each other. Not really.

She slid up onto the purple reclining tattoo chair and

watched me. "Come on. We haven't got all day. We've got dining furniture to shop for. Pick what you think would look good." She smiled and it lit up her face. Right then I would have done anything she'd told me to do.

I shook my head in mock exasperation. I'd choose because she asked me and not because I wanted to. Maybe because I *wanted* to be something to her. "Okay, lie down, Princess, and I'll come up with something."

One of the binders was open on the wooden desk at the back of the room and I began to flip through it. What should it be? A quote about art? She'd said I should pick what *I* liked. Did she trust me that much?

I glanced over my shoulder at her and she was watching me as I watched her. I wanted to go over and touch her, kiss her, hold her.

I took a breath. I knew what the tattoo should be.

Lowering my voice so she wouldn't hear, I explained to the tattoo artist what I wanted. Just two words in cursive font. It wouldn't take long and shouldn't hurt too much.

"You want yours where I have mine?" I asked. She nodded and turned on her side as she lifted up her blouse, revealing the side of her ribs. Her alabaster skin was so perfectly flawless. It shouldn't be marked. "Are you sure you want to do this?" I asked. "I told you, I'll buy whatever you want."

"Yes, I want to do this."

I pulled up a chair. "Can I dare you not to?" I didn't want her to do this for *me*. Or not because I'd asked her, not as a deal anyway.

"No," she said. "I'm committed."

"What happens if I've asked him to tattoo a gigantic turd on your ribcage?"

I expected her to laugh but she just looked at me. "I trust you."

My heart twanged. She trusted me so easily—too easily. The buzz of the machine starting up interrupted my inner conflict.

"Are you ready?" I asked.

She took a deep breath and nodded. Underneath her delicate exterior was a strong, feisty woman made of steel.

The tattoo artist stood at her waist, and I sat to his right, opposite her head.

I leaned forward and took her hands in mine. "Squeeze tight."

As the pen touched her skin, she crinkled her nose, shutting her eyes, but she didn't make a sound. The tattoo I'd chosen wouldn't take long.

"Grace," I said. "Look at me." I wanted her to see the confidence I had in her.

Our eyes locked and with every moment that passed, the connection between us grew. I willed her pain away and she trusted me to do that for her.

"There you go," the artist said as he turned off the machine a few minutes later. "All done."

Grace grinned at me. "I can't believe I got a tattoo."

I couldn't believe it either. And she hadn't made a sound, hadn't complained even a little bit about the pain. Strong as steel.

"How does it look?" she asked.

I stood and leaned over her. Her skin was slightly red but it looked beautiful. I wanted to reach out and trail my fingers over the marks. They suited her so much. Each word had meaning to me. The text was small and neat and *pretty*—just as I'd asked.

"You want to see?" I asked. "I can take a picture on my phone."

I took out my cell, took a shot of the tattoo, then stepped back and snapped one of her face. She looked so gorgeous, I couldn't resist.

"Hey," she said. "Give me that."

I swiped so the photo showing her tattoo was on the screen and handed it to her.

She trailed her fingers over the words as she whispered, "Ultimate bliss." Glancing up at me, she said, "That's lovely, Sam. Where does it come from?"

"You're all done," the artist said as he finished dressing the tattoo. Grace sat up and I gave him some cash.

"No, Sam. I'll pay." She had that same look in her eye Angie got when I'd offered to pay for her IVF.

"No you won't. I persuaded you to get a tattoo, and I got to choose the design. I'm paying."

After I handed over the cash, we stepped out onto the sidewalk.

"Thank you," she said.

"It really was my pleasure." I liked that I'd spent money on her.

"Ultimate bliss?" she asked. "What does it mean? You didn't say." She looked up at me as we began to walk north.

I shoved my hands into my pockets. It just fit her—as if it were meant for her. "It's from a book."

"You're quite the reader," she said. "Is it the same book that you got your quote from?" she asked.

I nodded. "It is, actually. From the same passage, even. You said you wanted me to choose and for it to be like mine." As I said the words out loud, I realized our two tattoos bound us forever in a way, even though I spent a lot of effort on making sure I didn't have any ties. She'd always have my choice on her skin. I ran my hand through my hair. Perhaps I should have chosen something less important to me.

"I like it," she replied. She seemed genuinely pleased. It wasn't the reaction of a princess at all. Maybe being connected to her like that wasn't so bad.

The sounds of the city filled the silence between us as we walked, to where, I had no idea.

"You're not going to tell me which book?" she finally asked.

"*The Count of Monte Cristo*," I replied. I didn't want to tell her how that book was the story I'd clung to in foster care. Or that it had given me some glimmer of hope that things would eventually get better.

As if she knew I couldn't give it, she didn't push for more of an explanation.

"You'll tell me more. Soon," she said.

I wasn't sure if it was a question or not but I glanced across at her and nodded.

———————————

"You look beautiful," I said to Grace as she locked the door to the gallery while I waited on the sidewalk.

I'd chosen my suit carefully that morning. And I'd made sure I was on time to pick Grace up. I knew going to the exhibition this evening was a job for her, but for me tonight was about spending time with her. Was this what dating felt like?

"Thank you, Sam Shaw." She looked at me from under her eyelashes and her cheeks pinked a little in a way where I wanted to reach out and feel their heat. "We'll walk. It's just a block from here."

I stuffed my hands into my pockets to stop myself from reaching for her as we started off along the street.

"How's your tattoo?" I asked.

"Actually, it's kinda great. The redness is gone. From a distance, you can't see it at all, but then as you look closer, it almost seems to reveal itself in layers. First you see it's writing, then you read it, then you understand it."

God, I really liked the way she saw the world. I really liked *her*.

"You know what I mean?" she asked, beaming up at me. Every time she smiled I had to resist an urge to kiss her.

I nodded, but didn't say anything. I wanted her to keep talking. I wanted to know more about her.

"I'm reading your book. I hope you don't mind," she said, her eyes fixed ahead of her. The street was busy with people pulling down roller shutters and walking to the subway, but we existed in a bubble, where it remained calm and peaceful and all the noise and activity was separate from us.

"My book?"

"*The Count of Monte Cristo.*"

"Oh." I swallowed. She was reading it. "It's not my book, Princess." It wasn't like I had ownership over it or anything.

"Maybe it's not. Maybe it is."

Maybe? I wasn't following her. It wasn't my book—millions of people had read that book.

"I've never read it before," she said. "I kind of knew of the story—the young man, falsely imprisoned for a crime he didn't commit—that he fights to survive, to escape." She squeezed my hand. "Reading it, I understand why you like it."

Before I had a chance to ask her what she meant, we'd arrived.

"Here we are." She nodded at a group of people at the entrance of a store. "This is us. If you don't like it, we can leave. Just let me know."

The place was full of people and their clothes seemed to be unusually bright. Perhaps I was just used to suits. People gripped drinks in jam jars, as they talked animatedly and periodically glanced at the walls. The guests were much younger than at the auction, although the glasses and moustaches were similar. It was a far cry from the auction and that smell of old money.

"It's quite the crowd, isn't it?" Grace looked up at me as we made our way toward the back of the gallery. I placed my arm around her waist to keep her close.

"Popular guy, I guess," I replied.

"Yeah. Buyers will be put off, though. Someone lost control of the guest list, but that could be good for us.

Plenty of pieces without red dots."

"Isn't more people good for sales?"

"Only if they're here to buy rather than take advantage of the free bar."

"What do you think?" She spun around three hundred sixty degrees and faced me. "Just give me your gut instinct."

I scanned the room. The paintings had an industrial feel to them. They were masculine and looked like they could have been set pieces from *Alien* or *The Matrix*, lots of black and dark green and dark blue. I tried to pick one out from another but they all seemed quite similar. They didn't seem like Grace's taste. "You like them?" I didn't like to say that it seemed like a case of the emperor's new clothes. How hard could painting like this be? I was pretty sure if someone handed me a paintbrush and a canvas I could come up with something that wasn't too different.

"Let's take a closer look," she said instead of answering. We moved toward one of the smaller pieces surrounded by fewer people. She stared at the canvass intently, first close up, her long neck straining forward and then stepping backward, her head tipping from one side to the other. To see how it would look on a wall? I should have been looking at the painting, but all I could concentrate on was Grace and the way each of her movements were so uncensored but they still showed her body off as if she were being photographed.

"I don't feel it," she said, clutching her fist at her stomach. "I think maybe I should, but I don't. Do you?"

What was I supposed to be feeling? "I don't think so," I

replied honestly.

"You know when you saw the Lautrec? How did that feel?" she asked.

I tried to think back. "I thought they were colorful and clean and . . . straightforward. They weren't trying to be anything they weren't."

She laughed and I cleared by throat, wanting to cover up my embarrassment. "No," she said, grabbing my arm with her two hands. "That's good. I'm laughing because you're describing everything these paintings aren't. And I agree with you." She squeezed my arm and the sparkle in her eyes relaxed me. "But even if I didn't agree with you, you're allowed to like art for whatever reason you like it. Don't ever feel judged."

I twisted the arm she was gripping and took hold of her hand, wanting to keep her close.

"But now we're here, let's try those over there," she said, looking over the heads of the crowd at some paintings on the other side of the room.

We made our way toward the far wall.

I was beginning to think it wouldn't be such a bad thing if tonight was a date.

"Technically, the artist is quite talented," she whispered. "But I'm not sure that's enough if neither of us are feeling it."

"But he's talented?" I wasn't sure how she knew he was talented. I was still pretty confident I could knock out some paintings like these in a couple of hours.

"Just the way he layers the color and uses the illusion of light. You see here." She pointed to the top right-hand corner of the canvas, which had several splashes of yellow paint flecked across it. "It's promising—like a homage to Rothko and Turner. But it's too clinical—there's no passion."

I liked the idea that she didn't like painters if they lacked passion. She had so much, the art she bought should at least be able to match hers. "So, we should go?" I asked, desperate to be away from all these people, for it to be just the two of us again.

"I'm sorry," she said, wincing.

I squeezed her hand. "There's no reason to be." I moved her toward the door.

"I should have checked it out before bringing you."

My chest tightened. I kept forgetting—this was a job for her. We got out into the fresh fall air, but I didn't let go of her hand as we walked toward Seventh. I wanted to remind her we'd been more than just client and art consultant. "I enjoyed coming tonight," I said. I wanted to know if she'd had a good time. Was it really all work for her?

"We were there for twenty minutes. You probably left the office early and—"

"Grace, I was happy to come. In fact, I was thinking maybe I need some more furniture." I'd found myself enjoying *her* company tonight. The art hadn't been important to me. And despite me knowing better, I wanted an excuse to see her again in an environment where it was clear it wasn't just about work.

"I think most places are closed this late," she said.

I ran my thumb over hers. "Not today, but if I were to say you could buy anything you wanted for my place . . ."

147

I paused, as if I was having to steel myself to take the final step off the cliff. "Would you come on a date with me?"

"A date?" she asked. Always a question with a question.

"Yes," I replied. "A date."

"I thought nothing happens after the sex?" she asked. I wanted to be able to give her a reason for me asking. I wanted her to understand this pull I had toward her. Every movement she made was completely mesmerizing to me, the way she talked so passionately about art was so compelling I wanted to listen to her all day. Even though I'd spent my adult life avoiding connection and relationships, somehow Grace had slipped under my radar and now I felt as if I were on a one-way street—as if I didn't have a choice other than to go deeper, spend more time with her.

"What can I say? I'm breaking my own rules." I tried to make light of my change of heart but the low rumble in my gut told me there was nothing light about this one-way street I was on.

"Well, I guess I'm going to have to help you—shit." Something had caught her attention in one of the windows. She stopped, then walked toward a glass storefront. Twisting her hand out of mine, she placed both her palms on the window. "I can't believe they sold it."

"What is it?"

"My painting. They sold my painting," she said, staring into the darkened shop, her voice trailing off.

"This was one you had in your gallery?" I asked. She walked backward, looking up to read the store name.

"It's Renoir. Isn't it the most beautiful thing you've ever

seen?" she asked me as she stood transfixed at the window. I moved closer. "Look at her face." It was a painting of a young girl looking up from her mother's skirt, her hair tied with a red ribbon. She looked straight at us.

"It's pretty," I said, unable to think of anything else to say. The painting reminded me a little of the woman writing at the desk—the La Touche I'd bought from Grace. It had the same mystery about it. But Grace seemed almost upset by this picture. I wasn't used to people being emotional around me. "You think I should buy it?" I asked.

She didn't answer. "Come on, let's go." She turned and continued up the street.

"Grace," I said as I caught up with her. "Talk to me."

"I don't want to talk about it." She sighed. "It was mine . . . for a while. Now it's not. I did what I had to do, and now I need to leave." She sped up, keeping her head down, staring at the ground.

"Hey," I said, grabbing her elbow.

"No. I'm done talking. I want to go home."

It was like a punch to the gut. I wanted our evening to continue. I wasn't ready to give her up.

Her arm shot out to a passing cab that screeched to a halt at the curb. "I'm sorry. I have to go."

I shoved my hands in my pockets as she pulled the door closed, leaving me on the sidewalk.

For the first time in a long time, I'd allowed myself to want more from a person, and here I stood in the taillight of Grace Astor's cab. Not only had she not agreed to date me, but she'd run off within a few minutes of me asking. I glanced back at the picture that seemed to get her so upset. I wanted to make it better for her.

Chapter Twelve
Grace

Sam was supposed to be all about business. Yet here I was, sitting next to him in a limo, driving into the city on a Saturday night for our date. Was it a dare? A quid pro quo for the furniture buying? I'd lost track.

"I'm going to furnish your entire apartment. You know that, right?" I asked. "Office furniture, bedroom furniture, bathroom, rugs, light fixtures, the whole kit and caboodle."

"Whatever you need to feel better about agreeing to this date," he replied and grabbed my hand in his.

"That was our deal," I said, grinning at him. "You can't back out now."

"I'm not. But you told me you don't do anything you don't want to. So, I know you want to be here, just like you wanted to get the tattoo."

He was right, but I wasn't about to tell him he was right. "Whatever you need to keep your ego ticking over, Mr. Shaw."

Sam took my teasing in stride, as he seemed to most things. Despite my head telling me I should have said no to something more with Sam—a proper date—when he turned up in Brooklyn with a car and a driver, I'd been pleased rather than put off. He was trying to impress me and it was cute.

The car slowed and pulled up a couple of blocks away from his apartment. I hoped he wasn't expecting to get laid—not that I wouldn't sleep with him, but I was hungry.

"You're going to make me walk?" I asked as he opened the door and helped me out onto the sidewalk.

"We're just here," he said, pointing at the building in front of us. "If your feet get tired, I'm sure I can give you a piggyback."

This didn't look like a restaurant. There were no lights, no people. We were on a pretty deserted street. I glanced around. Where exactly were we? I looked up at the huge mansion. Wasn't that the Frick—one of my favorite places in the world? I wasn't used to seeing it at night. It had the most beautiful art collection. I'd always liked to imagine arriving for dinner here, ready to swap stories with Teddy Roosevelt and Edith Wharton, as if I wasn't a visitor but a guest at the grand house.

"I'm sure you've been to this place a million times, but I wondered if you'd share it with me?" Sam asked as he took my hand and led me up the stoop.

I'd assumed we'd have dinner at some fancy restaurant. A tour of this place was so much better, but the black heels I'd put on with my blue leather skirt and silk shirt weren't really designed for walking. I might have known Sam would surprise me.

"Those shoes are something else," he said.

I looked up at him, and he was staring at my legs. "Something else?" I asked, grinning.

Our eyes locked. "Yeah, you should come with a warning

152

sign," he whispered into my ear.

I wanted him to kiss me, but knew if he did, neither of us would be able to stop.

We entered the door to find a man holding a tray with two glasses of champagne. Sam picked up both drinks and handed one to me. "Here's to a lovely evening."

"Sam," I said and took a sip, "it was really nice of you to bring me here, thoughtful. But I might be a little underdressed. Is it a formal reception or something?" I asked, transferring my weight from one foot to the other.

"It's whatever we want it to be," he said. "I thought maybe you could show me your favorite pieces and then we'll have dinner in the dining room."

"The dining room?" He couldn't mean the dining room *in the Frick*. Maybe he meant a restaurant nearby?

"Yeah, they asked me which room, but since I had no idea what you'd like I went with the obvious choice."

"We're going to eat in the dining room, amongst the Gainsborough and the Hoppner?" He couldn't be serious. It was one of my favorite parts of the place.

"I couldn't tell you what's in the room, to be honest. Just that there are a lot of paintings in there. I thought you might like it."

"Like it?" I stared at him as he frowned at me. "I can't think of anything I'd rather do." The faint hint of a blush bloomed across his cheeks as I slid my hand into his. "Where should we start?"

He led me into the Garden Court. The place was surprisingly empty. The curved glass roof that normally let in the sun was dark but the fountain in the middle of the courtyard was still babbling to the surrounding palms despite the time of night. Were we the only members of the public here? "Sam Shaw, do we have this place all to ourselves?" I whispered as our footsteps on the stone walkway echoed around us.

"They don't normally open on a Saturday night. I thought it would be nice to be here, just the two of us."

When had any man in my life ever done anything so thoughtful for me? Okay, so to be fair, no one I'd dated since high school had money, but that wasn't what made tonight special. Sam had organized things because he'd thought about me, and what would make me happy. Just the thought and attention he'd given to the evening to make it feel special, make *me* feel special. I shivered.

"Is this what you do? Extravagance, blow women away with your thoughtfulness in order to get into their panties?"

He scraped his hand through his hair. "I've blown you away?"

I hadn't meant to say that, hadn't meant to make it so obvious I wasn't used to men treating me as if I were special, because if I did he might stop, and I didn't want him to. "Yeah. A little bit."

The corners of his mouth began to curl upward and he nodded.

"A lot actually," I confessed.

"Good."

"I'm going to kick off my shoes and make myself comfortable, if you don't mind," I said as we walked into the small, windowless Oval Room at the end of the Garden Court.

"I want you to be comfortable. If you wanted to slip the

skirt off and walk around naked, that would be just fine with me, too."

I laughed. "Naked at the Frick? Not with all these eyes on us," I said, sweeping my arm around at the portraits that lined the room. "We can save that for when we go to the Guggenheim."

Sam laughed. Why hadn't I noticed the smile lines around his eyes before? Perhaps because I didn't see him laugh that often. But a smile suited him. I could imagine Sam as a kid, tumbling about with his friends in the backyard, young and carefree. When had he become so serious?

We wandered from room to room, stopping at various paintings. Sometimes, I talked about what I liked about the works. Sam seemed content just to listen, squeezing my hand at various intervals.

"Is that Degas?" he asked, nodding toward a picture of ballerinas. "You said he liked to paint dancers."

A rush of pride surged within me. He'd been listening, interested in what I was saying. "Yes. Degas. This is very typical of him.

Sam leaned forward to read the title of the picture on the plaque. "*The Rehearsal*."

"Degas liked to paint what he saw as real life, rather than posed models, so it follows that theme." Sam stayed silent, studying the painting. "Almost half his work depicts dancers as they sold so well."

He straightened up and turned to me. "Ahhh, he was a businessman about his art. How do you feel about that, Grace Astor? You don't like people who just want to make money from art."

I laughed. It was a fair challenge. "I think it was a combination of head and heart for Degas. At least I like to think so."

We wandered into the West Gallery.

"I think this one is my favorite," I said as we stood in front of Turner's *Harbor of Dieppe*. "The way he can make the surface of the water look like glass like he does." I shook my head. "It gets me every time."

"Where do you mean?" he asked, his brow furrowing as he scanned the canvas.

"Look where the sun hits the water. You have to concentrate without looking too hard at the components of the painting. Look at the scene as a whole—"

"Oh wow, yes," he said. "I see it. And the light. It's beautiful."

His enjoyment seemed real and as much as I loved these paintings, seeing him love them gave me an additional level of pleasure.

"Some people criticized it as being too unrealistic because the light in his pictures is so beautiful," I said.

"People always find a reason to complain."

The man who had served us champagne interrupted us. "Sir, dinner is ready whenever you are."

"Are you hungry?" Sam asked.

"Sure," I said, though honestly, I wasn't. I felt full up with life, happiness. With the evening. With Sam.

"These paintings are just so romantic," I said as we entered the dining room. "Can you imagine what it must have been like to wear these outfits in eighteenth century Britain?"

Sam glanced around at the portraits of wealthy British land owners and their wives. "Don't you all dress like that in England now?" he asked, waiting for me to take a seat at the dining table set just for two in the middle of the room. "It must be part of your DNA."

I laughed. "Whenever we go back to visit family, I make sure I pack my silk gowns and powdered wigs."

"When did you move to the US?" he asked as two waiters filled our water and wine glasses.

"We came to New York when I was five. I don't remember much about England—I just swear in British, but that's because my dad's great at it. Where did you grow up?"

Sam's smile disappeared and his face went blank. "Jersey."

"Are your parents still there?" I asked.

There was a beat of silence between us, as if he were thinking about an answer to an almost impossible question.

"No. They died when I was twelve. I don't have any family."

It was as if he'd punched me in the stomach. A million words whooshed through my brain and then left before I could cling to any of them. I wanted to say the right thing so badly. In the end, I said, "God, I'm so sorry," and reached across the table. He moved his hand before I could touch him.

"It was a long time ago," he said as he put his napkin in his lap.

"You grew up in my apartment building?" he asked, changing the subject. I wanted him to know how sorry I was for his loss, to find a way to make it better. Despite his prickly exterior, Sam was a kind and generous man who deserved good things in his life.

"Sam, your parents . . ."

He cleared his throat. "I don't talk about it. Let's enjoy dinner. I thought if I got to look at you all evening, you should have something beautiful to look at, too." His words brought me back to our date.

"You're very sweet. But my view isn't so bad, even without all this art."

Sam smiled, a big boyish grin. "You totally want me."

I giggled. "You totally want me."

He shrugged. "Of course."

Dinner arrived and we didn't speak until we were alone again. We were content just to watch each other, our eyes joined as if we worried if either of us looked away, the other would disappear.

I didn't want to ruin tonight by pushing him to talk to me about his past. It seemed every encounter with him told me something more compelling, more heartbreaking, more loveable about him. I wasn't having dinner with another spoiled rich guy—Sam Shaw had known loss and overcome it. Nothing had been handed to him.

I wanted to know every last thought in his head.

Chapter Thirteen
Sam

We pulled up outside Grace's apartment building and I felt the loss of her warmth the instant I let go of her hand so she could get out of the car. "Let me get your door," I said. I quickly exited my side of the car, rounded the trunk and opened her door to find her again. She grinned up at me. God damn that smile of hers.

"You didn't need to," she said, but something in that smile told me she liked me opening the door for her.

We took small steps to the door of her apartment, prolonging every moment of our perfect evening.

I couldn't believe I almost hadn't asked her on a date. I'd been three seconds away from missing out on the best night of my life.

Grace put the key into the lock with her left hand, even though I knew she was right-handed. She didn't want to let go either. But we'd have to go our separate ways eventually.

She stepped inside and snapped her head around when I didn't follow.

"I think I should go." There were a lot of reasons I shouldn't cross the threshold. For one, I didn't want her to think tonight had all been about sex for me. I liked this girl—to talk to and spend time with, not just sleep with. I'd begun to want more from her. I'd *wanted* to blow her away—for her to be impressed. For her to like me, too.

And that terrified me.

I was in new territory without a plan.

"Oh." The smile in her eyes dissolved. "I get it," she said, her voice flat. She didn't get it at all. I wanted to stay. I wasn't rejecting her.

"I think maybe it's best." How did I explain that I didn't want to spoil anything by coming inside because I wasn't sure what happened after this? I had no experience, no way of navigating what came next.

Her gaze hit the floor. I'd created her disappointment and I hated that I had. "You want me to come in?" I asked. Was she sure? Did she know any better than me?

"Not if you don't want to."

Jesus. *Of course* I wanted to.

"I get it. It's fine."

"I really want to come in," I said, stroking my finger down her jaw and under her chin, lifting it so I could see those beautiful blue eyes. She looked up at me, her brows drawn together. "I just don't know how this goes." Could I not know what happened next and be okay with that? Could I want more from her?

I knew that wanting led to disappointment.

"You don't know how this goes?" she asked.

I shrugged and took my hand away from her face. Unwittingly, I'd shown her parts of myself no one ever got to see. I wasn't sure I was capable of giving her anything more. I was midway through a marathon I hadn't trained for. My muscles were weak and my lungs were empty.

Because it was what we did, she could have made a joke, given me shit. But she didn't. She seemed to understand where my boundaries were better than I did.

"Me either. Let's find out together," she said.

She turned and went inside and, as if she were my oxygen, I followed her. I couldn't do anything else.

"Grace," I called out.

"In here." I followed the sound of her voice, my feet sinking into the thick pile of the rug in her hallway. Her home was as sophisticated as she was. Modern chandeliers hung from the ceilings. The grays and silvers on the walls, floors and furniture blended together without matching in a way that expensively decorated places managed. It wasn't the apartment of any ordinary twentysomething living in Brooklyn. You could take the princess off Park Avenue, but you couldn't take Park Avenue out of the girl.

"In a bed this time." She stood facing me from the corner of her bedroom and kicked her shoes off.

"You're impatient," I said. She wanted me and that felt good. Perhaps it didn't matter what came next. We'd managed so far.

"I've waited all evening." She fiddled with the fastening of her skirt, but I stepped forward and batted her hand away.

"If we're going to do this, then I want to take my time." I slid one hand around her waist and cupped her face with my other.

"There's an *if?*"

There wasn't an if. Not now that we were here. I'd have her tonight, but it wasn't just about getting off, scratching an itch, and I wanted her to get that. "There's no rush, Grace Astor." I smoothed my hand down her neck, mesmerized by her milky-white skin.

Sitting on the edge of the bed, I pulled her between my knees. I could see her better like this. I unbuttoned her blouse, raising an eyebrow when she tried to help. She dropped her hands and let me work the small blue buttons through their holes. I parted the sides of her shirt to reveal a lacey white bra. "This, I like." I ran my forefinger under the edges of the cup opening, relishing the feel of the rough lace on one side of my finger and her smooth skin on the other. Her nipples pebbled and I resisted the urge I had to pinch, bite, suck. My dick pressed against the seam in my pants.

Fuck she was so sweet.

I tugged her shirt from her and reached under her skirt. "This room is so perfect. The carpet, the cushions, the comforter. We're going to mess it up a little bit. You know that, right?"

She pulled the corner of her bottom lip into her mouth, her body swaying slightly as I slid my hand up her thigh. "We're going to fuck every which way." I stroked the juncture of her leg with my thumb. My thumb slicked easily across her skin—she was so wet—teasing the edges of her panties. "Your juices are going to be everywhere, staining everything. Can you handle that?"

She nodded, her movement a little slow, her eyes a little hazy.

"And I'm going to come all over you. I'm going to stain your beautiful skin so I own you." I slipped my thumb beneath the lace and into her folds. She gasped, grabbed my forearms for balance.

"Yes," she said, her eyes fixed to mine.

I began to shift my thumb in small circles. The movements were wet and easy as slowly I edged up toward her clit. Her grip on my arms got tighter and tighter.

I was casting a spell over her, and the deeper under she fell, the more intoxicating I found her. The way she worshipped my fingers and what they could do was almost as good as if I were thrusting my dick inside her. I'd never experienced the euphoria that making someone else feel good could bring until Grace.

She pulsed beneath my thumb and my cock throbbed in response. Seeing her turned on, feeling her slippery wetness—I was being seduced. *I* was falling under *her* spell.

"I need more," she said, pulling the cotton of my shirt.

"More?" I asked.

"Of you." Didn't she know she had more than anyone ever had?

I removed my hand, sliding her panties down, then unclasped her skirt, followed by her bra. My hands on her waist, I moved her to the bed. "Lie back," I said, unable to look away for a second while I undressed.

"Yes." Her eyes flickered between my jutting cock and my face. She reached out her hand. "I like this."

"This?" I asked, kneeling naked on the bed.

"Us," she said sleepily, running her foot down my calf

then pulling me closer. "I like it when we're close like this."

My heart swooped. She was describing a pattern we had together. I wasn't used to having patterns with a woman. In the back of my head I knew I should run, but with Grace, my head always got overruled. This was how it should be.

"And naked."

I placed my lips over her small smile, grazing her soft mouth with mine. She hummed and the vibrations travelled straight to my dick. If she were any other girl, I'd have come by now. My cock strained for release, desperate for her tight, wet pussy.

I worked my way down her neck, kissing and sucking, wanting to devour her, wanting to make her as crazy with lust as I was.

I trailed a line of small kisses from one hip bone to the other, then dragged my tongue back to where I started.

She pushed her fingers through my hair. "My legs are shaking."

I skimmed my hand down the length of her thigh. "That's your body telling you how much you want me," I mumbled against the skin between her breasts.

She moaned.

"But I want *you* to tell me." I wanted to hear it. I needed her to know this was what she wanted.

"I want you," she whispered.

"Say it again."

"I want you," she panted. "I want you. I want you." She writhed underneath me. "*Please*, Sam."

I groaned.

Quickly, I ripped open the condom I'd pulled out of my wallet while undressing and sheathed my cock. "Are you ready, Princess?"

She looked at me from under her lashes and nodded.

"Flip over." Maybe if I didn't have to see her beautiful eyes fall half closed as I drove into her, I'd have a fighting chance of lasting more than five seconds.

She reached over her head and rolled to her stomach. Straddling her, I pulled her hips up, revealing her swollen pussy. Jesus. Five seconds would be a miracle. I pressed my dick against her entrance and had to pause. Just the wetness surrounding my tip was dizzying.

But something wasn't right. I needed to see her beautiful face, feel her heat against my skin. She wasn't someone just to fuck—we shared this experience together.

I slumped to her side and pulled her toward me, her ass in my lap, her shoulders on the bed. *Yeah.* I needed this closeness with her, needed there to be nothing between us. I sucked in a long breath, breathing the almost sweet smell of her hair. "Look at me," I said, and she looked up at me. *Fuck yeah.* I pushed inside her, right up to the hilt, and nearly came as she caught her breath.

"You okay?" I asked.

"More than," she replied, reaching for my ass as I pulled her closer. We were a tangle of limbs, every part of us interconnected.

I started to move in slow, small movements, hooking my arm across her chest and onto her shoulder, keeping her in place.

165

"Jesus," she choked out, her eyes drifting closed.

"Look at me," I said again. I needed to see her. For her to see me. I wanted to be reminded of our connection—to know it was real.

My thrusts became sharper. Her fingernails dug into my thigh. I hoped she'd leave a mark. Another rendition of ultimate bliss to add to my skin.

I found her clit and her lungs decompressed in a guttural cry, her mouth opening wide as I gently circled the bundle of nerves. Her muscles clenched around my cock.

We stared at each other, wrapped in wonder and lust and connection as the drag and thrust of our bodies wound us tighter and tighter. Our eyes never left each other's as thunder rumbled louder and louder until interrupted by a crack of lightning. Her orgasm hit her in a wave across her body that covered me a fraction of a second later.

It was as if we'd been on a journey, a quest, weathered a storm—sex had brought us closer, bound us together.

"Tonight was . . ." Grace paused and looked up at me as if I held the word she was looking for. "More," she said finally.

There was no denying she was right. "More" was exactly what tonight had been. More than I'd ever had with any woman. More than I'd ever dared to want. More than I ever felt possible.

"Thank you," she said. "Not for the—well, yes, for the orgasm, but—"

"Orgasms. Don't talk about the orgasm as if it's lonely all by itself."

She giggled and poked me in the chest. "Okay, thank you for the orgasms*sssss,* but also for the Frick, and for dinner. I'm not used to . . . It was all so thoughtful. It was beyond . . ."

"You're a princess, after all. It's what you deserve." I hadn't planned the date at the Frick because I'd ever considered what other men had done for her. I'd just thought she'd enjoy it.

"You think I'm some stuck-up Park Avenue princess, but—"

"Hey," I said, pulling her into my arms. "I'm teasing. I think you're very special and if you haven't been treated like a princess, then shame on the men who've taken you out."

"You have no idea," she mumbled.

I wasn't used to sharing stories with women, knowing their history. Angie knew everything but she wasn't a woman to me in the same way. Grace, mumbling into my chest, dropping her lips to my skin in an effort to distract me, made me want to ask a thousand questions of her. But what if she didn't want to answer? I'd shut her down when she'd asked something personal of me earlier. Would it sting if she did the same to me? I needed to learn how to open up to her—to give more of myself. It was only fair if that's what I was expecting from her.

It was worth the risk to get to know more of her. "Can I ask you a question?"

She stilled her fingers that were tracing patterns on the back of my palms. "What kind of question?" Before Grace did it to me, I didn't realize how answering a question with a question was a form of self-defense.

I pulled her closer and kissed her on the head. "Why do you spend time on men who don't deserve you?"

She shrugged, brushing me off, just as I had done her.

She needed me to share something first—I was asking for her to reveal her vulnerability without being prepared to do the same.

I took a deep breath. "My mother and father were killed by a drunk driver when I was twelve."

I swallowed, looking straight ahead and not at Grace. I didn't often say those words anymore, there was little need, but the rush of pain I braced myself for wasn't as brutal as I remembered the last time I did. It would always hurt, but the fear of the hurt was as much an obstacle for me as the pain itself. "I had no other family, so I went into the system."

She shifted in my arms so she was facing me. Cupping my face in her tiny hand, she brushed her thumb across my cheek.

Her touch gave me the strength to go on, to share more. "It was tough. I was old enough to understand what I'd lost. To have experienced a different life, a better life, and have it taken away." Telling her was almost a release and I managed to glance at her as she blinked away tears.

"It was a long time ago. Things are better now." I didn't want her to feel sorry for me. I wanted to be closer to her, not feel her pity. I just wanted to give her more because that's what I needed from her.

"I'm sorry," she whispered.

I exhaled and threaded my fingers through hers.

"I think you're so special, Sam Shaw," she said, dropping a kiss on our joined hands.

I smiled. "I think you're special too."

"So is that why you don't buy furniture? Or have any relationships?"

What was she getting at? I had Angie, an apartment on Park Avenue. I just didn't attach meaning to material possessions in a way most people did.

"Because you know how painful it is to have something and then lose it?" she asked. "You don't want to have to experience that again."

The ever-present pain in my gut I'd gotten so used to, sliced deeper. Was she right? Did I keep my life free from things and people so I couldn't be disappointed again?

"I'm sorry. I didn't mean to push. It just makes sense," she said.

I couldn't argue with her. It *did* make sense. I'd just never seen the connection before.

"Maybe," I said. "I don't know."

She leaned forward and kissed my stomach. "My mother cheats on my father. Always has. He knows, but for some reason he stays married to her," she explained, revoking her earlier shrug in the same way I had. She was confessing, letting me in, giving me more.

"And you're your father?" I asked. "Picking people who don't deserve your love?"

"Maybe. Maybe I just don't want to be my mother."

Had both of us approached life and relationships based on our past experience? Maybe everyone did. But I still didn't understand, why was I able to be caught up with her in a way I'd never let myself before? How had she gotten me wanting more when I'd spent my whole life determined to need nothing?

She circled her fingers over the place where she'd kissed my stomach, giving me a glimpse of the tattoo under her arm.

Ultimate Bliss.

I hadn't had much time to think about what her tattoo should be when she asked me to pick, but those two words had been the first thing to come into my brain.

Did my subconscious know something I didn't? The words of that well-read passage tumbled through my head.

There is neither happiness nor unhappiness in this world; there is only the comparison of one state with another. Only a man who has felt ultimate despair is capable of feeling ultimate bliss. It is necessary to have wished for death in order to know how good it is to live . . . the sum of all human wisdom will be contained in these two words: Wait and Hope.

Had she been what I'd been waiting for? What I'd been hoping for?

Was she my ultimate bliss?

CHAPTER FOURTEEN
GRACE

Saturday night had been special. Something had shifted between us. I had plans to spend Sunday in Connecticut with Harper and Max, so Sam had left early. When he called me on Monday and I realized he didn't have any specific reason to, I found myself grinning like a maniac into the phone. He'd just wanted to hear my voice. Talk to me.

It felt good. More than good.

I'd offered to oversee the furniture delivery the next day. He'd suggested we go to dinner afterward. Of course I said yes. I couldn't wait to see him again—have him look at me with that complete openness and honesty that seemed to permeate from him. He was special and I couldn't get enough. I practically bounced through the first two days of the week at the gallery.

I waited by the elevators at 740 Park Avenue, listening for the whirs and clicks to indicate the car was at ground level. I was impatient to get up to see Sam. He'd said he'd leave work early to make sure he was here. I wanted to know how things would be between us now, after Saturday when we'd shared so much.

The elevator doors slid open to reveal Sam, my mother

and father standing in front of him.

"Hello, darling. We didn't know you were coming over," my mother said, adjusting her mink coat. "We're just heading out."

My eyes flicked between Sam and my parents as they all trailed out. Sam made to move past us all, as if he were leaving. Was he?

"Oh, that's fine. I was here to see Sam, actually," I said. He stopped and pulled out the megawatt Sam Shaw smile I'd only seen on the rarest of occasions.

"How do you do?" Sam asked, taking my mother's hand. Oh Jesus. My mother would love manners like that.

"Sam's bought a number of works from my gallery," I explained as he and my father shook hands. "I'm helping him arrange them. Sam, these are my parents, Mr. and Mrs. Astor."

My mother's gaze flitted between Sam and me. "What did you say your surname was?" She was confused by Sam. She clearly hadn't come across him but he was wealthy enough to live in their building.

"He didn't," I replied.

"Shaw," Sam said. "My name is Sam Shaw."

My mother nodded and I could tell she was scanning through her contact list, trying to place him.

"And have you lived here long, Mr. Shaw?" she asked.

"Sylvia, we're running behind. We'll leave you to it," my father said, wanting to discourage my mother's nosiness.

"We have a few minutes," my mother said, clearly eager to spend a little more time in Sam's presence. I knew that feeling.

"No, darling. We're late already." My father wrapped

his arm around my mother's waist, guiding her toward the door. "And we'll see Grace for her birthday next week."

My mother's attention shifted from Sam to me. "Yes. I've left you several messages about the menu, but I've not heard from you."

I avoided my mother's calls ninety percent of the time. When she wanted to discuss my birthday, I nudged that figure up to an even one hundred.

"I don't care about the menu. It's the Four Seasons—I'm sure it will all be good." I hadn't spent a birthday with my mother in a couple of years, but I'd promised my father I'd make more of an effort. I glanced at Sam, who was smiling politely at nothing in particular. He'd lost so much and here I was, acting like a princess talking about the Four Seasons to my mink-wearing mother. My birthday dinner was so inconsequential.

"I just want to make sure you have a perfect evening." My mother's voice wobbled, as it always did when she wanted people to feel sorry for her. It had stopped working on me a long time ago.

"I really don't mind," I said, trying to keep my tone neutral.

"Come on, Sylvia. Let's leave Grace to get to work," my father said. "We'll have a lovely time. It's the company that counts. Will we see you there, Mr. Shaw?"

Had my father picked up on something personal between us? I kissed my dad on the cheek. "Have a great time. I have to go." I turned back to the elevator and vigorously pushed the up button.

Luckily, Sam was polite enough to just grin in response to

my father's question. The doors opened and I dipped inside, indicating with a sharp tip of my head for Sam to follow.

"Nice to meet you, Mr. and Mrs. Astor," he called, following me into the elevator.

He cornered me as the doors closed. "You didn't tell me it was your birthday," he said, his fingers wrapping around my waist, his breath on my cheek.

"It's not," I whispered, my body suddenly weak from being so close to him.

He pulled back to look at me and shook his head. "Next week is, and you didn't tell me."

Is that what we did now? We hadn't discussed how things stood between us. I was looking for him to acknowledge that things were different between us.

"It's just going to be a few friends and family. You can come if you like."

"I like," he said, kissing my neck.

"It will probably be boring."

"I don't care."

"Is this what we do now?" I asked. Were we a couple? I wanted him to tell me.

"Is *what* what we do?" He ran his nose along my jaw and I tipped my head and pushed my hips against him.

"Invite each other to things. Introduce each other to our friends. Are we doing that stuff?" My words were punctuated by pauses while I enjoyed his fingers, his lips, his warmth.

"Yeah, we're doing that stuff," he replied as the elevator doors pinged open at his floor. He straightened, grabbed my hand and pulled me out of the car. "We're doing all the stuff."

I pressed my lips together, trying hard to disguise my smile. We were doing this.

Sam

"Her mother was wearing a coat when I ran into them. Mink by the look of it," I said to Angie as we walked through Bergdorf Goodman, looking for a birthday present for Grace. I had no idea what Grace would like so I'd enlisted Angie's help.

"How do you know what kind of fur it was?"

"Because I do. She grew up in that building. We're so different." I liked Grace. To anyone else, saying that they liked a woman wouldn't be a big deal. But for me, I never really considered whether I liked someone or not—it didn't matter. It wasn't just that she was good in bed or that she was so beautiful it left me breathless, I actually *liked* spending time with her. But because that was such an unusual reaction, it led to questions—why did I like her? Would I feel the same next Thursday?

"Why do you care?" Angie asked.

I'd observed the successful before becoming successful, learning their mannerisms, their speech patterns, so when I got there I didn't stand out. Through trial and error and practice, I'd learned to associate with the well-heeled. I wasn't born one of them, but Grace had been.

We were from different worlds. Could people from contrasting backgrounds really like each other?

I followed Angie as she scanned shelves and displays, picking up things and putting them down.

"What about a scarf? Those Upper East Side girls love a

neckerchief." Angie laughed, holding up a silky scarf with orange streaks in it. She wasn't wrong. I just wasn't sure Grace was a typical Upper East Side girl.

"Don't scrunch up your face like it's made of dog shit— it's a seven-hundred-dollar scarf," Angie said, putting it back on the shelf.

"It's not right," I replied.

"Is she not a neckerchief kind of gal?" she asked as we moved toward some glass cabinets holding wallets.

I'd never seen Grace in a scarf. I'd never really thought about what she was wearing beyond how it showed off her body. "I don't think so."

Despite our differences, I found myself wanting more of Grace. More of her time, more of her body. I craved her thoughts on everyday things. I wanted to watch the way she blinked, slower and slower, as she climbed toward orgasm. I knew that she had an unaffected belly laugh and a polite, rehearsed smile. Even now, I was thinking about her when I should be paying attention to Angie. I was following Grace deeper along a dark corridor, not knowing what lay at the end. But I couldn't stop, couldn't turn back.

"Who uses a passport holder?" Angie asked, peering over the glass cabinet. "So what's she like, this girl who has you buying her gifts?"

"She doesn't have me buying her gifts." I wandered around the row of cabinets. There was nothing here for Grace. "She invited me to her birthday. It's polite to bring a present." Grace wasn't interested in my money. If she wanted to be with someone wealthy, she wouldn't have a history of dating penniless artists or be working in a gallery she'd financed herself. "She's not like that."

"Okay, Mr. Sensitive. You have to admit that this is a watershed moment. You've never agonized over buying a woman a gift before."

"I'm not agonizing," I said. "I just want to get something that will suit her."

"Then tell me what she's like. Maybe that will give us some ideas."

"She's nice." I shrugged and a smile tugged at the corners of my mouth. "Funny. Passionate about what she does."

"And when you say, 'what she does', you mean she does *you* passionately." Angie wiggled her eyebrows.

It should have been amusing, but it didn't sit right with me for some reason. "Don't say that."

"Jesus. Calm down. I'm making a joke. You've got it bad, my friend." She turned and walked left toward some other stands full of useless crap.

I caught up with her. "Sorry, I didn't mean to snap. I just want to find this present and get out of here. You know I hate places like this." It was true that shopping wasn't my thing and I didn't want Angie to get things out of proportion and think my dating Grace was anything more than it was.

She shrugged. "Fine. But there are plenty of pretty things here, Sam. You just need to pick one."

But I couldn't get just anything. When I'd taken Grace to the Frick, she'd seemed so happy with my choice, and I wanted to create that same look on her face. "I took her to the Frick for dinner on our first date and she seemed to like that. Maybe I could do something like that again? Rather than a gift."

Angie pulled her eyebrows. "What, like you took her to the visitor café?"

"No. I hired the place out on a Saturday night. We took in the paintings and had a nice dinner in one of the rooms."

When Angie didn't respond, I glanced back to see if she was listening, but she was just staring at me, her mouth slightly open as if I'd told her I was going to buy the Empire State building. "What?" I asked.

"You hired out the entire Frick?"

"Yes."

"For your first date?"

Had she not heard me correctly? "Yes. And she seemed to like it so—"

Angie snorted. "I bet she did. That's the stuff of fairytales. You really like this girl." She grinned so wide her face looked like it was cracking in half.

I started to head toward the door, but Angie caught up with me and shoved my shoulder. "Sam," she said, still grinning. "You *really* like this girl. The Frick? That's serious shit."

"It's no big deal. I just thought she'd like it and I didn't want to be bothered by the crowds."

"It is so a big deal. That's the kind of shit a guy pulls when he's in deep."

I pushed the door open and stepped out onto the street. "Well, I'm not in deep. You know me."

"I do," Angie said from behind me. "That's why it's so exciting. I think you may be falling in love." She squealed, which, added to her ludicrous ramblings, was more than irritating.

I shoved my hands into my pockets. "Don't be ridiculous." I turned north, not sure where I was heading. Angie followed, pulling her jacket tighter.

"It's not ridiculous. It's wonderful, Sam. I thought it may never happen. I'm so glad because it's such an amazing feeling—you deserve all the happiness."

I squinted at the sun that persisted despite the cold. "It's nothing like that. Don't get too excited. We're just hanging out."

"I can't wait to tell Chas. And the four of us can go on dates."

"Angie. Seriously, stop. I need to find a gift and you're being no help." I didn't want to buy Grace something just for the sake of it. She knew how little value I placed on material things. So if I bought her something expensive but impersonal, she'd know it didn't mean anything, that I hadn't given it any thought.

"Promise me I won't lose you." Angie stopped walking and grabbed at my coat sleeve. "I love my husband. He's a good man and we can talk about everything." Her eyes went a little glassy. "But what you and I went through can't be understood by anyone who hasn't experienced it." I knew what she meant. Chas knew the Angie who'd survived, not the girl who'd had to get there. I just didn't understand why she thought she'd lose me.

"What are you talking about? I've not been able to shake you so far."

"I mean it, Sam. What if Grace and I don't get along? We won't be able to spend so much time together; we'll gradually lose contact."

I held Angie's shoulders. "You're being crazy. I'm not in love with Grace and you and I will be friends until the end of time."

"I can't lose you." Her gaze dropped to the ground. "I want you to be happy, but I want to be a part of that."

I pinned her arms to her body and brought her close. "You're not going to lose me."

"You're hugging me," Angie said. "I've known you fifteen years and you've *never* hugged me."

"Just go with it."

She stood limply, me wrapped around her. "I will never leave you," I said. "You will *never* lose me."

And I wasn't in love with Grace Astor.

CHAPTER FIFTEEN
GRACE

I kept glancing at the doorway to the Four Seasons, hoping to find Sam. I'd asked him to bring Angie and her husband. Apparently her husband was busy but Sam and Angie were going to make it. It would be the first time I'd meet her, and I was nervous. I knew how much he valued her opinion. How she seemed to be the only person he listened to. If she didn't like me, then what? Would it affect Sam and me? It had been a little over a week since he'd told me about his parents' deaths, but I'd seen or spoken to him every day since and things were going so well, I just wanted Angie to give us her seal of approval.

"Is he here yet?" Harper asked from behind me.

I peeled my gaze away from the entrance. "No. You'll know when you see him. How's the baby?"

"The baby's a baby. She doesn't do much. I want to hear about Sam. Is he the first man you've dated with a real job? Does he know what to do with his tongue?"

"You know we're in public, right?" I asked.

She shrugged as her husband, Max, and her sister-in-law, Scarlett, joined us. "Happy birthday," Max said, kissing me on the cheek.

"Thank you."

"Happy birthday," Sam said from behind me. I shivered. Had I ever known a man whose voice could make my whole body react? With just four syllables, Sam had made my nipples hard and my knees weak. I looked over my shoulder just as his hand slipped around my waist. He grinned at me and kissed me on the lips.

We were really doing this.

And for the first time I wasn't making sure my boyfriend wasn't checking out other girls or annoying my friends.

He broke our kiss and pulled back. "You look beautiful." He grazed his thumb across my cheekbone, not even glancing at what I was wearing, just pulling me toward him so we were thigh against hip. "I'm Sam," he said to the group, "and this is Angie Jenkins." I hadn't seen the blonde girl next to him—when Sam was around, all I could focus on was him.

"Angie, hi," I said and tried to pull away to greet her, but Sam kept me pressed firmly against his side.

After everyone introduced themselves, we made our way to the long dinner table. I'd invited forty-two people. Some family. Some friends. I hadn't wanted a big party, just a quiet dinner. I sat in the middle. The table split quite easily into family at one end, starting with my dad next to me on my left and my mother the other side of him, and then my friends to my right. I hadn't seated Sam next to me, but as I sat down and the heat of his hand left my hip, I wanted to quickly switch the name cards.

Harper didn't even try to hide her delight with Sam and

as soon as they sat down, she peppered him with questions.

"So, your husband's working tonight? What does he do?" I asked Angie.

"He has a small construction company in Jersey." Her gaze scanned the room, taking in the restaurant and then settled on me. "He's working all hours at the moment on an office building they can't touch during the day."

"Oh, that's tough, but I'm really pleased you could make it. I'm just sorry it's for something like this and not somewhere where it's just us. I can't wait to get to know you better." I held my breath, hoping she'd feel the same.

"Don't be, it was nice of you to invite me. Sam really wanted me to come." She shifted a little to allow the waiter to fill her water glass.

"So, you live in New Jersey?" I asked.

She laughed. "Yeah, my whole life. Thought it would be the last place I'd want to spend married life but Chas will never leave, so I guess I'm stuck."

I knew she and Sam had been to high school together, and I wanted to ask her questions about him. Did he talk to her about his parents?

"I heard you grew up in his building?" Angie asked.

I nodded. "Yeah, I'm sure he refers to me as the Park Avenue princess."

Angie smiled and said, "I haven't noticed him say that, but then, as I'm sure you're finding out, he only says a fraction of what goes on in that big brain of his."

"That's for sure. I have to stop myself from asking him what he's thinking eleven times an hour." The waiters began serving our food and a murmur went around the table as plates were put in front of people.

"So, you're spending a ton of time together then?"

Only most nights since I'd come back from Connecticut. "Yeah, though I haven't known him long."

"You have to take care of him," she said, lowering her voice and leaning in to me just a fraction. "I've never seen him so taken with a woman. He likes you an awful lot."

I reached for my water glass and took a sip. I really wanted to put it against my cheek to get rid of my blush. "I like him an awful lot, too."

Angie smiled and squeezed my hand. "I hope so."

"You don't believe me?"

"It's not that. It's just that he's never liked anyone. And I imagine you've had other boyfriends . . ."

"It's different for me, too. Maybe not as much as it is for Sam, but he's not like any of my previous boyfriends. He keeps so much inside, and yet he's the most open and honest man I've ever met. I will do everything not to hurt your friend, I promise."

"Thank you," she said. "I'm sorry. I don't mean to come across as overprotective . . ."

"I don't blame you. It's nice that you look out for each other."

Angie laughed. "When I started dating Chas, he and Sam came to blows one night when Sam saw him talking to a woman at a bar. Sam didn't ask any questions, just saw red and punched him. We're a little protective of each other."

I knew it was irrational, but I couldn't help but feel a

tinge of jealousy. I wanted to have known Sam his whole life. There was still so much about him I didn't know. I couldn't imagine the cool, calm Sam Shaw punching someone. "Does he have a temper?" I asked, suddenly concerned.

Angie swallowed her water. "No, not at all. I've never seen him like that before or since. But there is so little he cares about in this world—I think he'd throw himself in front of a train for the things that matter to him."

I may not have known Sam long, but Angie was describing the man I knew—loyal and protective. Why the hell was I spending my birthday among all these people when I just wanted to be curled up on Sam's couch next to him? I ached for him, was lonely without him, even though he was just three feet away.

Angie excused herself from the table, and as she got up, Sam turned to find me staring at him. "You okay?" he asked quietly.

I leaned toward him, resting my hand on the warm leather of Angie's seat. "I'm sorry I didn't sit you next to me."

He tilted his head to one side. "Don't be sorry. I'm fine talking to Harper."

"No, I mean I'm sorry for me. I miss you."

He cocked his head, and narrowed his eyes. "You're not enjoying your conversation with Angie?"

"Oh yes, of course. She's so nice and clearly adores you. I just miss you."

"I'm here, Princess," he said, curling my hair behind my ear. "With you."

And he was. I felt him in my heart.

Sam

Grace telling me she missed me when I was two feet away made me want to grab her hand and pull her out of there so the two of us could be alone. But part of me enjoyed seeing her with her friends and family. It was confirmation of who she was—kind and generous. Funny. Sexy. Gorgeous. She wasn't a different person with them. The fact that she was a little uncomfortable with all the attention made sense, too. I liked being able to observe these things about her from a distance.

I also liked being able to talk to Grace's friends—they were such a reflection of her. Harper was sitting next to me and was feisty and charming. Her husband, Max, clearly worshipped her.

"So, are you serious about Grace?" Harper asked.

"Excuse my wife," Max said. "She's a total pain in the ass. Harper, don't pressure the poor guy. They've only been dating a few weeks."

I chuckled. "It's fine. You can ask me anything. If I don't want to answer, I'll tell you."

Harper turned to Max as if to say *See?* "You said you knew with me from the moment I walked into King & Associates," she told her husband. "I want to know if it was the same for Sam."

Max just rolled his eyes and Harper turned her attention back to me. "So, was it the same?" Harper asked.

"I'm not quite sure what you mean, but of course I thought Grace was attractive when I first met her."

"So you're not serious about her?" Her eyes narrowed as if she were a cop questioning a suspected felon.

I wasn't sure what *serious* meant. I liked her. I didn't want to stop hanging out, but it wasn't like I was in love with her, even if Angie thought otherwise. "Like Max said, we've only been dating a couple of weeks."

"But, you're official? You're her boyfriend?" Harper asked.

Had I missed something? Were we supposed to have a conversation about our status? I was happy with the way things were. I didn't need to put a label on it.

When I didn't answer, Harper asked, "Are you fucking other women?"

"Absolutely not." Her question took me by surprise and I answered on instinct. But it was true. Grace and I spent almost every night together, and even if we didn't, I had no desire to fuck anyone else.

"And she's not fucking anyone else," Harper said.

It didn't sound like a question but I wouldn't mind an answer. I hadn't thought about whether Grace was sleeping with other people—I'd just assumed she wasn't. I glanced at Grace, who was chatting to the other people around the table. Was there anyone else here that she was sleeping with? "I care about her," I spluttered out. It would bother me if there was another guy on the scene. I wanted her attention, her body, her analysis of her day.

"Well, I should hope so," Harper said. "She's very special. If you hurt her, I'll hunt you down."

"There's something you should know about me, Harper," I said, leaning toward her. "There aren't many

189

people in my life I care about, and I like it that way. Grace is an exception."

"What are you two talking about?" Grace asked, smoothing her hand over my back. Dinner plates were being cleared and people were leaving the table for the restrooms or a smoke. I shifted my chair, and guided Grace so she was sitting on my knee.

"You," I said.

"Harper, are you giving him a hard time?" she asked.

"No more than I deserve. She cares about you, and that's only ever a good thing," I said.

Grace's hand curled around the back of my neck and I exhaled in a long breath. It should have felt uncomfortable, someone touching me so casually in public, but instead it felt completely normal. Comforting, even. She wouldn't be doing that if she was fucking someone else. "You're so sweet."

"No, I'm not. But I do care about you, and so does Harper."

Grace looked up at me from under her lashes. "I care about you, too," she said.

"So, you guys will have to come up to Connecticut," Max said, sliding his arm around the back of his wife's chair, and leaning toward us.

"Yes!" Harper said. "If you can put up with a houseful of crazy, that is. We'd love to have you. Next month when the pool house is finished. Then you can have a reprieve from the madness when you need it."

"Well, I don't know," Grace said, glancing at me. "Maybe."

I'd speak to her later about being *official*. In the

meantime, a weekend away with her best friend sounded good. I dipped my head to catch her eye. "I think that would be great."

Grace's eyes widened as she nodded. "You do?"

"Absolutely."

There was nothing fake about the smile she replied with.

"That's settled then," Harper said.

I didn't encourage or accept social invitations, but if that's what Grace wanted, I'd go along with it.

"You know these girls will drink too much and leave us to handle the kids," Max said.

"I think we can handle it." I'd heard of Max King, but never met him before. He had a reputation as a ballbuster, but he seemed laid back as he spent the evening with his wife. I'd never had social time with guys like that. The only man I could call a friend was Chas and that was only because of Angie.

The girls continued to discuss dates for the Connecticut weekend until dessert was served and Grace went back to her chair. My body was cold where she'd been. Couldn't she have eaten on my knee?

Harper glanced at me and lowered her voice. "Grace told me she saw the picture when she was with you." Her hand went to her throat. "Was she very upset?"

"Who?" I asked.

"Grace," Harper explained, "when she saw the painting."

I clearly should know what she was talking about, but despite scrolling through my memory at warp speed, I had no idea. "The picture?"

"The Renoir in the front window of a gallery a few stores down from hers."

Oh, she meant the portrait Grace used to own. "She said she loved that picture." I hadn't realized it was such a big deal.

"That was the picture her grandfather gave her as a child—she loves it. It's what started her obsession with art."

Had Grace told me that? There was so much I was learning about her.

"She sold it so she could open the gallery. Handpicked the buyer because she wanted someone to love it as much as she did. Then the weasel up and sold it on within six months, can you believe it?" Harper turned to her husband. "She's heartbroken about it. Almost asked her father for the money to buy it back, but of course, she won't." Why hadn't Grace told me? "She's so desperate not to be her mother, but this painting is emotional for Grace—it's not about the money, never is with Grace." Harper explained.

It was part of the reason I liked her so much.

It was part of the reason I was agreeing to weekends away in the country.

It was part of the reason I was pretty sure I'd still like her next Thursday.

———————————

Grace held open the door to her apartment while I carried in the two bags filled with presents we'd brought back from the restaurant.

"Thank you," she said, grinning at me.

"You're very welcome." I paused at the door to kiss her on the lips. It was difficult to go more than a few seconds without touching her when she was so close.

"You have a lot of gifts," I said as I put down the overflowing bags.

"I'm sure you don't approve." She poked me in the abs, but smiled before she went into the kitchen.

"Why would you think that?" I asked, following her.

"I know how you feel about material things." She set down two glasses on the counter and filled each of them with seltzer. There were so many things to appreciate about this moment. The fact that she now bought the water she knew I liked. That she was making me a drink without asking, because she already knew what I wanted, even before I did. I'd spent a lifetime avoiding this kind of interaction but I found myself enjoying it.

"You know that it's not that I think material things are frivolous. Just that they don't hold meaning for me." I certainly didn't judge Grace for having a fully-furnished apartment and expensive clothes and accoutrements. It just wasn't something I needed.

She handed me a glass and pressed her hand against my stomach. "It's fine."

"I haven't given you a birthday gift yet," I said. "I did go shopping—I took Angie."

She tilted her head to one side. "I didn't expect anything."

"I got you something very small, for now. I want to get you something else—I think I know what, but I haven't had time." I pulled out the square package from the bag of gifts

I'd brought in. "This one I wrapped myself."

"You did?" She stood on her tiptoes and I kissed her quickly.

"You haven't opened it yet." I handed her the gift.

"I don't need to. I like that you wrapped it yourself—that's the best thing you could have said."

We moved to her couch and I took off my jacket, laying it on the chair. She beamed at me as I took a seat next to her. Christ, I wish I'd bought her diamonds or a horse or something. She looked at me as if I'd just given her the moon.

"Go on then," I said.

She tore open the paper like a five-year-old on Christmas morning and looked up at me when she saw what it was. "Oh Sam, I love it," she said, flipping through the coffee-table book I'd bought of the Frick.

She ran her hand over the glossy cover. "That's so thoughtful."

My heart thumped against my ribcage as she curled her fingers around the top right-hand corner of the book and opened to the page where I'd written an inscription.

I want for nothing with you in my world.

She traced over the words in silence. Was it too much? Not enough?

She stared at the page. "I feel the same, Sam."

I ran my hand over hers and lifted her fingers from the paper, drawing them up to my mouth, kissing the back of her hand. "I didn't know what to buy."

"This is perfect," she whispered as I pulled her onto my lap.

"Harper asked me if I was sleeping with other women." Grace's face froze and her smile wilted. "I told her of course I wasn't."

I wanted to ask her if she could say the same. I knew she wasn't, but I needed to hear it. We both stared at each other before she answered my unasked question. She sucked in a breath. "Neither am I."

I tried to bite back my grin before she pressed her lips against mine, soft and certain. I cupped her face.

I should have been roaring in delight. Instead, the flecks of fear over caring about someone—having them care about me—seemed to embed more deeply.

Her mouth on my jaw brought me back to her, back to the joy. She smelled like cherries—ripe and sweet. I shifted her legs over mine.

"I know we haven't been together long, but there's something about you that fits with me."

I knew exactly what she meant. It was as if we'd been separated and found our way back to each other. But it didn't eradicate the fear I felt. Much as I cared about her, those feelings brought fear along with them.

"I feel very lucky to know you, Grace Astor."

"The feeling's mutual, Sam Shaw."

Her giggle vibrated against my chest and I pulled her closer. "Tell me about the painting that we saw in the window. Harper said you sold it to pay for the gallery and that it was the piece that started your love of art. Is that true?"

She pulled her hands from my face and shrugged. She relaxed against my chest, moving nearer. "It's been sold. I found out yesterday. I walked by the gallery and it was gone, so I couldn't help but ask what had happened to it. Some buyer from the Middle East apparently."

I circled her with my arms. "I'm so sorry, Grace."

"As much as I loved it, it gave me my gallery. I shouldn't be sad."

I stroked her back, the joy draining from me, replaced by frustration that I couldn't erase her loss. "I wish I could make it better."

She placed her hand on my cheek and dropped a kiss next to it. "Harper shouldn't have mentioned it."

"I'm glad she did. I want to know what's troubling you." I might have spent my whole life since my parents died trying to avoid caring about anyone, but Grace had broken my stride. I'd do whatever it took to keep her happy and safe.

She twisted in my arms so she was facing me. "Other than being a complete busybody, how did you like Harper?"

"I love how much she cares about you."

"Did she threaten violence? I think Angie might have. Subtly."

I chuckled. Angie wasn't violent, but she was protective. "Did she?"

"She told me the story about you punching her husband because you thought he was cheating on her." She lifted my hand and placed her palm against mine.

"That was the last time I hit someone."

"Have you punched a lot of people?" she asked, cocking her head.

"I've done what I've needed to protect myself and Angie." At Hightimes I'd kept to myself most of the time. There was a group of four boys who had terrorized the place, but after I'd broken the nose of their leader, they'd left me

196

alone. The Kung Fu lessons I'd had before my parents died had been useful.

"I'm sorry, Sam. I wish I could make it better," she replied.

I buried my face in her neck because I didn't want her to see my expression. This was new to me, having someone care about me. I wanted to shout from the top of the Empire State building how incredible it felt, but a nagging sense of fear kept me from sprinting to Fifth Avenue.

Would I always worry, or would Grace chase that from my life?

Chapter Sixteen
Grace

His fingers trickled across my leg as we sat contentedly on the couch, my back to his front. I couldn't remember ever having a better birthday. Sam made everything better. Unlike previous men I'd been with, he'd overcome real hardship on his own. He hadn't looked to anyone else to solve his problems or make his life better. I was finally dating an adult. But dating felt like too slight a word for what was happening between Sam and me.

"You know what would round this birthday off kinda perfectly?" I asked and grinned up at him.

"What's that, Grace Astor?"

I shrugged. "An orgasm."

"Oh, I see." He nodded. "You're expecting me to put out."

My laugh was interrupted as he slid his hand down my leg and gripped the hem of my dress. "It *is* my birthday."

"Did you really think I would have an evening with you and not spend the whole time wanting you naked and under me?" He pulled up the fabric, his hand rough against the skin of my thighs, and every cell in my body tightened.

The atmosphere shifted and I tried hard to steady my breathing. Just a few cursory words and his fingers on my thighs had me ready to beg for more.

"You think I don't notice how your breathing changes when I touch you. Tonight, when I first saw you at the restaurant, you think I didn't see your nipples harden as I put my hand around your waist?"

I could hide nothing from this man. I didn't want to.

His fingers pushed into my underwear.

"I understand how much you want me. Because I want you that bad too. *Every* second. You can't think for a moment I'd not want to feel this." His finger pushed between my folds and I gasped, partly in pleasure but mostly in relief that he was here with me, making me feel so good in every way. "That I don't want to feel you wrapped tight around my cock."

I gripped his thighs on either side of me and pushed my hips up, wanting his finger deeper.

I tugged at my blouse, needing to feel his hands everywhere. The buttons were stiff and I was impatient. His fingers stroked me up and down, as he unfastened the buttons with his free hand. I sank back against him as he took over.

"Why would you think I could do without this any more than you could?" he asked.

And that was why he was so different to anyone that had come before him—we were equals. We'd had very different lives but we wanted each other for the same reasons and just as badly.

He pulled my bra down and I cried out as my nipple grazed against the lace. He groaned from behind me, removing his hand from my underwear. Before I had a chance to complain, he'd stood up, taking me with him, me still facing forward.

"Stand," he said. And he let go of me and moved away. Starting with my shirt, he peeled everything I was wearing from my body until I was totally naked.

I felt his hands at my feet, sliding up to my ankles. He must be kneeling behind me. "I want every part of you." His palms pushed up my legs. His movements weren't fluttering or tantalizing. They were sure and possessive. He ran his hands up the back of my thigh and then gripped my ass—squeezing and kneading. "And your beautiful ass, Grace Astor. That's mine too."

As much as it felt good, he was touching me for him, not me. And I loved it.

"Yes," I breathed.

"And this." His hands slid over my hips. He was standing now, pressing his cheek against mine. "This beautiful pussy," he said as he roughly pushed his finger against my clit. "That's all mine too. Everything. Every part of you."

My knees weakened. It was true. My body responded as if I'd been waiting for him my whole life and now I'd found him. It was awakening properly for the first time ever.

His other hand grabbed my breasts and I wanted to melt into him, become part of him. "Tell me I have all of you," he whispered.

I reached over my head behind me, threading my fingers through his hair. "You do."

His hand left my clit and it was only the sound of his zipper that made me feel better.

"Condom," I managed to choke out.

He pulled me back toward him. "I got it."

His fingers slid lengthways between my butt cheeks, skirting the puckered asshole and making me shiver. "So wet, Princess. I get you so wet." I was over my embarrassment of how much he turned me on. There was no point trying to hide it. As he said, he saw it all.

"You got me so hard."

And then I felt him. The tip of him. The hot, hard end of him.

Sam just slid his cock along my sex, between my cheeks, making me wait.

"Sam. Don't torture me. It's my birthday."

"Do you want it so bad it hurts yet?" His voice was deep and raw. "That's what you do to me. I want you so bad right now it hurts."

Before I had time to absorb what he was saying, he was inside me in one swift movement.

It was relief, pleasure, desire all mixed into one. And my knees buckled.

"Hey, beautiful," he said, holding me at the waist. Me impaled on him. "Is it too much?"

It was.

"Sam," I said. I couldn't think of the words in the right order. I couldn't tell him how good it was.

He pulled out and guided me to the couch. I sat astride him. "We can take it at your pace. We can do it how you like it."

I realized I had my eyes closed, lost in a trance. I opened

them and he was looking at me. He had a slight sheen to his forehead and I reached out and stroked his hair. "I like it every way with you."

He lifted my hips and pulled me on to him again. My body was still weak, but the couch and his hands supported me, and I placed my palms against his chest.

He blinked lazily as he kept his focus on my face and began to lift my hips, just slightly, and then pull me back onto him. I let him move me, watching his jaw clench when he hit the end of me. He was so deep and it was so good.

I concentrated on the press of his thumbs below my hips, the hard muscles under my palms. Anything to stop myself from coming because I wanted this to last forever.

His eyes flickered from my face to my chest and the sway of my breasts as they lifted with each thrust.

"You look so beautiful," he said.

I shuddered and he groaned as I involuntarily squeezed him.

"Jesus, Grace." He picked up his pace, lifting and pulling.

I bit down on my lip to stop myself from crying out, but it didn't work and I screamed out a plea. For more. For Sam. For this moment to never end.

I began to move my hips a little more, increasing the push and the pull, speeding up the pleasure as it circled us both.

I wanted him as much as he wanted me.

I wanted this moment.

I clung to his chest, my fingernails digging into his

skin, and he sat up, pulling us chest to chest, his mouth finding mine.

His kisses were jerky and staccato as if he were using any energy he had left to pour into me. His breathing was labored and he groaned. "I can feel you. So tight. You're almost . . ." Before he had time to finish his sentence, I was spiraling into orgasm and he was following, pumping his hips from the sofa. His expression was equal parts tight and soft as we gazed into each other's eyes through our climax.

I wanted for nothing with Sam Shaw in my world.

———————

"They're both great—the perfect combination of soft and firm," I said, staring at Bergdorf's ceiling as Sam wriggled next to me. We were furniture shopping—bed shopping more specifically—and we'd narrowed it down to two. "You should make the decision. It's your bed."

"You'll be sleeping in it as much as I will," Sam replied.

I turned to face him, making no effort to hide my grin. In the weeks since my birthday, there was no longer any discussion of whether we'd see each other that night. We were together *every* night, but he came to Brooklyn because I refused to sleep on his mattress. I might deny being a princess, but a mattress on the floor was just a step too far. "Well, why not buy both of them? You have four bedrooms to fill, after all."

Other than not having a bed to sleep on, part of the reason we didn't spend much time at his apartment was because it felt odd to be back there. Park Avenue was the symbol of everything I hadn't wanted to become. I didn't want to be a Park Avenue princess, didn't want to marry a man I didn't love because it was a so-called *good match*. I didn't want to cheat on him to get an escape, but stay with him because I liked the trappings of my life. Trappings that just didn't matter.

I didn't want to turn into my mother.

In so many ways, 740 Park Avenue seemed like my past, not my future.

"My place is closer to work for both of us," Sam said.

He'd never really brought up the fact that we always stayed at my place in Brooklyn, so I hadn't realized it was a problem for him. "You'd prefer we stay at yours?"

He sat up, swung his legs over the side of the mattress and began bouncing up and down. "It makes sense. It's closer."

"I guess," I said. "And we don't have to spend every night together." Things had moved quickly with Sam and me. It had been an intense couple of months and although everything seemed right—perfect even—it probably was a good thing to have a bit of space. I really liked him—like, lightning bolt out of the clear blue liked him—but I'd been let down enough to know I should be holding back a little. I was sure now that I'd suggested it, he'd jump at spending some time apart.

Sam stopped bouncing and turned to me with a frown. "You don't want to stay at my place?"

I shrugged. "I like Brooklyn."

"Because it's your place, or for some other reason?" He

held out his hand, offering to pull me up.

"Park Avenue isn't really my thing anymore," I replied, keeping my hands by my sides. "I'm not the princess you think I am." Wasn't he happy I wasn't demanding to see him every night?

Sam stood and rounded the bed so he was standing over me. "I feel like I'm missing something." He stared at me as if he were trying to soak up an explanation from just being near me.

"You're not missing anything," I said. "Don't you want some time apart?"

He frowned. "I like things how they are." My body sagged into the mattress. Why did he have to be so cute? Every time I gave him an opportunity to let me down, he doubled down and made me feel even more adored. This guy could really break my heart one day.

"It's just easier for me to stay at my place. I have all my clothes in Brooklyn. Occasionally I even have food in the refrigerator and—"

"And we're sleeping in a bed where other men have been before me."

I just stared at him. Sam was the least insecure man I'd ever met, but he didn't like anything to do with my previous boyfriends. "Okay. So I'll buy a new bed." It wasn't jealousy that made Sam see red, but the fact he didn't think any of my exes had been good enough for me.

"You don't think it's easier to come to my place?"

Everything was easier on Park Avenue because no one could live there without a ton of money.

I wasn't going to be taken in by all that. I wanted to like Sam because of the way he was so sincere about everything—the way he never seemed to hide any part of himself when he was with me. I didn't want to be with him for his apartment or because it was close to my work.

"Okay, well we can keep sleeping in Brooklyn if that's what makes you happy."

Sam had changed my future. He'd shown me things could be different. He may have money, but it didn't define him . . . and I shouldn't let it define me.

"I think you and the apartment are just perfect. And I think I prefer this bed," I said, sitting up.

Maybe being back at 740 Park Avenue might be more of a rebellion than a surrender to a life I didn't want.

Chapter Seventeen

Sam

"You got along with Max, right?" Grace asked as we turned off I-95 toward Max and Harper's house. The journey had been slow—first with traffic and then because the roads had grown icy as we'd gotten farther out of the city.

"Sure," I replied, glancing across at her. "Why wouldn't I?"

She'd never asked about my friends other than Angie and Chas, but I supposed as I never mentioned any, she knew there wasn't anyone else in my life. Apart from her. Grace had unexpectedly changed things in small ways and big ways. I now had a bed and a sofa and I'd increased the number of people I cared about in the world by fifty percent.

"Should I buy a car?" I'd rented a Range Rover for the drive out to Connecticut. "I have a parking space in the building."

"Mr. No Possessions wants to buy something that won't make him money? You're becoming quite the shopper. I had a car I never used, so I sold it. You think you'll use it?"

I liked the way this one drove, but I wasn't really interested in buying a car. What I wanted was to take my mind off a weekend in the country. It hadn't seemed significant when I'd agreed. I'd been content to make Grace happy, but as the city drifted away, the scenery became disturbingly reminiscent.

I'd never been back to my old neighborhood in New Jersey. Hightimes was thirty miles from the house I'd grown up in, and although Angie and I had travelled into the city, we never went back to my childhood home. As an adult, I never wanted to be reminded of my parents' deaths. The good memories weren't worth reliving the bad.

I put my hand on Grace's knee. I was doing this for her and she was worth it. She slid her palm under mine and squeezed my fingers.

"This weekend is a lot of firsts for us," she said. "First trip away together. First time I have to deal with your driving." She laughed as I pulled a shocked face. "First time staying with friends. First evening with Max and Harper on our own. I mean, I have no idea who we are in public." She seemed anxious, and as much as I was, too, her anxiety was more troubling to me than my own.

"What are you talking about?" I asked.

"Well, are we one of those affectionate couples who can't stop touching each other? Are we the type who bicker? Do we laugh at each other's jokes even though we've heard them before? Who are we?"

"You're crazy. Let's just be who we are. You're still you. I'm still me. Even in public."

"You make it sound so easy." She sighed. "I hope you're right. You never know, I might not think you're so hot in the Connecticut light."

I started to chuckle. "You're so funny. Let's pull over and

get naked so I can convince you that you'll still think I'm hot." I pulled over, then turned on the hazard lights.

She grabbed my forearm. "No, that's their house on the corner. We've arrived already."

"We can turn around. I want to be sure you still find me attractive."

She shook her head in exasperation, so I pulled out and turned into the driveway.

A teenaged girl stood in the drive with a baby on her hip. She waved.

"That's Max's fifteen-year-old daughter, Amanda," she said and I waved as well. "The baby is Amber. Lizzie, the youngest, is probably sleeping."

That seemed like a lot of kids.

Harper came out to greet us as we got out of the car, her arms outstretched. "I'm so excited you're here." She pulled us both into a hug.

"Harper! I need your boob," Max shouted from inside the house.

"If only that were true," she muttered as she guided us in. "Oh, how I long for the days when Max was first in line for some boob action."

"She's breastfeeding," Grace explained.

"Sometimes I feel like a cow," Harper replied. "I just exist for my milk and wonder if I'll get slaughtered when I dry up."

Grace laughed at Harper's dramatic drawl. "Welcome to Connecticut, Sam."

Harper turned and grinned. "Yes, welcome. You'll be

happy to know you won't be required to breastfeed during your stay."

"I appreciate it," I replied.

As soon as we got through the door, Max kissed Grace on the cheek and then handed the baby to Harper before shaking my hand.

"Let's have a beer. I need to celebrate doubling the number of men in the house," Max said as he dove into the fridge, bringing out a bottle of wine and two beers.

"I've been expressing milk all week so I can have a drink tonight," Harper said. "Then we're all happy, right?" she said, cooing to Lizzie. "You're fed and I'm drunk. Perfect."

I wasn't sure if it was appropriate to laugh about breast milk, so I tried to keep my face neutral.

"Can I have a drink, Dad?" Amanda asked. "In France, kids my age have wine with dinner, you know."

"Well, we're not in France," Max replied.

Amanda rolled her eyes and handed Amber to Grace, who puckered her lips. Amber kissed her. They were clearly comfortable with each other. This was a side of Grace I'd not seen before.

"Down," Amber said, wriggling in Grace's arms. Grace bent and put her on the floor.

She glanced up at me. "What are you thinking?" she asked, slipping her arm around my waist.

"He's thinking this seems a lot like a zoo," Harper said.

Not exactly, but it was noisy and chaotic and the relaxed, family atmosphere stirred something hidden deep within me.

"Why don't you start on dinner?" Max suggested.

"Amanda's making lasagna."

"But you're going to help, right?" Amanda asked, turning back to her dad.

"I'm going to be here, but you can do this. You've watched me make it a thousand times. You're going to college in a couple of years. You need to learn how to cook. I spoil you."

I remembered my dad cooking on the weekends. He would run my mom a bath and then prepare dinner, standing me on a stool next to him until I was big enough to reach the counter on my own and we'd talk about school and I'd stir things and shred cheese and generally think I was helping. Amanda was a few years older than I had been the last time I'd cooked with my father.

"You mean I need to learn how to cook because I'm a girl."

"No, you need to learn because you should be able to feed yourself decent meals. Stop being a pain." Max sat on one of the bar stools opposite the counter. "We'll sit here and watch," he said as Amanda tied an apron to her waist.

Had my father had the same kind of love for me I saw in Max's eyes?

I knew the answer. I recognized the expression Max wore as one I'd seen on my father's face every time he looked at me.

"Get everything you'll need out on the counter," Max said, then turned to me. "How's business?"

Grateful for the distraction from the whirring inside my head, I said, "Good actually." Grace and I took seats next to Max. "The market is tough at the moment, but I think that's an opportunity. It stops people from playing the real estate market like it's a game of blackjack, which can't be a bad thing." I took a swig of beer.

"I saw you're developing that site by Battery Park."

"Yeah. It's such a great location. It's underutilized at the moment."

For a very long time my social interaction had comprised of Angie and Chas. I wasn't used to new people and I wasn't used to being with so many voices in a non-work environment. The memories of my own childhood were growing stronger. I tried to convince myself that Connecticut with Max and Harper wasn't anything like my childhood home because I'd never had any brothers and sisters. All the noise—babies crying, people laughing—and the child paraphernalia littering every room in the house were all alien.

But there were too many similarities for me not to remember my parents.

I'd forgotten the sense of family, of love. I'd buried the memories of times with my parents and stomped on the ground so they never surfaced. For nearly fifteen years they'd remained there, still and unmoving. But now the earth had cracked and the ground was shaking.

I was trying like hell to hold it together.

"Grace, is Sam better than your other boyfriends?" Amanda asked as we watched her prepare supper. "Harper said you date losers."

"Harper!" Grace called over to the couch. Max rolled his eyes and I smiled because I knew he expected me to.

"What?" Harper asked as she placed a sleeping baby

Lizzie into the crib at the end of the couch.

"You said I date losers?" Grace asked.

Harper came into the kitchen, opened the refrigerator and took out a bottle of wine. "You can't deny it's true." Harper looked up at me as she filled a fresh glass. "You're the first decent guy she's ever dated. Don't fuck this up."

"Harper," Grace protested.

But Harper was right. I had to get this right and I wasn't sure I knew how. I'd spent every day since my parents died deliberately trying not to want anything—Grace had been right. I didn't want to lose anything important to me again. It had been hard, at first, difficult to stop coveting things. And even now, it was almost impossible not to be jealous of those with loved ones, but it had become easier. It hadn't happened overnight, but slowly, a hardened shell had grown around me and become my armor. After that, every day was easier.

"What? It's true," Harper said.

I'd realized pretty early on that her previous boyfriends weren't worthy of her. I was no angel, but it was no effort for me to put Grace first, where she deserved to be. But could I do that forever? Grace looked comfortable here, happy amid the family and the love. And she should have that for herself. I just wasn't sure I could give it to her. I'd shut down my emotions a long time ago—ruled out the possibility of this kind of future for myself. For the first time in a long time I'd allowed myself to covet someone. I'd had no choice. Grace had broken through my armor and not given me a say in the matter. But a family? A home? I couldn't risk that.

I took a swig of my beer, trying to swallow down the

anxiety threatening to drown me.

"Your problem," Harper told Grace, "is that you're a fixer."

Grace snapped her head around and caught me forcing down a chuckle. It was one of the many things I loved about Grace, and it was exactly how I'd described her in one of our first encounters. She scowled and placed her hand over my mouth. I grabbed her wrist, kissed her palm and twined her fingers in mine. "I didn't say a word, Princess."

"She's always taken men on like projects. Guys that need fixing, or nurturing," Harper said.

"*Harper*," Grace complained. I knew she didn't like hearing herself described like that.

"You give and give and give," Harper continued, ignoring Grace, "until you're bled dry. It's like you're permanently breastfeeding these losers! You've been dating children."

Grace sighed.

"Well, *I* don't need fixing," I said, though I knew it wasn't true. But I also knew that nobody, not even Grace, was capable of fixing me. No one had the power to go back in time and stop that drunk driver. But did Grace know that? Or was I just another one of her boyfriends who needed *nurturing*?

"We all need a little fixing," Grace said in a small voice as I smoothed my hand over her back.

Perhaps I should have walked away from Grace, but now that I was here, I didn't have the strength to let her go. "I *think* Harper's trying to tell you that you're kind and generous and loving," I said.

"In the way only Harper can," Max said.

"Of course that's what I'm saying," Harper said as she began to shred cheese. "Did I just turn into your commis chef without realizing it?" she asked Amanda, who just shrugged.

"She has us both wrapped around her little finger," Max said.

My mother would have said the same about me.

"Just grate enough for the topping," Amanda said.

"Yes, ma'am," Harper replied, then turned back to Grace. "Look, what I'm trying to say is you are one of the kindest, sweetest, most generous and loyal people in the world . . . and I don't think the men you've dated so far have come close to deserving you."

"I'm *so* happy we're talking about this in front of Sam. I really am," Grace said, and although she was smiling, her tight jaw told me she was uncomfortable. I stroked my thumb across her wrist wanting to calm her.

"It's nothing I didn't already know," I said.

"So you approve of Sam?" Amanda asked Harper. "You think he deserves Grace?"

I was sure I *didn't*.

"So far, so good," Harper said.

"Don't take that personally, Sam. She says the same thing about me," Max said as he moved off the stool and kissed Harper on the head as he made his way to the fridge.

"How can you tell?" Amanda said.

"Tell what?" Harper asked.

"That he deserves Grace," Amanda replied.

"Well, from what Grace tells me—and from what I see."

Harper glanced at me as she handed a plate of shredded cheese to Amanda. "He's thoughtful and caring and makes her laugh."

Grace smiled and turned her head toward me. I raised my eyebrows. Did I do all that?

"Remember, you have to judge men on what they do, and not just what they say," Harper said.

"Amanda doesn't need dating advice, but thank you, my sweet," Max replied.

"I wish someone had given *me* that advice sooner," Harper said. "No, that's not what I mean. I wish I'd *followed* that advice sooner."

"I think things worked out just about perfectly," Max said, grabbing Harper.

Amber started screaming from the living room and Harper pulled out of Max's arms.

"Drink your wine," Max said. "I'll get this. She's getting tired and needs to have a bath."

"And that is why I married the guy," Harper said. "He's a total DILF."

"Harper!" Amanda shouted.

Harper just shrugged and Amanda rolled her eyes.

"Are you okay?" Grace asked me under her breath.

I nodded and smiled, tucking her hair behind her ear, allowing my finger to continue across her jaw.

I looked up to find Amanda watching us.

"Are you going to marry Sam?" Amanda asked, looking at Grace. Even though her question wasn't directed at me, it caught me off guard.

Grace laughed. "Maybe."

"Why only maybe?" Amanda asked.

Loving Grace hadn't been a choice, but marriage? I hadn't thought about it. Ever. Marriage was for other people, people who'd had a normal life. People who knew how to be a husband, a father—people who knew how to love.

"Amanda, you shouldn't ask people such personal questions," Max said.

"Why not? It's just Grace. She asks me much more personal questions."

I curled my hand around the edge of the countertop, hanging on to I didn't know what. I needed something solid—something to be sure of. The ache for something that had gone before grew and grew.

I tried to refocus on the conversation around me.

"You're right. I do ask you personal questions and there shouldn't be a double standard," Grace replied. "Sam and I haven't known each other very long, but maybe someday."

Surely Grace understood I wasn't *that* man, the one who could commit. I couldn't give her three children, a house filled with love and laughter and chaos. It was too much to be responsible for.

Too much to lose.

"Excuse me," I said as my stool scraped against the slate floor of the kitchen. "I'll get our bags out of the car." I needed some air. Some distance from a life I could never give Grace. I wasn't the man who deserved her.

I was anything but.

"I'm sorry for saying that earlier," Grace said as we shut the door to the pool house. "About marriage, I mean. I know we're going a million miles an hour and—"

"Hey," I said, pulling her into my arms. As much as what she'd said had unsettled me, she shouldn't be apologizing "You have nothing to be sorry for. I like knowing how you feel about these things." I moved us toward the bed and pushed her onto her back.

She pulled at my shirt until I was leaning over her. "Did I freak you out?"

"You didn't say anything wrong. Why would I freak out?" I wanted to protect her from my fears.

She grinned as she scraped her nails over my scalp absentmindedly. Her touch went straight to my cock. Every. Time. I had to slow this down—tell her I couldn't give her what she wanted.

I groaned, rolled away and presented her with an opportunity. Straddling me, she settled on top of me, and my dick hardened four layers beneath her pussy.

"Are you telling me you've thought about marrying me?" she asked as she moved her hips back and forward.

"No, I haven't." It was the truth and she deserved that. Her smile faltered, just a fraction. "But you're the only woman I've ever cared about in this way."

She stopped rocking and tried to move, but I grabbed the tops of her thighs and held her in place. "Talk to me. Is marriage what you're looking for?"

"Not for the sake of it," she said, her gaze fixed to my chest.

"I don't understand. Do you want a family, the children, the chaos—all the responsibility? Is that what you see for yourself?"

"For myself and the man I love." She looked at me from under her eyelashes. Was she saying she loved me?

"No, Grace." I released her thighs and moved her off me and sat up. "I'm not a man you should love." I pushed my hands through my hair. Didn't she understand? That wasn't what this was between us.

"What do you mean, you're not a man I can love?" she asked from behind me. The bed moved as she shifted and I felt the warmth of her hands on my shoulders. I stood to avoid her touch.

I couldn't do this. I didn't know what I'd been thinking getting involved with a woman—allowing myself to care about someone, for someone to care about me. I'd known it could only end in disaster.

"Surely I get to choose who I love?" Her voice was harder than before, her tone more challenging.

I couldn't look at her. Instead I pulled out my overnight bag and began to pack. I needed to leave. Get back to my apartment—be on my own. "I'm just saying you can't chose me. And if you do . . ."

"What? You're going to leave me? Because I love you?"

The hints were gone. She'd said it. "Don't say that. You can't love me. And I can never love you."

Something hit me on the head—a shoe maybe. "You're an asshole, Sam Shaw." Her voice cracked on my last name. "You've spent the last few months being the best man I've ever known after my father." It took all my strength not to look at her as she began to sob. I wanted to make her feel better, to pull her into my arms and tell her that everything was going to be okay, but it wasn't. I stayed silent.

"What am I supposed to do? Just ignore how wonderful you are—how special you make me feel? I love you. And if you don't love me then we'll go our separate ways, but you can't tell me not to love you."

The more she used that word—love—the weaker I became. I hated that I liked hearing it so much. She slammed the bathroom door and I could hear her sobbing on the other side. *Our separate ways.* Her words woke something in me. I wasn't sure I could give her up.

I dropped the jeans I was holding and sank onto the chair at the end of the bed, clutching my head. As much as I didn't want it to be true, the fact that Grace loved me hadn't caused my world to come tumbling down—not yet. But it would eventually, right?

Her sobs echoed around the bathroom. I hated hearing her crying. More, I hated I had caused her tears.

Shit. What was I going to do? I owed her the truth. I had to tell her how I felt.

I stood and headed to the bathroom, gently knocking on the door. "Grace," I called, "I'm sorry." Should I open the door? We'd never argued before, not like this. "Can I come in?" She didn't answer, which wasn't a no. I turned the knob, sagging in relief that she hadn't locked me out. Not physically, anyway, though that might have been better for both of us.

Grace sat on the edge of the bath, her head bowed. I hated seeing her sad. I wasn't used to it. I loved basking in her confidence and smiles, loved the way she'd wickedly flick her hips or cock her head to one side in a challenge. "Grace, I'm not trying to fuck you over here."

She stayed completely still.

I sat next to her, pressing my thigh to hers. Even though it had only been seconds without feeling her, it was still too long. "I'm sorry. This is just—"

"Too much. I knew it." She got up abruptly and I grabbed her wrist.

"Let me finish. I know I've upset you, but you have to let me explain. Coming here . . . it's brought up a lot of stuff for me."

Her body went limp and she stood expectantly in front of me.

"Stuff about my parents. Things I never even think about because the memories cut like thousands of tiny blades."

"What kind of things?" she asked, her voice neutral, as if she were keeping herself limber and ready to run in whatever direction would protect her best.

I wanted her to know everything, but I didn't want to have to tell her, didn't want to go through the agony of saying the words. It was why my friendship with Angie was always so easy. She knew, and always had.

"Being here reminds me of my childhood home. The place I lived before my parents died." I took a deep breath, wanting to steady myself. "It's just brought up some memories that I've spent a long time trying to forget."

"You never talk about them," she said, her body relaxing slightly against mine.

223

"I know, but it's not just you. I don't talk with anyone about this anymore. My parents aren't ever coming back, so it always seemed easier to forget they were ever there in the first place." I rested my elbows on my knees and my head in my hands. I didn't want to do this, but she deserved to hear it. "When I think about what I had—everything I lost—the pain comes back."

Her thigh brushed against mine again and she smoothed a hand down my back. It was such a gentle touch, but it ripped me open.

"I lost my whole world when my parents died. I felt like I was being punished for something I didn't do, sent to jail for crimes I hadn't committed. Their deaths were unjust and the consequences just as unmerited."

She pressed her lips to my shoulder, soothing me with a simple gesture. She'd become so special to me. How had I let that happen?

"Forgetting about them was my escape. I never wanted to go through anything like that again—and I've made sure I haven't. Unwittingly, I made a vow never to love anyone again."

"But you care about me, Sam, I know you do. I feel it."

I reached for her hand, still unable to look at her but wanting to reassure her anyway. "I do. But it wasn't something I was looking for, and it wasn't a choice."

"I'm sorry," she whispered. "I shouldn't have brought you here."

The last thing I wanted to do was make her unhappy. "Of course you should. I had no idea seeing Max and Harper's family would bring back so many memories for me. And seeing you with them—you deserve the same kind of happiness."

"You don't want marriage or a family?"

Just the words sent my pulse spinning. "I've never thought that would be my journey."

The silence between us grew, but neither of us moved until she released my hand and began grabbing at my shirt. "Lift your arms up," she said, pulling the fabric over my head. "Here." She traced my tattoo with her finger.

Wait and hope.

"That's who you are. I know you're an orphan, a victim, a child in mourning. But you're an optimist, too. Don't you see? The thing about the Count is that he might have had to wait years, he might have had to dig tunnels and fight pirates, but he finds his ultimate bliss at the end. Life is a storm, my love."

Life is a storm, my young friend.

You will bask in the sunlight one moment, be shattered on the rocks the next.

What makes you a man is what you do when the storm comes.

You must look into the storm and shout as you did in Rome

Do your worst, because I will do mine.

"Storms will come, Sam, but I want us to face them together."

I turned to her. "I want us to face the storms together too." It was the only thing I was certain of. I didn't know if I could give her a family, or a home like the one I'd had. But I could try.

———

225

I'd never gone fishing before, but now that Max and I were sitting in chairs on the riverbed, sipping beers and enjoying the fresh Connecticut air, I wondered why. "The peace is nice," I said.

Max laughed. "Yeah. The house is so chaotic sometimes, it's good to spend a couple of hours in silence."

"But you like it," I said. "The chaos?"

"Of course. I love my family, but that doesn't mean I don't still like to escape the crazy. That's why we're out here when it's so damn cold."

I glanced back at the clapboard house in the distance. The land Max and Harper's home was built on led down to a river on a gentle slope. The leaves on the trees were gone, but their branches provided a chestnut-colored canopy over the clear calm water. It was a beautiful spot.

"My father and I used to come fishing to escape the three girls back home. Sometimes Violet joined us, but normally it was just me and my dad."

"Does Harper mind?"

"Not at all. She counts the minutes I take out here and makes sure she gets her alone time, too."

I laughed. "That seems fair enough."

"It works for us both. But I also make sure Harper and I spend time together—it's so easy for it to become all about the kids."

Max shared his experiences as if he believed it was inevitable that Grace and I would start a family. For so many couples, it was the natural course of events. As much as I wanted to try to open up with Grace, I just didn't think it would be easy after a lifetime of doing everything I could to avoid personal entanglements.

"It's a lot of pressure." I mumbled almost to myself.

"What is?" Max asked, snapping shut his box of fishing tackle.

"Clearly, having three kids has logistical challenges, but do you find yourself worrying about losing it all or something happening to one of them?" Were my fears irrational, brought on only because of what I'd experienced, or did everyone go through it?

Max's brow furrowed as he tipped back his beer. "Every day. Amanda going to high school nearly killed me—all the exposure to drugs and alcohol, you know?" He squinted in the sunlight as he glanced across the water. "She'll be driving in just over a year." He sighed. "I have to try not to think about what the hell could happen to the babies. Harper may seem like she's super cool with everything, but she's anything but. A few weeks after Amber was born, I insisted on taking Harper to dinner while my mother was visiting." He sat back in his chair. "Now, my mother has had three kids of her own, and she had Amanda with her. She can drive, use a phone and is far calmer than either Harper or me. But still, Harper cried all the way to the restaurant because she was terrified something horrible was going to happen to Amber in the two hours it was going to take us to eat dinner."

He bent and fiddled with the fishing rod. "Being responsible for another human being is the scariest thing you'll ever do, but it's also the most rewarding." Max smiled. "It's a legacy, and infinitely more important than any business you might build."

I took another gulp of my beer, finishing it off, and set the bottle down in the grass. I understood what he was saying, but I doubted he'd ever had to endure time in a group home. He would never understand the freedom that financial security brought—and that's what my business had given me. "But I can control the success of my business to a certain extent—I can make decisions that keep my money safe. The same's not true of people."

Max didn't say anything for a while. We were both content to watch the surface of the water, and the bob of the floats. "You a football fan?" he asked after a few minutes had passed.

I shook my head. "Nope."

"Baseball? Any sports team?"

"Hockey. New York Rangers. You?"

"The Red Sox."

"Really? In a land of Yankee fans?" I bet he kept *that* quiet in the office.

"What can I say? I like to take risks. I mean, Jesus, you're a *hockey* fan. Anyway, you don't follow a team knowing they're going to win every time, do you?"

"Definitely not if you're a Red Sox fan."

He chuckled. "That's life, isn't it? There are no guarantees. But it's something else when your team wins, right? You know you're not going to win every year. You still support them through the rough times. Kids are the same. You know a lot of it is going to be hard, and you're going to worry *a lot*. But it's all worth it when they smile and tell you they love you. Trust me."

My parents must have worried about me all the time. But they'd never let it show. They'd still taught me to ride a bike and cross the street. They knew they couldn't protect me from everything and they didn't try and stop me from going out into the world because they knew it was dangerous. Still, I understood now that my happiness was always their priority. And I was sure that if they were still alive they'd still want that—want me to love and be loved.

Had I been letting them down by keeping myself so closed off all these years?

And even if I was, could I risk my sanity, my heart, my life, with no guarantee life wouldn't snatch everything I loved away from me? Again?

One thing was for sure, I'd survived loss once, but I wasn't strong enough to do it twice.

CHAPTER EIGHTEEN
Grace

"It's so good to be home." I kicked off my shoes before the door was even closed. The drive back from Connecticut had been almost twice as long as on the way out and I was ready for a bath and my bed.

"You didn't have a good time?" Sam asked, taking my coat and hanging it up for me.

I grinned at what had become a habit of ours when we got back to Brooklyn. "Of course. But I'm always happy to come home."

"Do you know what I missed?" Sam asked, stopping me from going into the kitchen and circling his arms around my waist, pushing his erection against my stomach.

"How long have you been in that state?" I asked.

He dipped his head and kissed my neck. "All weekend," he replied. "It's been torture."

I giggled. "Thank you for not dry humping me in front of Max and Harper." After our argument, sex hadn't been on the agenda. But despite the lack of physical intimacy, after our discussion in the pool house about Sam's parents, I felt we were closer than ever.

"Well, my control is up." He walked me backward toward

the bedroom. "I want to show you what you've been missing."

As we walked, he pulled off my top and unzipped my skirt. I bounced as my ass hit the bed and watched as Sam stripped off in double time before me.

"What are you looking at?" he asked, standing on one leg as he peeled off his socks.

I shrugged. "Some guy."

"Some guy who thinks you're the most beautiful woman on the planet?" he asked as he stood naked, sliding his finger behind my knee. How could one touch in such an innocuous place get me so wet?

"Maybe," I breathed. I'd told him I'd loved him and he'd freaked out. I could settle for him calling me beautiful for now. I knew he cared about me, and I had to be sensitive to how different our relationship was for him.

He leaned over, forcing my back to the mattress. Rather than drive me away as Sam had feared, the things he'd told me about his past only made me love him more. To have endured what he had as a child and be the man he was, floored me. I was in awe of him. "Some guy who is *the* most special man."

"Some guy who's going to work really hard at being the man you deserve," he said.

My body and mind turned to jelly.

He placed small kisses from my stomach up between my breasts, then yanked down my bra straps, enveloping my hardened nipple with his tongue. My fingers threaded through his hair as he sucked and scraped, bit and licked. I twisted my hips in frustration. I needed him to know how wet I was. His palm spanned my belly, holding my hips to the mattress.

He released a nipple and looked up at me. "Is that the way your pussy asks for attention?"

I nodded, a little embarrassed.

"Don't hold back. I like you needy," he said as his fingers dipped beneath my panties, his middle finger finding my clit. Infuriatingly, he just rested his finger lightly on my nub and went back to work on my other nipple.

"Please," I cried out, tilting my hips in an effort to create some friction against his finger.

"There," he said, slowly circling my clit. "I like to hear everything. Even if it means we fight and then make up. I want to know everything that's going on in your head, my princess."

"Kiss me," I said with a smile. "But don't move your hand."

He grinned and pressed his lips against mine, his tongue delving deeper.

"You feel so good, like coming home," he said as he pulled back to look at me. It was the biggest compliment Sam could have paid me. I understood how difficult it must have been to let me in, but I knew he wanted to, and I would do anything in return. I swept my hands down his back.

I unhooked my bra and tossed it away while Sam pulled off my panties. I clasped my hands over his shoulders. I liked the feel of him under my fingers. He was so solid, so safe.

In one swift movement, he slid me to him, my back to his front, and lifted my leg up and back so it leaned on his.

I loved the warmth of him enveloping me in this position. "You ready, Princess?" he asked as he teased my sex with the tip of his cock.

"Always," I said. I waited as he slipped on a condom.

"I've wanted you so bad all weekend. We have a lot of catching up to do." He thrust into me, his hand on my hip, pushing me onto him. My body sagged in relief at having him inside me. This was how it should be. Always.

"I've missed this," I said. "Missed you."

"You never need to miss it." He dragged himself out and thrust up again. "I'm going to try, for you, Grace."

His tender words coupled with his hard fucking were the perfect combination. Had he meant what he said?

My mind went blank as my body began to buzz from the inside out with the beginning of an orgasm.

"Fuck," Sam yelled, then pulled out, rolling to his back. "I was so close—too close—I want to make this last," he said.

I liked that he'd only been in me a few seconds before his need to come had overtaken him. I shifted to face him and placed a kiss on his sticky, hot chest.

"I'm sorry," he said, stroking my back. "I have no control around you."

"That's okay."

He swept his hand down my body, his fingers finding my clit. He stared deep into my eyes as he circled and circled. His gaze made his touch all the stronger. The buzz built in my stomach this time. His movements were steady and small, as if he were patiently and carefully pulling my orgasm from me. I gripped his arm, keeping him in position.

I let out a groan and he took my bottom lip between his teeth, then slid his tongue into my mouth in strong, possessive strokes, as if to remind me I was his. I groaned and seeped onto his fingers as my body shook and then dissolved into my climax.

"Jesus, I love it when you come," he said, pushing me to my back and sliding over me.

I couldn't speak. Just smiled and cupped his face with my palm.

As he pushed into me, pleasure crept up his face. Giving him that sensation was so powerful, I felt myself grow wetter, despite just having come.

"Christ," he called out. The muscles in his neck tensed and I stroked a finger over them. "Fuck, Grace."

I gasped as he slipped his hand underneath my ass and pulled me up, increasing his rhythm. I was vaguely aware of my headboard cracking against the drywall as his thrusts became more urgent.

I lifted my legs, wanting to give him more, to pull him closer. He thrust deeper, his breaths heavy on my neck peppered with "You're all mine" and "Forever."

"I think we should definitely get a car," Sam said and I turned to look at him as I was locking the door to my apartment, checking to see if I'd heard him right. "And a driver."

Was I reading too much into him saying *we*? "A driver?"

"Yeah. We get cabs every day anyway. A driver can drop me at work, then take you to the gallery. If either of us need it, we have it. You agree?" He took my hand, despite the fact that going down stairs side by side was slightly awkward.

He was talking about a future together—I'd never heard that from him before. "Well, I am a Park Avenue princess, so of course I agree."

The air was chilly as we stepped outside, an icy wind tunneled down the street. Some early snow had settled while we were away, but most of it had disappeared. "I think it might snow again," I said as Sam craned his neck looking for a cab. "Let's walk to the corner." I pulled on his arm.

"The trip won't be as far when we're on Park Avenue," he said. "And we won't have to wait in the cold for a cab."

There was that word again. *We.* I grinned.

Before long a cab pulled up and Sam opened the door for me to climb in.

"The bed arrives tonight," he said as he sat next to me. "Where do you want to stay?"

"Tonight?"

"Yeah. Tonight. Tomorrow."

If I didn't know better, I would have thought he was on the brink of suggesting we move in together. Although I'd detected a shift within him since Connecticut, I wasn't expecting it to be freewheeling from now on.

"We could have Angie and Chas over on the weekend," he said. "Maybe even Harper, Max and all the kids."

"Maybe." I didn't want to push him, or bring back painful memories if he wasn't ready. I was determined to give him some time and space to process everything.

"I really like them. We should invite them." He squeezed my hand and looked out the window.

"Just here on the left," he said to the driver as we approached the gallery.

The cab stopped and Sam put his hand on mine. "Hey. Before you go. I . . . about that thing you said in Connecticut?"

I held my breath, unsure what he was going to say, but so hopeful it was what I wanted to hear. I'd not repeated my *I love you*—I didn't want to trigger anything. I nodded.

"Well," he said, then took a deep breath. "Yeah, well I feel the same."

CHAPTER NINETEEN
Sam

I'd known I'd loved her since our argument in Connecticut. It was part of the reason I was so mad—she'd managed to make me love her despite all the odds, and despite my every effort not to.

She narrowed her eyes as if she hadn't heard me correctly.

"You know," I said, wanting to say the actual words but finding it a struggle to push them out. She squeezed my hand. She wasn't going to make me say it but she deserved to hear it.

"I love you," I said.

Her eyes became watery and I reached to cup her face. I didn't want her to be sad.

"I love *you*, Sam Shaw."

I nodded and tried to bite back a grin.

The cab driver cleared his throat. "I better go," she said.

"I don't want you to." I wished I'd told her last night and I could have spent hours just holding her close.

"I'll see you tonight. Maybe try to leave early and we can have dinner."

I turned to the driver. "I'm just going to say goodbye. Hang on." I wanted to wrap my arms around her before she left for the day, even it was just for a second. Grace opened the cab door as I set foot on the street.

There was a squeal of brakes, a yell from our driver and then I got thrown back into my seat.

What the hell? The cab stilled and I turned my head.

"Grace?" Her passenger door was closed and deformed, and the shattered windshield of another car faced me. Broken glass covered everything.

We'd been hit.

"Fuck," I said, scrambling out of the cab. "Grace!" I shouted, but didn't see her. As I rounded the trunk, I expected to find her arms outstretched toward me. But she'd disappeared. "Grace," I screamed when I found her, lying on the asphalt, her hair sprayed out against the road. It felt like it took hours to get to her. I sank to my knees. Her eyes were shut and her legs twisted awkwardly.

My heart pounded. Panicked, I stroked her cheek. "Grace," I said, looking up to find someone standing over me, staring. "Call 9-1-1," I bellowed then turned back to put my hand on Grace's chest. An inch of me relaxed as my hand rose and fell with her ribcage.

What was I supposed to do? I wanted to scoop her up and run to the nearest hospital, but something stopped me from moving her. I shrugged off my coat, pulled my phone from the pocket then draped the coat over her. I called 9-1-1 myself, unsure if the bystander had done as I'd asked. Grace needed help as fast as possible.

I kept my hand on her cheek as I spoke to the operator, telling her the address over and over again. Why did she keep asking me the same questions? I hung up at the same time the sirens started to wail. It was going to be okay. It had to be. I couldn't lose her.

I lifted Grace's hand just slightly off the road and slid mine underneath it. That's when the scent of metal hit me. It wasn't the engine. It was more subtle than that. I kept seeing images of my old family car.

Blood coated my fingers. Jesus. Where was she bleeding? How could I stop it? I scanned down her body, unable to see an obvious cause.

I closed my eyes, willing time to rewind, wanting to see how in an alternate universe, I had forced her to get out of my side of the cab.

"Sir, you have to move out of the way." The words were so slow I didn't understand until I'd been moved.

"Grace," I said when someone asked her name.

They spoke to her, telling her what they were doing as they wrapped her neck in a support and three of them put her on a stretcher. But all their voices overlapped. I tried to separate them, wanting to hear what each one of them said, desperate to know if she'd be okay. Because that's what I had to hear.

But I knew what faces looked like when the news was bad.

I didn't love people. I *couldn't* love people.

Bile steamed up from my stomach and I vomited over the car parked next to the cab. Acid continued to rise, coating my throat and my mouth. It felt selfish, getting sick while the best person I knew was dying on a stretcher.

I wretched again, until finally nothing came out. I

241

wiped my mouth and straightened, trying to see what was happening with Grace. A man in a uniform led me over to the ambulance. I couldn't hear what he said. I saw his lips move, but I couldn't focus. I just kept looking back and forth between him and the ambulance.

I stumbled toward the back and took a seat next to Grace.

I wanted to do something, anything to save her. I should have taken a first aid course or something. I looked around, but no one was doing anything.

I should call someone. I didn't have her parents' number but I did have Harper's. She'd know what to do. I dialed.

"Harper. There's been an accident. Get Grace's parents."

"What? Is she okay?"

I couldn't answer that question. "Call her parents. Tell them to come to the hospital."

"Where are you?"

I glanced out of the window. "In an ambulance."

"Fuck, Sam, which hospital?"

I had no idea. "Which hospital are we going to?" I asked the woman next to me.

"Mount Sinai West," she replied.

"I heard. I'm on my way," Harper said.

"Grace . . ." I wanted to hold her so badly. I'd swap places with her in an instant if God would let me. An oxygen mask obscured her face, and her arms lay straight at her sides. I slid my fingers over the smooth skin of her arm. Where was her coat? I glanced down her body. Her legs. They'd been twisted and covered in blood when I'd seen them.

"Where is she bleeding?" I asked, but didn't catch the

response through the fog in my head.

I fixed my stare on Grace, willing her to wake up, willing her to be okay, willing my life force into her.

The ambulance stopped and the doors swung open. I followed the paramedics, who slid Grace's stretcher out onto the street. As my foot hit the asphalt, my legs weakened and I fell to one knee. Someone lifted me under my arms and I found my footing, chasing after Grace's gurney.

As I got through the doors, someone's hand pushed at my chest, trying to stop me. "Sir, you can't go through there. They need to perform an exam. Take a seat and someone will come to check you over." She handed me a clipboard.

"I'm fine," I said as I strained to see where they were taking Grace.

I dared not blink in case I missed news of her.

Finally, I sat, ignoring the clipboard. I waited. And waited.

"Sam."

I looked up to find Harper standing over me.

"Is she okay?"

I shook my head. "I don't know. I don't think so."

"Sam," she yelled, pushing at my shoulders. "Where is she?"

Thankfully, one of the nurses came over and answered Harper's questions.

Helplessness, a feeling I'd spent so long trying to avoid, consumed me. I didn't want to listen to Harper—I wanted to see Grace. I slumped forward, my head in my hands, my elbows resting on my knees. Why had I insisted we take a cab? If we'd taken the subway, we wouldn't have been on the road. Or if I'd hired a driver, or just been sitting on the other side of the taxi . . .

"Sir, can you follow me? I need to do an exam," said a nurse in pink scrubs as Harper took the seat next to me. I didn't want to; I wanted to sit here and wait for Grace. I needed her to be okay. Even if I were fighting impossible odds, if I sat here, maybe there was a chance.

When my parents died, no one had told me anything. I never saw them in the hospital, never saw them stretchered off into the ambulance. I remember being at the hospital, on a bed behind a curtain, and then being taken overnight to a stranger's home. I wouldn't let that happen this time, this time I'd get to say goodbye.

"No. I'm staying here," I said.

"We'll have to perform the exam here. You've been sick and you're likely in shock. I have to insist—"

"Okay, fine. But I'm not going anywhere."

As the nurse poked a thermometer into my ear, I spotted Grace's parents at the reception desk.

"Harper," I said, nodding at them.

She went over to Grace's mother, then gave her the clipboard, as if the responsibility for Grace's welfare had been passed from me to them.

That was how it should be.

I had no business in Grace's life. I'd taken things too far.

The electric doors opened for the first time since Grace had gone through them. I stood to speak to the person who walked through, but it was only a courier and of no use to me.

"Sit down, sir," my nurse said, pushing me toward my

seat and handing me a white plastic cup of water. "Take small sips."

She shouldn't be here, wasting her time on me when there was Grace to look after. "Can you see about Grace?"

"They're still doing tests," she said, resting her hand on my shoulder.

As she left, her parents approached me. What could I say to them? I'd failed to keep their daughter safe. "Are you okay?" her mother asked me.

"I'm sorry," I stuttered.

Harper moved down a chair and Grace's mother sat beside me and patted me on the knee. Her father paced in front of us.

"I should have stopped her."

"It wasn't your fault. Harper said a car ran into the side of the cab," Grace's mother said.

How did Harper know that? Had I told her?

I nodded. "She was getting out. I should have made her get out of my side."

"Hush," she said. "There's nothing you could have done. Have they given you an exam? You should insist on a CT."

"I'm fine. It's Grace—"

"Shhh," she said, "everything's going to be okay."

She spoke with authority and if I hadn't understood what came with death, I would have believed her. Nothing was going to be okay if Grace didn't make it.

Seconds, minutes, hours passed. I resisted every urge I had to burst through the doors and find Grace. What were they doing?

Finally, the doors slid open again and this time a nurse came out, clutching a clipboard. "Grace Astor," she called out.

The four of us surrounded her, desperate for information. "Grace is doing well. She's lost some blood but she's conscious and asking for Sam."

It was as if I hit the drop of a roller-coaster ride—fear and excitement tumbled about in my belly. "She's alive?" I asked.

"She's a little banged up, but fine," the nurse said. "Her CT was clear."

She was going to be okay.

"She's bruised, and has a mild concussion. She's broken her leg in two places." I heard Grace's mother cry out but I smiled. A broken leg? That was it? "They'll reset the break this afternoon, then do the cast. We've given her something for the pain. She's conscious and you can see her, but no more than two of you at a time. Sam, shall I take you through?" I should have been magnanimous and offered to let her parents go first, but I had to see Grace, to know for sure she was okay. I followed the nurse without looking back.

We passed down the first corridor and then turned into a bay of beds. I scanned the room, looking for Grace. The nurse led me to a curtained-off bed and for a split second, before she pulled back the partition, I imagined I'd find someone other than Grace in the bed. I couldn't quite believe she was okay. They must have mistaken her for someone else.

I steeled myself as the curtain went back, but almost threw up again when I saw that it *was* her. Her eyelids fluttered and, finally, Grace opened her eyes and looked at me. "Sam," she said, her voice croaky.

I rushed forward, then stopped. I wanted to pull her toward me, but I was almost too scared to touch her. I stepped forward and she lifted her hand. I glanced back at the nurse.

"She's fine," the nurse assured me.

I slipped my palm under hers and kissed her on her forehead. As I pulled back, she winced. "I'm so sorry, Grace." For the kiss, for the accident. I wanted to take away her pain.

She gave me a small smile. "I love you."

Just a few hours earlier, those words had sent my soul soaring. Now they felt inappropriate. She shouldn't love me, because I *couldn't* love her. It wasn't how it was meant to be.

I pulled a chair up so I could sit beside her. I needed to study her beautiful face, remember how warm her hands were, memorize her smell.

But I couldn't protect Grace, and I had to protect myself.

For a moment, I'd allowed myself to love her, thought it possible for me to be loved. I should have known better. I wasn't strong enough.

I had to walk away.

CHAPTER TWENTY
Grace

I looked down the bed, amused by the different sizes of my legs. I remembered being told my leg would be reset, and then nothing after that until I came around in a different room.

I'd never broken a bone before.

"Are you okay, sweetheart?" my mother asked, holding out a cup of water.

I shook my head. "I'm fine. Where's Sam?"

My mother glanced at my father on the other side of the bed. He patted my hand. "Just relax."

"I'm perfectly relaxed. The drugs are taking care of that. Where's Sam?"

"I don't know, honey," my mother said.

He was here; I remembered from before they reset my leg. "Harper?" I asked. "Is he hurt?" She was sitting on a chair by the window, playing with her phone.

She looked up at me and put her cell down. "No. Not at all. I think he went to collect something. I'm not sure. I'll try to call him." She stood up and left the room.

Where would he be? The Sam Shaw I knew would want to be right by my side when I woke.

"How are you feeling, darling?" my mother asked me.

"I'm fine, Mom."

"You're not fine. We were very worried."

"I was lucky," I said. When I was coming back from the anesthetic, I'd heard Harper say that if the car had stopped a few inches later, things would have been much worse.

But it hadn't and they weren't.

I had a broken leg that would heal.

The only thing wrong was the fact Sam wasn't with me.

"Can someone give me my phone?" I asked, trying to move to sit myself up.

"Stay still," my mom said. "I don't know where it is. Harper's gone to call him. You need to concentrate on getting better."

No one was listening to me. I wanted Sam. "Will they let me go home tonight?" I didn't like the thought of staying here overnight. Sam and I were supposed to be spending tonight in his apartment. The bed was arriving. Shit. The bed. Had Sam gone to take delivery? Surely he wouldn't leave me like that. Where was he?

"I don't think so. They want to keep you here for observation."

"The nurse said they did a CT scan, so what's the problem?"

Harper walked back into the room, her eyes glued to the floor.

"Did you speak to him? Where is he?" I asked.

She glanced at my parents and then back at me. Whatever it was that she had to say, she didn't want to say it in front of my mom and dad.

"Dad, would you mind getting me a magazine or a book

or something for me to read when you're gone?"

"Of course, honey. Your mother and I will go do that now."

My mom scowled at him. "I'll stay here. You go."

He pulled at her elbow, knowing that I wanted to speak to Harper in private. "No, come on, Cynthia. She'll be fine here with Harper."

My mother rolled her eyes but grabbed her purse. My dad winked at me. *Thank you*, I mouthed.

Harper continued to avoid my gaze as my mom and dad left the room, closing the door behind them. As soon as they were gone, I said, "You need to tell me what's going on. Where's Sam? Is he okay?"

Harper's chest rose as she took a deep breath. She finally looked at me as she moved from the chair by the window to the one closer to my bed. "I don't know, Grace. I really don't. I've got Max trying to call him."

"I don't understand. He was here before, wasn't he?" I was sure he'd been by my side before my leg had been reset. He'd kissed me on my forehead and held my hand and told me he loved me.

"Yeah, but when he'd seen you he told me that he had to leave."

"Did he say when he was coming back?"

She shuffled her chair closer and clasped her hand over mine. "I'm sure he'll be back soon. I think he's feeling bad about the accident—guilty."

Why would he be feeling bad? He hadn't caused it. "It wasn't his fault."

"I know," she said. "But you know how guys are. They

like to think they control the universe." She shrugged. "And they like to protect the people they love."

And Sam only had Angie and me.

He was feeling *bad*, not guilty. The accident would have been a trigger for him, bringing back all the memories from when his parents died.

Shit. He would be hurting far more than I was. I needed to see him, to comfort him, make him feel better.

"His parents died in a car accident. It must have brought back some memories for him." *More* memories. Connecticut had been hard enough. "Do you have my phone? I need to call him."

"I don't. Maybe Sam has it?"

"Harper, I need to see him. Tell him I'm okay. He's hurting, and he doesn't have anyone. I need to be there for him." I needed to get discharged. I tried to pull myself up using the rails of the bed.

"What are you doing?" Harper asked.

"I need to find Sam."

She stood up and pried my fingers off the bed. "Lie back. You're not going anywhere. You've just been in a serious car accident and you should relax. Are you crazy?"

"Are you?" I asked her right back. "I *love* him, Harper. I need to find him."

"He'll be back. Just give him some time to cool off."

Something deep in my gut told me that giving Sam time was the last thing I should be doing. If I knew Sam like I thought I did, he was shutting down. Shutting me out. He'd said he'd had no choice in how he felt about me, but what if the accident had changed all that?

_____

"Have you seen my phone?" I asked Harper as she came back into the living room from putting the babies to bed. Harper had collected me from the hospital, insisting I go straight back to Connecticut with her as soon as I'd been discharged.

"Would you like a glass of wine now that you're just on Tylenol?" In the three days since I'd last seen Sam, I kept expecting him to turn up, explain that he'd had to take delivery of the bed and take me from the hospital.

But he never came.

"Yeah, that would be nice, but have you seen my phone? I thought I had it right here."

My purse, with my cell and wallet, had been returned to me in the hospital. I wasn't sure how and I didn't care enough to question it. I was just grateful to have it back, even if Sam wasn't answering my calls.

"You think Sam's phone was damaged in the crash? Maybe that's why I can't get through," I asked as Harper handed me a glass of wine and my cell.

She shrugged. "Even if it was, why wouldn't he have come back to the hospital?" Harper had stopped asking if I'd heard from him since we'd been back in Connecticut.

"It's totally understandable that he needed a break from everything after the accident. It must have been a lot to take on considering what happened to his parents and the car crash. Don't you agree?" I wanted to know he'd come back to me—I needed to know it was going to be okay.

"Do you need a hand?" she asked as I leaned forward.

My stomach lurched at her so obviously avoiding the question. Surely it was understandable that he would freak out. "No," I said, pushing myself up. "I'm fine when I'm up. It's just standing in the first place that's hard. I'm not used to balancing on one leg." I took a few tentative steps. "Walking on crutches has got to be good for my core, right?" I was trying not to just sit down all the time. The doctors had told me I was going to be in a cast for a couple of months, so I had to get on with my life. I'd hired a temp to keep the gallery open this week, but I wanted to be back at work on Monday.

"Who cares? I don't have a core. My children ripped it from my body along with my dignity when I gave birth."

I laughed and then swayed a little on my crutches. "Stop it. You love your girls."

She grinned. "I do. But they need to understand the price I paid to have them."

"The problem is when I'm hobbling on crutches, I can't drink because I have no free hands." I leaned on one of the kitchen stools by the counter and Harper brought my glass over and sat down. "You think he's okay? He could have had an accident . . ."

"I don't think he's been in an accident, Grace, and neither do you, if you're being honest." She took a sip of her wine.

"You think he's being an asshole?"

"It's pretty weird that he's left without so much as a word. And it's been days. You've been discharged and he's still not here for you."

"He's hurting."

"Maybe," she said. "But so are you. This accident could have been a lot worse."

"But it wasn't."

"I just think you should prepare yourself for the fact that you may never hear from him again. He seems like he could be ghosting you."

A stab of pain hit me in the chest.

"Are you okay?" Harper asked.

I nodded and steadied myself against the counter. She thought Sam's silence was him walking away. Ending it. For good. I'd just assumed he was hurting and couldn't share whatever he was going through with me. I'd expected that in a couple of hours or a few days, he'd come around. But I was getting impatient. And Harper clearly thought he wasn't coming back.

The thought that I may never see him again, speak to him, touch him, kiss him—it was horrifying. I finished off my wine. "Can I get a top up?" I asked. It wasn't possible, was it? He'd said he would try to build a future with me. That's what I thought he'd said. He couldn't, wouldn't just walk away from that . . . would he?

"We're happy together, Harper. Why would you think that he'd just disappear and never want to speak to me again?"

"You know as well as I do that logic doesn't apply when it comes to men."

"But Sam's not like that." Other than my father, Sam was the best man I'd ever known. He was thoughtful and kind and cared about what should be important in this world. He'd been through so much in his life yet remained decent and honest at his core. He was special. And he loved me. He'd told me and I knew what a huge thing that was. He wouldn't let me go so easily, would he?

"Come on. We all think they're not like that until they are. You haven't known him that long."

Harper was right, Sam and I hadn't known each other very long, but she didn't understand how far we'd come. We were committed to each other—he said he'd try for me. That he wanted to be the man that deserved me.

I knew I just needed to see him, to reassure him. "I need to go to Manhattan," I said as Harper poured more wine into my glass.

"Let's see how you feel on Sunday. And when you do go back you should stay at my apartment in the city. Cab fare will be a lot cheaper than if you go to Brooklyn. You can't take the subway for a while."

I shouldn't need to take a cab at all.

Sam was supposed to be hiring a driver.

Why was I having to make plans that didn't include him?

"I want to go into Manhattan to see Sam."

"Grace, I don't think that's a good idea. He'll call you or he won't. You're in no state to be running after him. You need to be concentrating on getting better."

"You don't understand how I feel about him. This is *it* for me. I will never love any man the way I love him." I twisted the stem of my wine glass, the alcohol lapping at the edges, trying to get free. "Will you come with me? Or do you think I'm being such an idiot that—"

"Idiot or not, of course I'll come with you."

"Monday then." Monday would mark a full week since the accident. A full week since I'd seen Sam. "We can go to his office and I can prove you wrong." I tipped back my glass. "But if you're right and he's walking away from me, for whatever reason, then he's going to have to say it to my face."

CHAPTER TWENTY-ONE
Sam

"What is it?" I barked into my phone as I walked into my apartment. I'd spent as little time as possible here since the accident. I couldn't avoid thinking about Grace when I was here—from the art to the sofa. The place was all about her.

Christ, I could smell her. I thought the scent would have waned by now. Thoughts of her were still as strong as ever, but those I could shut down. I'd done it before and I could do it again. That way I'd survive, and she'd go on to have a happy life without me.

"So you're not dead. Thank you for finally answering your God damn cell." Angie had no right to be angry. I was the one who should be pissed.

She'd been calling me and messaging me on and off since the accident. I hadn't wanted to speak to anyone. I'd needed to be alone. I'd walked from the hospital for hours and hours until I'd found myself at the diner. I vaguely understood that time was passing but it hadn't applied to me, as I'd disconnected from the rest of Manhattan going about their daily lives.

"I'm busy, Angie. What is it?" I shrugged off my jacket, throwing it on the floor, and went into the kitchen. I was anything but busy. I'd called in sick. I never took any time off, not even for vacation, so no doubt people were starting to get jumpy. I'd have to go back. I put my phone on speaker and found my calendar.

Tomorrow. I'd go back tomorrow. It was Monday and I could just pretend that the last week hadn't happened. I'd erase it from history.

"Are you fucking kidding me? You and Grace were in a car accident on Monday and you didn't think to tell me?"

"How did you find out?" I opened the kitchen cabinet and pulled out the first thing capable of holding alcohol.

"Not from you, that's for damn sure."

I took the bottle from the counter and unscrewed the top single-handed. "Angie, I don't have time for this."

The whiskey glugged into the white cup emblazoned with the logo of a commercial real estate agency on the side.

"Grace told me, you idiot. And speaking of idiocy, why the fuck are you ignoring her calls?"

I took a big gulp, enjoying the burn down my throat as I swallowed. The pain was soothing, distracting.

"Do you have an answer or are you just being a gigantic dick?" Angie asked.

On the surface, not picking up my phone to Grace or Angie looked like a dick move. I'd gone dark on Grace and hadn't responded to any of her calls or messages. But I needed to pull up the drawbridge, reestablish my defenses. I'd had an ugly reminder of how frail life was and how close to the edge I'd been.

"I'm fine, Angie. Grace is fine. We're just over. That's all.

It's no big deal."

I don't know how Angie had become some kind of exception to my isolation. I should have cut her loose long ago.

There was a pause on the other end of the line. Had I gone too far? Good. Perhaps she'd get the message and leave me the fuck alone.

"Sam," she said quietly.

I topped up my mug of whiskey and stalked out of the kitchen, clutching my drink only to be hit with the sight of the La Touche on the wall.

Fuck, she was everywhere.

"Sam, I'm worried about you."

I put my drink down on the coffee table Grace and I had bought. Why the fuck did I have a table to put my fucking whiskey on? Anger boiled up inside me and I flung the table over. My cup of whiskey flew across the room, liquid raining in an amber arc across the couch, the crack of the table leg breaking providing the sound track.

"What was that?" Angie asked.

Now I'd have to pour myself more whiskey. "Nothing. I dropped my drink." I stooped to collect the white mug. The handle had snapped off but I could still drink out of it. I headed to the kitchen to get the bottle.

"Are you okay, Sam?"

"I told you, I'm fine. Not a scratch on me. And Grace is fine. She's been discharged."

"And how would you know that? She said she hasn't heard from you since she woke up."

I didn't respond. I had nothing to say. I couldn't deny

what Angie was saying and I had no reason to try and excuse it. But I had to put my survival above everything else. It was the only way. I'd made a mistake by caring about someone. I couldn't handle the pain of even the *thought* of something happening to Grace. It was easier for both of us to walk away now.

I might miss her wide smile and generous heart. I might miss her warm touch and light kisses. I might miss the way she made me feel, but it was better this way.

I may have survived my parents' deaths, but it had sliced a crack straight through me that constantly threatened to break open.

Walking away now, I had a chance.

This way I was safe.

And alone.

"Come in," I said to the knock at my door. I'd specifically told my assistant, Rosemary, that I couldn't be interrupted. I had a lot of people to catch up with after being out for a week.

Rosemary poked her head around the door. "Sorry to disturb you but I thought I should let you know that there's a woman in reception who wants to see you. When I explained you were busy all day, she just told me she'd wait and took a seat."

My heart began to pound. I knew exactly who it was. Couldn't Grace take a hint? Jesus, she was stubborn.

"I don't know what to do," Rosemary said with a helpless shrug. "She looks like she might sit there all day. Do you want me to call security?"

"Did you get her name?" I asked, even though I knew damn well.

"Grace Astor. I think she's been here once before."

I stared at the screen and nodded, trying to pretend that hearing her name hadn't affected me. "Show her in and I'll see why she came."

"Okay." She paused. "Can I help in any way? Is she waiting for payment? She wouldn't tell me anything."

"I have no idea what she wants, but I'll deal with her."

I watched out of the corner of my eye as Rosemary went to say something else, then thankfully thought better of it and closed the door behind her.

I closed my eyes.

Breathe, Sam. Breathe.

Being cruel to be kind was in her best interests as much as it was my own. It might hurt to start off with, but it was pain that could be survived.

I opened my eyes at the sound of the door handle turning but I didn't look away from my computer screen.

"Grace Astor," Rosemary announced as Grace hobbled in on crutches. Why the hell hadn't I been the one to take the hit? Why had it had to happen to the only woman I'd ever had any hope of a future with?

I kept my eyes facing the screen but all I could focus on was Grace—so small and fragile.

I could almost hear the ticking of a clock in the fraction

of a second I didn't acknowledge her.

As soon as the door shut behind Rosemary, Grace used her crutches to step toward my desk. I stood, shoving my hands in my pockets, my gaze fixed on the door to her left.

"Sam, look at me."

I wanted to. I really did. I longed to take in every inch of her, commit her to memory before I'd never see her again. But at the same time, I wanted to go to her, scoop her up in my arms, tell her I was sorry and that everything was going to be okay.

"Why are you here? You should be resting at home," I said.

"Why am I here?" she asked softly. "Where have you been?" Her voice grew louder. "Why haven't you answered any of my calls or messages? It's like you just disappeared."

I had to do this. I had to make the wound sharp and deep or she'd never accept it was over. I turned my head and looked her straight in the eye. "Things got too heavy too quickly between us." That much was true. Her love had run me over like a herd of buffalo. "I've had a chance to re-evaluate." My ears began to buzz as if my words were coming from someone else.

"I don't believe you," she said, her eyes narrowed in confusion.

I'd tricked myself into thinking that I could be happy. That I could love. That I could live like other people. Grace's accident had reminded me that could never be my life.

"It's been a week. What could have changed so much?" she asked.

I shrugged. "I'm sorry if I led you to believe our brief

fling was something it wasn't." I tried to keep my voice even and detached, as if I were negotiating the purchase of a new building, but what I was saying cut deep, each syllable a separate blow. There was nothing about my love for Grace that was brief or could be described as a fling.

"Sam, don't talk like that. I know you don't mean it. You're just scared."

I clenched my jaw. "I don't want to get serious with you, so I'm scared?" I snorted. How dare she pretend to know me better than I knew myself? She'd never experienced what I'd been through.

"Yes, Sam. You're scared of opening yourself up. Scared of loving me. But I'm here, by your side, and we're going to weather the storms together. Don't you remember? You said you'd try."

I wasn't scared.

I just knew how vicious life could be.

I was a realist.

I took my hands out of my pockets and leaned forward, placing my palms flat on my desk. I looked her straight in the eye. "I'm not scared of anything. I just don't have feelings for you. You need to accept that."

Her eyes welled with tears and her knuckles whitened where she gripped her crutches. "Well, I don't accept that."

I straightened up and put my hands back in my pockets. "There's nothing I can help you with. Don't make a fool of yourself."

She gasped and it was as if someone had their hands around my heart and was squeezing and twisting.

265

The creak and stretch of her crutches filled the room. She shouldn't be on her feet. I'd offer her a seat, but I needed her to leave. Every moment she was here, beautiful and warm and the woman I'd always love, I could feel myself weakening. "You should go, Grace. Can I call a car for you?"

I walked around her, keeping as much physical distance as I could between us as I made my way to the door. That didn't stop her scent from filling my lungs. I fisted my hands, digging my nails into my palms, hoping the pain would be enough to distract me from what my heart was telling me to do. Comfort her, soothe her, love her.

My back to her, she screamed, "Sam!"

Fuck, why was she making this so difficult? I'd been mean to her. Cold. Nasty. She should throw me away and get on with her life.

I stopped, facing the door. "You need to leave."

"I know you're hurting, and I know that the accident must have been horrible for you," she said. "But I'm fine. You're fine."

I didn't move. Despite my abandoning her, even though I'd said such awful things to her, she was still trying to give me the benefit of the doubt, trying to see things from my point of view. She was an amazing woman, but I couldn't be the one who told her so.

"I love you," she whispered, her voice cracked and small.

My hand went to the door handle. I had nothing I could say. If I looked at her now, I knew I'd go to her because I loved her too, and eventually it would be the destruction of us both.

I turned around to face her for what I knew would be the final time. I needed to deliver a knock-out blow. "I've told you I don't feel the same. You should go."

"Sam." Her voice was full of tears and she leaned on her crutches as if they were keeping her afloat. "Please don't do this. I need you."

Those final three words gave me the strength I needed to open the door.

She shouldn't need me.

And I couldn't need her.

"Good luck, Ms. Astor." If she wasn't going to leave, then I would. I walked out of the office and away from the only woman I'd ever love.

CHAPTER TWENTY-TWO
Grace

"Please just drive," I said to Harper as I closed the door. Somehow I'd found the strength to leave Sam's building and met Harper waiting outside.

Harper pulled out and turned north on Madison. "Can we go through the Upper West Side? I just can't . . ." There were too many memories on the other side of the park—the Frick, the apartment. I wasn't up to a look-what-your-life-could-have-been tour.

"No problem," Harper replied, grabbing my hand with hers and squeezing. "I'm so sorry."

Her sympathy unleashed the floodgates and I began to sob, deep bellowing sounds I'd never made before.

Harper didn't pull over, didn't comfort me. She understood the only thing that would make me feel at all better was to get as far away from Manhattan, from Sam, as I could. She'd agreed to drive me into the city, but from her reaction, she'd known my turning up at his office wouldn't go well.

How could I have been so wrong? Oh, I knew he loved me. I wasn't wrong about that. But I'd thought that would be enough. I thought that now that we'd found each other, both of us were committed to doing whatever it took to be together.

We had no strength at all if we'd been blown off course so quickly and so badly.

"Maybe he just needs more time," I said.

Harper glanced at me. "Did he say he needed more time?" she asked, knowing damn well he hadn't.

Tears began to roll down my cheeks again. "No, he told me he didn't love me, but I know that's not true."

"Does it matter?"

"Of course it matters. If he loves me then—"

"It takes more than love," she said. "If he's telling you he doesn't love you, you have to take him at his word."

"But don't you see? He's doing it to protect himself. He doesn't *want* to love me—he doesn't want to love anyone in case he loses them and has to go through what he did when his parents died." I hadn't told Harper about Sam's lack of furniture or social circle, but I understood so clearly now that those things were borne out of a fear of losing something he'd grown attached to. It made perfect sense. Sam had nearly lost me in the accident, and now he was pushing me away to protect himself. I understood.

"Don't *you* see? It doesn't matter."

"What do you mean? Of course it matters." He loved me. It was too late to erase that—pretend it wasn't true. Surely.

"The outcome's the same. Whatever his reasons, he's ended it."

"Don't say that," I whined as I tried to catch my breath between sobs. "He'll come around. I just need to give him time."

"You need to give *you* time. And then you should get on with your life." Harper's voice was soothing and sympathetic but her words were sharp and jagged. How could she think

I had a life to get on with without Sam?

"Now's not the time for your tough love. I have to believe Sam will come back to me." Even though we'd been together so little time, I'd waited my whole life for him to come along. "I can't just give up on him."

"Look, I believe in the fairytale. I really do. Look at my husband, for crying out loud. But, you're my best friend and I can't bear to see you hurting like this. Whether or not he loves you, he's not with you, showing his love. And if you can't see it, can't feel it, then I'm not sure it matters what he feels deep down."

I didn't like the fact that her words made sense. I didn't want to believe what she was saying was exactly what I'd say to her if she were sitting in the passenger seat.

"You don't know him like I do." The words sounded weak even as I said them. Had I become one of those women who excused the behavior of their boyfriends and husbands by explaining other people just didn't know the real him? How pathetic.

"Of course I don't, but I know what I see—a man who abandoned you when you needed him most. That rejected you when you gave him the benefit of the doubt and went to his office to tell him you loved him." She sighed. "And that's the only side of him I need to see."

I sat, silent and defeated.

"We should make a plan," she said, forcing some cheer into her voice. "Let's have a fire in the pit tonight and make s'mores. We'll put the patio heaters on and wrap up in blankets. What do you say?"

"Does this plan involve wine?"

Harper turned and smiled. "Wouldn't be a party without the wine."

I nodded. "Sounds good."

"Have you spoken to Natalie?" Harper asked, blatantly trying to shift my focus from my past to my future, to the gallery and my temporary assistant.

My gut churned. "I messaged her this morning. Everything's fine. I think she likes being left to her own devices. I'll probably go back and she won't let me in."

Harper laughed but it was a little forced. "Maybe while you're in Connecticut you should think some more about your plan for the place. I know some of the work you love most you don't really sell. You know, the more traditional stuff. Have you thought about splitting the gallery in two and doing both?"

I didn't have head space for this conversation. Seeing Sam but not being able to touch him, the thought of never seeing him again—it was all so exhausting. "It won't work. I don't have the right contacts to get the traditional art in the gallery. Or the money."

"Remember you said you could never have a gallery of your own without your father's money and look how that turned out."

"But I had to sell my Renoir." I started to cry again at the thought of losing that painting to some unknown buyer in the Middle East.

"You sold that painting to get Grace Astor Fine Art. Don't take your foot off the gas now. If you let it, the gallery could be a great focus."

She was talking as if what I was experiencing was a normal breakup, as if I just needed to take my mind off things, channel my energy, and I'd bounce back in no time. Didn't she understand that I'd always love Sam?

"Don't you think?" she asked.

I nodded. "Sure."

"Maybe Max can introduce you to some of his rich clients. In fact, why don't you start running parties in your gallery? Maybe Max can host something there?"

I shrugged. I understood Harper had my best interests at heart, but I couldn't focus on anything other than what I'd lost.

I wasn't ready to move on and I didn't think I ever would be.

"Yes, bring it in this side," I said to the two men who were delivering new pieces I'd bought from a couple of Max's clients. He was happy for me to sell them on his behalf, taking a commission. Being as determined and stubborn as she was, Harper's idea about Max throwing a client party at Grace Astor Fine Art had come to fruition three weeks after she'd first mentioned it. She'd been right to push me to focus on work. I'd made a ton of contacts and booked three more parties since.

It was keeping me busy, but despite it being seven weeks since I'd seen Sam, I still thought about him every moment.

We had our third business event tonight and I wanted

this new work on the wall before people started to arrive. The aim of the parties wasn't about the art at all. It was just a backdrop for a networking evening combined with a speech by a high-profile person in business or sports. Max had given me some suggested names and with what I was making on the venue hire, I used it all to pay the right person. Tonight it was some baseball player.

I waved at Scarlett as I saw her cross the street toward me, her almost-black hair so dramatic with her red coat. "Hey," I said. "How are you? You look beautiful."

"Stop it. You invented beautiful." She glanced behind me. "I brought you lunch—I figured if I didn't you wouldn't eat." She held up a paper bag.

"You're good to me," I said. "But I need to finish up with this delivery first."

"No problem."

"Hey, do I look cool?"

Scarlett frowned. "Cool?"

"You know, like it's just another day and I'm not going to explode with excitement." I grinned at her.

She laughed. "Yeah, babe, you always look cool. Are you excited?"

"Hell yes." I nodded toward the delivery truck. "There's a freaking Gauguin in this lot. Can you believe that?" All the incoming pieces were beautiful and a step up from the work I could normally stock, but a Gauguin? I was going to pee my pants. Art like this would put me on the map.

"Hey, I've heard of that guy. Isn't he like in museums and shit?" Scarlett asked, smiling at me. "I knew that this place would be a smash."

"Well, I'm not sure smash is the right word . . ." For the first time since I'd opened I felt like I had a bit of momentum.

"You should be so proud of yourself, Grace."

"It was all Harper's idea. She was trying to give me a focus after . . ." I shrugged. "You know." I didn't like talking about Sam. I tried not to even think about him. He ignored every single one of my calls and messages. He'd made his decision. Whatever his motivations, as Harper said, the outcome was still the same.

"Yeah, but you took it and ran with it. You made it all happen."

What I hadn't expected was that people would actually buy art during the events. I'd hoped to pass my card around and maybe people would think of me around bonus time or on their wife's birthday. "I've gotten great sales on both the nights we've had these things—I hope we do again tonight."

"Well, that's because people can't resist your good taste and charm. Speaking of, are any of the men dating material?"

"I thought you had your hands full with Duncan?" I asked.

"Not for me, silly. For you. I'm sure a couple of them have asked you out."

"Oh, not really." I opened the door to let the next delivery through. I'm not sure I would have noticed if I'd been hit on.

"None of them your type?" she asked.

"Honestly, I'm not looking for anything right now. I just

want to concentrate on my business." Just the thought of another man touching me was enough to make me want to throw up. Seven and a half weeks since I'd last seen Sam, and the thought was still unconscionable. My cast was off but my heart still bore the scars of that accident. I wasn't sure those would ever disappear.

"Duncan has a friend who'd like to meet you. You'd like him."

"Thanks, but I'm not dating anyone at the moment." History said that people got over heartbreak and maybe one day I might want to date again, have someone kiss me again, but I couldn't imagine that day was very close. "Can we drop it?"

"Hey, Grace," Mark, an artist I'd be featuring soon, said from across the gallery. "I'm done in the back and going to head out."

I glanced at Scarlett, who was looking at Mark as if he were naked—eyes wide, mouth open. "Okay, did you leave them in order?"

Grinning, he walked over to us. So much for the suffering artist vibe—Mark looked more tickled than tortured. And the way he looked at me was so intense it was uncomfortable—as if I could provide all the answers to the questions he had. "Mark, this is Scarlett. Scarlett, Mark is one of the new artists who's going to be exhibiting with us."

"Nice to meet you," Scarlett said, her eyes sparkling as she held out her hand. Mark shook her hand briefly but all his attention was fixed on me. The old Grace would have loved Mark. He was talented, and although his exhibition at my gallery wouldn't be his first, he was still relatively undiscovered. And he was handsome in a pretty kind of way, and utterly charming. A few months ago, I would have eaten him up with a spoon. But my appetite had left me.

"Thanks for letting me have input on the curation, Grace, I really appreciate it."

I smiled, trying to be professional. "No problem. It's really great to get your view."

"I was wondering if I could take you to dinner as a thank you?"

Out of the corner of my eye I saw Scarlett raise her eyebrows, and as subtly as she was able, turn her attention to the painting right behind her.

"There's no need to do that," I replied. "All part of the job." I didn't date guys like Mark anymore. I'd grown up. Experienced what it felt like to have someone really love me. Now I understood the difference between wanting to fix someone and loving them. Even if I'd wanted to, I couldn't fall back into my old cycle.

He looked genuinely disappointed. "I understand. Let me know if there's anything you need, otherwise let's speak next week."

"Sure," I said, waving as he left.

Scarlett spun around. "Grace, he is gorgeous. Why on earth did you turn him down? I thought he was just your type."

Funny how Sam had changed me so completely and fundamentally, yet no one seemed to get it—there wasn't anyone else for me but Sam.

"No, he's not my type. Not anymore."

"Dinner wouldn't hurt though. A girl's gotta eat. You might like him if you spent a bit of time with him."

"I told you; I'm not dating." The delivery guys came through the door with the next piece.

"I don't think you should shut yourself off from men completely. It's been months."

"Please, Scarlett, I asked you to drop it."

She tucked her arm around my shoulder. "Sorry. I just want you to be happy."

"And I appreciate it. So make me happy by telling me what you brought us for lunch. Does it include alcohol?" I asked. "Because I could do with a little buzz to get me through this afternoon."

She laughed. "Yeah, I'm not sure my employers would be so lenient on me for day drinking."

"Maybe not. You're in charge of the money, after all." I elbowed her in the ribs and she squeezed me tighter before releasing me.

"We'll have to make do with pine nut, arugula and goat cheese salad."

Truth was, I'd lost my appetite.

I'd gotten past the stage where everywhere I went, I thought I caught glimpses of Sam. I went whole days without crying over him. But I was nowhere close to being able to think about him without pain trickling through my body. I was desperate for my longing for him to disappear. I was ready to be over him. It just wasn't happening.

I wondered if it ever would.

CHAPTER TWENTY-THREE
Sam

"Coming," I shouted at the pounding against my hotel room door. I stalked over—Jesus, room service was impatient— and slung it open only to find Angie instead of my food. Fuck. I should have checked the peephole. "What are you doing here?" I barked.

She didn't answer, just pushed past me into my suite. I couldn't be in the Park Avenue apartment without memories of Grace surrounding me—she'd picked out the furniture, the art. It was too much.

I let the door slam shut. "How did you find me?"

Angie sat on the couch, crossed her arms and stared straight ahead. "I'm resourceful. When your best friend disappears for eight fucking weeks, you find a way."

"I didn't disappear."

"You moved out—I sat outside your door for twenty-four hours, so I'd be sure. And you stopped answering my calls."

"You're here now. What do you want?" *I* wanted to be left alone—I didn't need Angie interfering.

"I want you to explain what the fuck you're trying to do by ignoring my calls. Presumably you're avoiding me ripping you a new asshole because you've abandoned Grace when she needed you most."

My heart lurched at the thought of Grace needing me. I tightened my hands into a ball. That was why I'd walked away. I couldn't open myself up like that.

"There's no avoiding this conversation, Sam. We're family. And family tells each other when someone's making a huge mistake."

Family. That was such a loaded word. It was what I'd lost when I was twelve. It was what I'd been on the verge of having again with Grace. But Angie was right—most of all it was what I'd had with her since we'd found each other in foster care.

I didn't respond. Instead I bent over the glossy wood cabinet by the sofa and pulled out a bottle of whiskey and two glasses. I poured two drinks and sat down next to her.

I tried to hand her a glass, but she knocked it away. Rivulets of whiskey coated my arm and the glass clunked as it hit the carpet.

"Jesus. You could have just said no." I took a sip of my drink.

"It smells disgusting," she said, folding her arms in front of her again.

"It absolutely does not. It smells like expensive whiskey." She had such a temper.

"Well, it smells like dog shit to a pregnant woman."

I tried not to smile. This was what she and Chas had been wanting for well over a year. "Congratulations. I'm really happy for you."

"Fuck you."

"What? I'm happy for you. I mean it." Wow. Angie was having a baby. She deserved it all.

"You're going to be the godfather, asshole."

I pushed my hands through my hair. "No, Angie, I'm not." I needed less to care about in my life, not more.

"I'm not giving you a choice. You're the only person in my life I totally trust—the person who knows me the best." She turned and looked at me for the first time since she'd arrived. "I have no one else to ask. So, there's no disappearing out of my life, out of our lives. Do you get that? I can't handle it. I need you."

I stood up. "It's not a good idea. You can't *need* me, Angie. I'll just end up disappointing you. Or one of us will die and—"

"Just stop it," Angie said. I glanced at her and she rolled her eyes. "You're so dramatic."

I paused and then chuckled. In our darkest hours, Angie had always shown me the funny side.

I sat back down beside her.

"And now I need you more than ever," she said. "I have this tiny human parasite in me and it's going to arrive in seven months. I have no idea what I'm doing and I'm sure I'm going to melt down at least once a day. The only thing I learned from my mom was how to be a crack whore. I want to save those lessons until my daughter's eighteen."

"You're having a girl?" Angie would be a terrific mother despite her start in life.

The corners of her mouth curled up. "Yeah. Can you believe it?"

I shook my head. "It's amazing."

"I *need* you, Sam."

"You have Chas."

"I need him, too. But don't you get it? You're my family. I've been abandoned once—don't do it to me again." She started to cry and I grabbed her hand. I hated the thought that I'd left her like her mother had. "And you can't do it to my daughter, either. She's going to need you, too."

I squeezed her hand. "I'm right here." Angie would always be in my life, for better or worse. It was just too late to change that. She was family. "I'm so sorry for disappearing."

"I know you are."

Just like that, I was forgiven. We were Sam and Angie again.

"So, you ready to be an uncle to this kid?"

"Not even a little bit." I smiled at her.

"All you have to do is love her. That's all I ask."

"I think you're asking the wrong man." I wasn't capable of doing things other people took for granted—things like loving people. It just wasn't that easy.

"You can't live without love, Sam. If you try, you might as well have died in that car right alongside your parents."

I tried to twist my hand free from hers, but she wouldn't let me. "Don't say stuff like that." I knew how lucky I'd been.

"I know you don't like to talk about them, but I also know the man you are. Not the guy people see from the outside—not what your parents' deaths did to you—the man who's left when everyone else except me is gone." She leaned over and poked me in the chest. "I know what's in here. I know who your parents created while they were alive. A man who would lay down his life for me. Loyal. Determined. Fierce. Someone who's capable of giving great love."

Even though they'd left me so early in life, I was my parents' legacy. Angie was right—all the good inside me was them. "You're going to be an amazing mother."

"If I'm not, it's all your fault. You convinced me I could do this. And I'm determined I'm going to do my best by this kid. I owe it to my daughter, to Chas, but most of all to me. You told me I shouldn't let my past determine my future. But neither should you, my friend. You deserve Grace."

I rested my head back on the cushion and closed my eyes.

"That's what your parents would want for you, Sam. A great love. Someone who deserves you. Someone like Grace. I think they would have loved the way she loves you."

I was sure they would have loved Grace. And she them. The inside of my nose burned as images of what might have been formed in my imagination.

"She doesn't love me. Not anymore." The thought hit me in the chest with a sledgehammer. "And that's the way it should be."

"No, Sam, that's not how it should be at all. What you and Grace have doesn't come along that often."

As much as I might want to deny it, I couldn't. What Grace and I had was special. But it wasn't enough to protect me if the worst happened. I stared up at the cracked ceiling. "What if something happened to her, if she left me somewhere down the line? I just wouldn't handle it."

"Be the guy she's never going to want to leave and let the

universe decide the rest."

"The universe? That's your answer? That's no guarantee. I wouldn't *survive* losing her. I know I wouldn't." Even now, after not seeing Grace for weeks, if I heard something had happened to her, it would kill me.

"I think you're the strongest guy I know. You can survive anything. Let your parents' deaths teach you that. Let it have been a demonstration of your strength. Don't let their deaths make you live in fear. Honor your mom and dad by living your best life, and loving as hard as you can."

I leaned forward, putting my head in my hands.

I knew my parents would want me to be happy. But they'd understand how I had to protect myself. Wasn't surviving enough?

"I don't think I can."

"Let me ask you this: would you have preferred not having those first twelve years with your parents? Never to have known them at all?"

I groaned in response to the pain that ripped across my chest. I couldn't imagine anything worse than never having known my parents. Those years had been worth all the pain and suffering that came later. I would have endured anything to have had them in my life, even for a shortened time.

And then I knew—I had to love Grace for as long as life allowed me to do so.

———————————

I watched from across the street as people funneled out

the gallery door. The evening was almost over. I'd done my research in the days since Angie'd ambushed me. Tonight Grace was hosting a party for a Wall Street investment bank I happened to do a lot of business with. A brief phone call to a contact there had secured an invitation. It had taken more than a phone call for the next part of my plan to fall into place, but I was nothing if not tenacious. I always got what I wanted. I hoped tonight wouldn't break my streak.

I grasped the brown paper package I'd brought in both hands and headed across the street.

"Sam Shaw," I said to the security guy at the door. He swiped his fingers over the screen of an iPad and nodded at me. I waited for a group of four men to leave, then stepped into the gallery.

I scanned the faces of the guests, trying to find Grace. I didn't want to disrupt her evening, so my plan was to hang around until everyone else had left. In the meantime, I had a delivery to make.

I made my way to the back of the gallery, trying to get to the secret area where she kept her favorite pieces. But something had changed. The layout was different, not as big. She'd put an additional wall down the middle of the gallery and the hidden area had disappeared. *Shit.* What was I going to do now? That was where I'd wanted to leave my gift.

From where I stood, the gallery looked smaller. The art was bold and modern and it ran the length of the space. I turned my head to see a pass-through, larger than a doorway, in the middle of the wall. She'd split the store? I looked around but there was still no sign of her, so I headed toward the opening. The other side was Grace through and through. I could tell this was the art she really loved. I grinned. I saw her in every piece. Her secret collection wasn't so little anymore, and it certainly wasn't secret.

Good for her. She was doing what she loved. Even though I had no right to be, I was so proud of her.

I crouched, set down my gift, and tore at the twine. I'd deliberately tied the wrapping with string so I could get it off quickly, but now the knot wouldn't loosen.

I twisted the string, trying to soften the knot, but the light was dim and I couldn't see what I was doing properly.

"Sam?" Grace asked from behind me.

I dropped my hands and stood, steeling myself for my first look at her. Even though I'd prepared myself, when I turned around the sight of her was almost too much. I'd forgotten how her generous spirit showed on her face, how her warmth was infectious.

"Hi," I said. "You look . . ." *Like the love of my life.* "Beautiful."

"What are you doing here?" she asked, stepping back as I moved toward her.

"I came to apologize and explain. I just need a few minutes." I didn't expect her to forgive me, not right away, but I had to believe I had another shot with her. Whatever happened, I'd keep loving her my whole life.

Her expression was blank but she wasn't asking me to leave. I had to take my chance. I took a deep breath. "You're the first woman I've ever loved and the only one I ever will. I messed up." And I would pay forever if she didn't forgive me. "If I'd known I'd meet you, that I'd feel how I do, I'd have practiced. Made my mistakes, gotten them out of the way before you came along. But I had no idea what love could feel like. You are beyond my imagination, Grace Astor."

My eyes flickered down her body. She wasn't giving anything away. But while she would let me, I would continue to state my case. "You taught me to see myself as an optimist. And I know myself to be a fighter. I'm not giving up on you. Ever. I love you."

Her chest rose as she drew in a breath. "I brought you this," I rushed out, indicating the painting, half opened and resting against the wall. I had to put off her inevitable rejection as long as I could.

Grace shook her head. "Sam, no, I don't need anything."

Christ, she didn't even want to receive a present from me. "It's yours."

"No, you don't have to buy—"

"It's yours. Whatever happens, it's yours."

CHAPTER TWENTY-FOUR
Grace

Sam's gift was so unnecessary. All I wanted was him—to see in his expression that he still loved me. His eyes were wide, his hair mussed and longer than I'd seen before, but he was still *my* Sam. He always would be. Through everything, I'd never doubted Sam's feelings for me. So I'd waited, hoped and prayed and *believed* he'd come back to me. Back to us.

"Please, Grace, just open it."

I kneeled and slid the string off the brown paper. The edges were hard, like a frame. Had he brought me a painting? I discarded the paper, then the bubble wrap and tissue that was the last layer of packaging. Just a glimpse of the frame told me what he'd done. Tears began to roll down my face as I revealed the canvas. How had he found it?

"My Renoir," I said, my gaze flitting about the piece, trying to take it all in. "You brought it back to me. How did you find—oh, Sam, the cost."

"Shhh, please don't think about it. It was always yours. And so was I."

"You know, it's funny," I said, looking up at him. "I always thought I'd get it back one day. I was devastated when I had to sell it, but even when I delivered it to the buyer, I believed it would be mine again one day. A bit like you, Sam Shaw."

"But . . ." His mouth fell open as he struggled to find the words.

"I don't need the big speeches and the expensive paintings—just you. I only ever needed *you*," I said.

His eyes glistened with tears. "I don't deserve—"

"You *deserve* to be happy," I replied. "And I deserve to be with the love of my life. Which is you. I know that. I've always known that. But I need you to understand that you can't run from me when the storm comes, Sam. We have to stick together."

He nodded. "I get it. Really, I do. I'll never leave again."

I reached for his hand. "Good. I hate being without you."

His hand curled around mine and he pulled me toward him.

"You never have to be. Honestly, Grace, I want to prove it to you. I want to give you everything you want and deserve."

"And what do you want?"

"I want *you*. I want you to move in with me tonight. I want to make up for lost time. I want to marry you tomorrow."

"You want to marry me?" I asked, fighting for breath.

"Of course I want to marry you. You are the love of my life—I want it all."

"Is that a proposal?" I asked, the chatter of the gallery fading away, leaving just Sam and me in each other's arms.

"Do you want it to be?"

I slid my hands over his. "I just got you back."

"So, today your answer's a no—but I'm going to keep

asking until you're ready. If it takes a hundred years, one day, Grace Astor, you will be my wife."

"Oh? And what makes you so sure of that?"

"Because," he said, tilting my chin up for a kiss, "you taught me the most important lesson in the Count's story. 'Happiness is like those palaces in fairytales whose gates are guarded by dragons: We must fight in order to conquer it.'" He smiled down at me. "I won't ever stop fighting again."

Epilogue

Sam

"Marry me?" I asked as I walked out of our bathroom, a towel around my waist, combing my fingers through my wet hair. Grace watched me from beneath the covers as she always did after my shower.

Morning, noon and night, I loved Grace Astor, but she always took my breath away first thing in the morning—her sleepy face, soft limbs and croaky voice. She owned me. Despite her wanting to take things slowly, we'd not spent a night apart since I'd gone to the gallery nine weeks ago.

She grinned at me and sat up in bed, smoothing her hands over her bed hair. "No. You marry me."

I froze. Had I heard her correctly?

She bit the corner of her bottom lip, trying to stop her smile. I stalked across the room and pulled her down next to me. "What did you say?"

As we lay opposite each other on the bed, she traced her finger over my nose and across my lips. "I said *marry* me."

"Are you asking me to marry you?" I asked, propping my head up with my hand.

She nodded.

"You're finally saying yes?"

"No."

I was confused.

"*You're* going to say yes. I hope. I'm asking *you*."

I chuckled. "Okay. I'm saying yes."

"You're saying yes?" she asked, her smile widening. Could she really think that she'd get a different answer?

"I've asked you every day for the last fifty-eight days—were you expecting me to say no?"

We laughed and I pushed her to her back and kissed her, taking my time to explore her warm, soft mouth, enjoying her fingers combing through my hair.

"This means we're engaged," I said.

She nodded. "I need a ring."

"I bought three."

"You have *three* engagement rings?" She tipped her head back and laughed. "When?"

I kissed her again, lingering over her lips. "Fifty-seven days ago. Want to see?" I started to move, but she pulled me back by the arm.

"In a little while. Right now, I'm good with you in nothing but a towel, kissing me."

I pulled down the straps of her top and placed a kiss on each shoulder. "Kissing you where?"

She tugged at the bottom of her top and lifted it up and over her head. "Everywhere."

No man was luckier in this moment than me. The best woman I'd ever known had promised to spend the rest of her life with me. Life didn't get better than that.

I kissed down her belly, tugging at her nipples and

making her gasp. I grinned at the sounds she made. *I* did that. I could make her feel that good. And I'd keep doing it forever.

I hooked my thumbs into the edges of her underwear and pulled them down, kissing from one juncture of the thigh to the other, licking the dip in her skin where her leg began. Her skin smelled of ripe cherries.

"Sam," she called, her voice raspy and breathless but content. Certain. Of me. We'd come a long way.

I smoothed my hands over her inner thigh, pressing her open, getting her ready. I wasn't sure who felt the anticipation of what was next more—her or me. She arched her back and I slid my tongue over her clit. Already, Grace was wet enough for me to drink and I was always thirsty for her.

My erection pressed into the mattress as I lapped down her slit. She groaned, pushing out her little demands in a breathless flurry of *please, don't stop, yes, just there.*

I pushed my hand over my cock. I wondered whether the taste of her, the sounds she made, would get me this hard forever. I grinned against her as she continued her chatter. *Yes.* No question. She'd always get me hard.

She grabbed my shoulders. "Sam, I need you."

Those words used to scare me, send me running. Now, there was nothing more I wanted to hear. That someone so beautiful, generous, kind and loving would need *me*. It was nothing short of an honor.

I kissed her clit and moved up the bed. "You need me, Princess?"

She reached for my cock. "Yeah," she whispered as she dove for my mouth, hungry and ready for me. I rolled on top of her and pressed my dick to her entrance. She responded by curling her legs around my hips.

"This is our first time making love as an engaged couple," I said as I pushed into her. She groaned, her palms flat against my chest.

I closed my eyes for a second, just to steady myself at the feel of her.

"No," she said. "I don't think so."

I bent to kiss her. "Did I miss something?"

She grinned. "All engaged means is that we'll spend the rest of our lives together—and I think that's been the case from our very first time."

The drag of her around me as I pulled out combined with her words took my breath away.

"Yes," I replied as I pushed back into her and began my rhythm. She was right. She'd been mine from the moment I touched her. I'd been hers before I'd ever met her.

We molded together like magic. The heat from our bodies enveloping us, binding us. As I rocked into her, gazing at her, she cupped my face. "I love you," she said as my orgasm began to rumble in the distance. "I love you," she repeated, the rumble growing louder, and she started to pulse beneath me.

"I love you," I said and she gasped as if it were the first time she was hearing it.

"Sam," she called, her unsteady voice telling me she was close. "Oh God, I love you, Sam." She arched her back and milked my cock, pulling my orgasm from me as I began to spiral, my pulse banging in my ears. I bent and kissed her shoulder, sucking, tasting, breathing her in, wanting as much of her as I could get as our orgasms joined, drawing out the pleasure.

Our breathing slowed and I rolled to one side, sliding her toward me, our legs entangling. "*You're* my ultimate bliss," I said, quoting Dumas. "I get it now. Without even knowing it, even through the darkest grief of my life, I waited and hoped. For you."

She trailed her fingers over my tattoo. "I think I waited and hoped for you my whole life, too."

"The day you appeared, a part of me knew it was always meant to be you."

"Your soul," she said. She never ceased to amaze me. "I highlighted that passage." She smiled. "'There are two ways of seeing: with the body and with the soul. The body's sight can sometimes forget, but the soul remembers forever.'"

"I love you, body and soul," I replied.

Grace

"She's the most beautiful thing I've ever seen, don't you think?" Sam said, leaning over his daughter as he changed her diaper.

"You only just realized?" I asked, wrapping my arms around his waist.

He chuckled. "I guess I get reminded every now and then."

Lauren kept her gaze focused strictly on her daddy, as if reminding him he better do her diaper right.

"She's never this still when I change her," I said.

"I think she knows I can't get shit on my tux."

I laughed. "Can you imagine the wedding photos?"

We'd walked the block to the Frick from our apartment. Lauren in her stroller, pushed by Sam in his tux, me in a red silk organza gown—who got married in white?

It seemed like the most perfect way to arrive at our wedding—with our whole world strolling along a New York avenue.

Sam fixed Lauren's diaper and pulled up her tights. I'd managed to wrestle a headband of pink flowers around her head to match her dress.

"She looks like a sugarplum fairy," I said.

"Did you hear that, sugarplum?" Sam lifted her upright and kissed her on her fat cheek. Lifting her onto his hip, he turned to me. "Are you ready?"

I smiled and nodded.

The museum had suggested we hold the ceremony in the West Gallery, but we both thought it was too big. We hadn't invited many people and wanted it to feel small and intimate, so they'd set things up in the dining room where we'd had our first official date.

Smiles and cheers greeted us as we walked in. Sam wrapped his arm around my waist, our daughter on his other hip, not wanting the three of us to be separated. I wouldn't have it any other way.

"You look incredible—a real Park Avenue princess," Harper said, kissing me and then Sam.

"I'm just happy I found my prince," I responded.

Scarlett and Violet pushed Max out of the way before he had a chance to kiss me. I just grinned at him as he rolled his eyes.

"You look stunning," Scarlett said.

"And you can tell Lauren is your daughter. She's such a cutie," Violet said as she stroked Lauren's cheek.

Sam moved us on and I blew them a kiss.

"Hey, Daddy," I said as we approached my mother and father. Sam kissed my mother on the cheek.

"I don't think I've ever seen you look so beautiful," my dad said, his eyes misty with tears.

"I'm marrying the love of my life. What could be better?" I asked.

"I did the same forty years ago and I don't regret a moment," he replied. "She's made me very happy—I can only wish you the same."

"Thank you, Daddy."

"That's one hell of a dress," my mother said. "You look gorgeous."

Sam kept us moving toward the registrar.

Angie stood when she saw us. "I'm so proud of you," she whispered to Sam as she hugged him, the embrace awkward because Sam refused to let go of me even for a second.

I waved at Chas, who was feeding their daughter, Morgan, in the front row. He grinned.

When Angie went to sit down I turned to Sam. "Are you thinking about your parents?"

"Always," he replied. "But I feel them in my heart." He dropped a kiss on my lips.

We had no bridesmaids, no best men, no bouquets and no speeches. It was just Sam, Lauren and me with a few of our friends celebrating our love and our lives . . .

Our ultimate bliss.

The End

COMING SOON
SCARLETT'S STORY

Books by Louise Bay

King of Wall Street

THE KING OF WALL STREET IS BROUGHT TO HIS KNEES BY AN AMBITIOUS BOMBSHELL.

I keep my two worlds separate.

At work, I'm King of Wall Street. The heaviest hitters in Manhattan come to me to make money. They do whatever I say because I'm always right. I'm shrewd. Exacting. Some say ruthless.

At home, I'm a single dad trying to keep his fourteen year old daughter a kid for as long as possible. If my daughter does what I say, somewhere there's a snowball surviving in hell. And nothing I say is ever right.

When Harper Jayne starts as a junior researcher at my firm, the barriers between my worlds begin to dissolve. She's the most infuriating woman I've ever worked with.

I don't like the way she bends over the photocopier—it makes my mouth water.

I hate the way she's so eager to do a good job—it makes my dick twitch.

And I can't stand the way she wears her hair up exposing her long neck. It makes me want to strip her naked, bend her over my desk and trail my tongue all over her body.

If my two worlds are going to collide, Harper Jayne will have to learn that I don't just rule the boardroom. I'm in charge of the bedroom, too.

THE NIGHTS SERIES
(a series of three, full length, stand-alone novels)
Parisian NIGHTS

The moment I laid eyes on the new photographer at work, I had his number. Cocky, arrogant and super wealthy— women were eating out of his hand as soon as his tight ass crossed the threshold of our office.

When we were forced to go to Paris together for an assignment, I wasn't interested in his seductive smile, his sexy accent or his dirty laugh. I wasn't falling for his charms. Until I did.

Until Paris.

Until he was kissing me and I was wondering how it happened. Until he was dragging his lips across my skin and I was hoping for more. Paris does funny things to a girl and he might have gotten me naked.

But Paris couldn't last forever.

Previously called What the Lightning Sees

Promised NIGHTS

I've been in love with Luke Daniels since, well, forever. As his sister's best friend, I've spent over a decade living in the friend zone, watching from the sidelines hoping he would notice me, pick me, love me.

I want the fairy tale and Luke is my Prince Charming. He's tall, with shoulders so broad he blocks out the sun. He's kind with a smile so dazzling he makes me forget everything that's wrong in the world. And he's the only man that can make me laugh until my cheeks hurt and my stomach cramps. But he'll never be mine.

So I've decided to get on with my life and find the next best thing.

Until a Wonder Woman costume, a bottle of tequila and a game of truth or dare happened.

Then Luke's licking salt from my wrist and telling me I'm beautiful.

Then he's peeling off my clothes and pressing his lips against mine.

Then what? Is this the start of my happily ever after or the beginning of a tragedy?

Previously called Calling Me

Indigo NIGHTS

The only thing better than cake is cake with a side of orgasms. Dylan James has no expectations when it comes to relationships. He uses women for sex and they use him for his money and power. It's quid pro quo and he's good with that. It works.

Beth Harrison has been burned. She's tired of the lies and the game playing that men bring and has buried herself in her passion—baking which keeps her out of the reach of heartbreak. As she begins her career as a TV baker, a new world opens up to her.

Dylan and Beth both know that casual sex is all about giving what you need to get what you want.

Except that sometimes you give more than you need to and get everything you ever wanted.

The Empire State Series

Anna Kirby is sick of dating. She's tired of heartbreak. Despite being smart, sexy, and funny, she's a magnet for men who don't deserve her.

A week's vacation in New York is the ultimate distraction from her most recent break-up, as well as a great place to meet a stranger and have some summer fun. But to protect her still-bruised heart, fun comes with rules. There will be no sharing stories, no swapping numbers, and no real names. Just one night of uncomplicated fun.

Super-successful serial seducer Ethan Scott has some rules of his own. He doesn't date, he doesn't stay the night, and he doesn't make any promises.

It should be a match made in heaven. But rules are made to be broken.

The Empire State Series is a series of three novellas.

HOPEFUL

Guys like Joel Wentworth weren't supposed to fall in love with girls like me. He could have had his pick of girls, but somehow the laws of nature were defied and we fell crazy in love.

After graduation, Joel left for New York. And, despite him wanting me to go with him, I'd refused, unwilling to disappoint my parents and risk the judgment of my friends. I hadn't seen him again. Never even spoken to him.

I've spent the last eight years working hard to put my career front and center in my life, dodging any personal complications. I have a strict no-dating policy. I've managed to piece together a reality that works for me.

Until now.

Now, Joel's coming back to London.

And I need to get over him before he gets over here.

Hopeful is a stand-alone novel.

love unexpected

When the fierce redhead with the beautiful ass walks into the local bar, I can tell she's passing through. And I'm looking for distraction while I'm in town—a hot hook-up and nothing more before I head back to the city.

If she has secrets, I don't want to know them.

If she feels good underneath me, I don't want to think about it too hard.

If she's my future, I don't want to see it.

I'm Blake McKenna and I'm about to teach this Boston socialite how to forget every man who came before me.

When the future I had always imagined crumbles before my very eyes. I grab my two best friends and take a much needed vacation to the country.

My plan of swearing off men gets railroaded when on my

first night of my vacation, I meet the hottest guy on the planet.

I'm not going to consider that he could be a gorgeous distraction.

I'm certainly not going to reveal my deepest secrets to him as we steal away each night hoping no one will notice.

And the last thing I'm going to do is fall in love for the first time in my life.

My name is Mackenzie Locke and I haven't got a handle on men. Not even a little bit.

Not until Blake.

Love Unexpected is a stand-alone novel.

AITHFUL

Leah Thompson's life in London is everything she's supposed to want: a successful career, the best girlfriends a bottle of sauvignon blanc can buy, and a wealthy boyfriend who has just proposed. But something doesn't feel right. Is it simply a case of 'be careful what you wish for'?

Uncertain about her future, Leah looks to her past, where she finds her high school crush, Daniel Armitage, online. Daniel is one of London's most eligible bachelors. He knows what and who he wants, and he wants Leah. Leah resists Daniel's advances as she concentrates on being the perfect fiancé.

She soon finds that she should have trusted her instincts when she realises she's been betrayed by the men and women in her life.

Leah's heart has been crushed. Will ever be able to trust again? And will Daniel be there when she is?

Faithful is a stand-alone novel.

Let's Connect!

Sign up for my mailing list to get the latest news and gossip.
http://eepurl.com/bjHtfH

I love hearing from readers – get in touch!

Website

www.louisebay.com

Twitter

www.twitter.com/louiseSbay

Facebook

www.facebook.com/louiseSbay

www.facebook.com/authorlouisebay

Instagram

www.instagram.com/louiseSbay

Pinterest

www.pinterest.com/Louisebay

Goodreads

www.goodreads.com/louisebay

Google+

plus.google.com/+LouiseBayauthor

Acknowledgements

This time last year I wrote the acknowledgements for Indigo Nights. Doing it again almost exactly a year later makes me look back at the last twelve months. I can't believe so much has happened—good and bad but mostly good and I'm thankful for that. I go into 2017 working my notice from my day job. In a few weeks I will be a full time writer. I couldn't have imagined that when I started out just a few years ago—it's not even three years since I pressed publish for the first time. Thank you every one of you who has bought my books—you made that dream a reality.

Some books are easy to write. And some aren't. For some reason this book was one of the more difficult ones. Some things get easier the more you do them, but I'm not sure that will ever happen with writing. I think I just become more aware of what I'm not doing and what needs to be stronger and better. But that's part of the reason I love writing—all that learning! Thank you for reading. Sam and Grace are very special to me. I hope you enjoyed their story.

Elizabeth – Whenever a book is difficult, we're always going to say, well at least it's not as bad as *that* book. And it wasn't. But you did have to talk me off that cliff—thank you. I'm glad Sam's your favorite but we won't tell anyone. He's not bad as heroes go. In fact he's pretty amazing and a huge part of that is thanks to you. I hope 2017 is a fantastic year for you.

Nina – I love you. And you'd make a super-fabulous art consultant—even if you did have Sam against the wall. I can't wait for that 2017 hug!

Jessica Hawkins – Thank you for being so awesome and supportive.

Karen Booth – Thank you blurb fairy. I can't believe we got to speak!! Yay!

To all the incredible authors that constantly give me help and support—I love this community and I'm so proud to be a member.

Najla Qamber – You totally nailed this cover. You're amazing and I appreciate every moment of yours that I get.

Jules Rapley Collins – Thank you for being such a great support babycakes. Megan Fields I know 2017 is going to be good to you.

To all my family and friends who have supported me over the last three years, including you Twirly, I love you. I hope to see a little more of you now I'm not juggling three jobs.

Thanks to all of you who blog, tweet, share, like and help spread the word about my books. I couldn't do it without you! Here's to book number ten!

Made in the USA
Las Vegas, NV
15 February 2021

17870852R00187